For Helen

First published in Great Britain in 2012 by Comma Press
www.commapress.co.uk

'My Mother and her Sister' first appeared in *The Mail on Sunday Magazine,* 1996, and was also broadcast on BBC Radio 4 Morning Story, July, 1996. 'Lucky' was first published in *Manchester Stories 2* (*City Life,* 1999), and *The City Life Book of Manchester Short Stories,* edited by Ra Page (Penguin, 1999). 'The Runaway' first appeared in *Matter 4,* 2004. 'Conception' first appeared in *Woman's Weekly Fiction Special, No. 47,* October, 2006. 'Conception' and 'My Mother and her Sister' were previously collected in *Ellipsis 2,* (Comma, 2006). 'Ped-o-Matique' was specially commissioned for *The New Uncanny* edited by Sarah Eyre & Ra Page (Comma, 2009). 'Hitting Trees with Sticks' was shortlisted for the BBC National Short Story Award 2009, was published in the official anthology (Short Books), and was broadcast on Radio 4 in December 2009; it was also published in the *Kenyon Review Fall 2010, vol XXXII, no 4.* 'Saved' first appeared in *Riptide Vol 5,* 2010, and in *Epoch Vol 59 i,* 2010. 'Morphogenesis' was specially commissioned for *Litmus,* edited by Ra Page (Comma, 2011), and benefited from the consultation of Dr. Martyn Amos. 'Red Enters the Eye' first appeared in *Epoch Vol 60 iii,* 2011.

ISBN 1905583451
ISBN-13 978 1905583454

The publisher gratefully acknowledges the assistance of Arts Council England. The author gratefully acknowledges the support of a Wingate Scholarship for work on the more recent stories in the collection.

Set in Bembo 11/13 by David Eckersall
Printed and bound in England by MPG Biddles Ltd.

HITTING TREES
WITH STICKS

by

Jane Rogers

About the Author

Jane Rogers has written eight novels including *Her living Image* (Somerset Maugham Award), *Mr Wroe's Virgins* (Guardian Fiction Prize runner-up), *Promised Lands* (Writers Guild Best Novel Award), *Island* (Orange longlisted), and *The Voyage Home*. Her most recent, *The Testament of Jessie Lamb*, was Man Booker longlisted and won the 2012 Arthur C. Clarke Award. She has written drama for radio and TV, including an award-winning adaptation of *Mr Wroe's Virgins* for BBC2. Her radio work includes both original drama and Classic Serial adaptations. She is Professor of Writing at Sheffield Hallam University, and is a Fellow of the Royal Society of Literature. Visit www.janerogers.org

Contents

Red Enters the Eye

BEFORE SHE WENT to Nigeria Julie bought twelve pairs of sharp dressmaking scissors. Good equipment showed respect. And buying things made it easier not to panic. She was afraid the women would resent her swanning in, setting herself up to teach them. She bought six pairs of pinking shears, ten packets each of needles and pins, thirty assorted reels of cotton. She had raised enough money to pay her airfare and to buy three reconditioned sewing machines from the Singer shop on Stockport Road. *So Sew Right* magazine had donated £150 in exchange for 'a young designer's fashion tips' for their next issue. Julie jazzed up her third year essay on colour.

Accessorise with red! There's nothing hotter than shiny red shoes teamed with a red satchel. Smoulder with a black dress, or transform jeans and t-shirt into something special. Remember, red enters the eye more quickly than any other colour.

By the time she landed in Jos she'd run out of fear. From the moment the female passport officer smiled and said, 'You are wel-come in Nigeria,' in her deep coo-ing voice, Julie's spirits rose. She loved the strong colours and designs on the women's wrappas, and their graceful posture. She loved the heat and the light and the exotic humid petrol-fumey air; the shrieks of invisible birds that sounded like monkeys; the reds and purples of hibiscus and bougainvillea.

The only disappointing thing was the woman from the refuge. Fran appeared as Julie was trying to prise her luggage from a surly official. 'I'm transporting sewing machines for a charity. They said there would be no charge.' Fran smiled absently and gave the man cash. When Julie started crossly hauling her cases onto a trolley Fran restrained her. 'The driver will bring it.'

'I don't understand why you –' Julie let her protest die away as Fran strode off to the car park. The driver was dragging two of Julie's cases with one hand and the really massive one with the other. Julie tried to take it from him but he shook his head.

They got into the back of the car while the driver laboured to fit the cases into the boot. Fran handed Julie a cool bottle of water from under the passenger seat and said, 'Please don't open the window.' There were lines like scratches around her eyes, and her hair was more grey than blonde.

'How long have you been working here?' Julie asked.

'Yewande and I set up the refuge in 2002. But I've been in Jos for years, I used to teach.'

Julie might have guessed. The driver got in. 'Simon – Julie. Simon is our driver and security guard.'

Simon gave a sycophantic little chuckle.

When they stopped at the lights, people from the roadside flooded in amongst the traffic - women with trays of oranges on their heads, boys selling cigarette lighters and mobile phones, a legless man on a trolley offering cans of drink. 'Miss Julie – window!' Simon shouted. A young girl had squeezed her fingers through the gap which Julie had rebelliously left open. Julie recoiled from the fingers, pinky-brown with blunt, bitten nails, waving at her like the tentacles of an octopus. Fran leaned over to rap sharply on the window and shout at the girl to go away. The waving fingers withdrew. Fran rolled Julie's window up tight.

'People get hurt. If their fingers are inside and the car moves on.'

The women's refuge was as Julie had expected, although she had not foreseen an armed watchman at the entrance to the compound. Fran confirmed it was a real gun. 'For his own protection as much as anyone else's.' In the courtyard children ran and fought and played football with a deflated ball while the women, most of them with sleeping babies bound elegantly to their backs, chatted and hung up washing and prepared food and braided their daughters' hair and sang along to a babbling radio. Some smiled at her. It could be any group of mothers and children, anywhere – but then there was the shock of the arm in a sling, the limp, the red wheals from a pot of boiling porridge.

Julie's room, like all the others, opened onto the courtyard. The narrow window let in a rectangle of sun which moved across the floor during the morning and vanished in the afternoon. Sitting on her bed and listening to the children chanting outside, Julie felt the butterflies dance in her stomach. This was it! She was really going to make a difference.

On her first evening Fran and Yewande invited her to their quarters. Yewande was younger and more smiley than Fran, but the way they both spoke was flat and deliberate, 'as if enthusiasm was a dirty word,' Julie later emailed to her friend Elspeth. At least Yewande was half-Nigerian, at least her clothes weren't as dingy as Fran's; but her top was too tight. You could see where her bra bit into her back. They both needed a makeover. As Julie sipped her cold beer and stared at their shelves of masks and primitive dolls with naked conical breasts, she decided they were probably lesbians.

They told her the rules. Keep the sewing equipment safe in your room, keep the door to your room locked. Try not to make favourites of any of the women. Tell Fran or Yewande at the first sign of any trouble, and don't discuss religion. Whoever's in charge must sign in the security guard, when Obi relieves Zacchaeus, or Simon relieves Obi, or Zacchaeus relieves Simon. The outside gate should only ever be opened by the guard. Never let in anyone you don't know.

'Men, you mean,' said Julie.

3

'Never let in anyone who doesn't already live here.' Fran's voice plodded like two flat feet.

'But how do new women come?'

'Via hospital or through the churches —'

'I thought this wasn't religious?'

'We have no tribal or religious affiliation,' said Yewande quickly. 'Absolutely not. But the churches sometimes provide a haven.'

'And we work closely with my old school,' said Fran. 'They often refer —'

'But surely if someone's in danger —?'

Yewande shook her head. 'We can't take in people off the street, it's too risky. Some of these women's husbands walk past every day.'

'Has one ever come in?'

'A man with a machete. But Fran stopped him.' Yewande laughed.

'How did you do that?'

'I told him to go home before I called the police,' said Fran flatly.

Pretty soon Julie understood it all. Really the place ran itself. Fran and Yewande held a kind of surgery in the mornings, dispensing health and legal advice; Yewande also ran a literacy class. And in the afternoons they would have sewing.

Nine women gathered round the long dining table on the first afternoon. The stately woman whose name began with R said she had already sewed many garments. 'Some of these women know nothing,' she told Julie disdainfully. 'Some of these women are ig-nor-ant.' Fran announced that Miss Julie was giving them an opportunity to make clothes for their children and to learn a marketable skill. She told them they must always ask permission before using the machines. The scissors and pinking shears and needles, all this equipment which had been brought from England specially for them, must be counted in and out at the start and end of every class.

Julie stared at her feet, hoping the women would not think it was her idea to patronise them so.

At last Fran finished and Julie plunged in. They were going to make squares from fabric samples, then sew the squares together into patchwork bedspreads. They would practise hemming first by hand, then by machine. She demonstrated the first stages; measuring six inch squares, cutting, folding and pinning the hem on four sides.

'Oh this is very easy!' said R, whose name was Rifkatu. Some of the women laughed – whether in agreement or because they thought Rifkatu was boasting, Julie could not tell. Some remained silent, glancing quickly under their lids at Julie then away, as if afraid that she would see them. If they could sew already, this exercise would insult them. She put the samples on the table and tried to smile – 'Choose a colour you like.' Two women reached for the same red flowered rectangle, and laughed. Someone flipping through the pile found them an identical one. Everyone measured and cut and pinned – two with practised ease, the others more slowly. They spoke to one another softly in their own language. At the far end of the table a thin woman with yellow-brown skin and hollows under her eyes fingered her cloth. Working her way around the table, Julie offered to help her.

'She cannot understand you.'

'No English,' said the others.

'Can you translate?'

The women laughed.

'You can?'

They shook their heads. 'No one speak this language.'

'Ig-nor-ant,' said Rifkatu.

'OK,' said Julie, 'What's your name?'

The woman watched her carefully.

'I'm Julie, what's your name?' Julie did the embarrassing miming-pointing thing. When the woman whispered her name it was a hiss of consonants Julie could not reproduce.

'OK, I'll show you.' Slowly she demonstrated again, the

measuring, the cutting. The woman's eyes followed her moves. 'You try?' She held out the scissors to the woman, who flinched away sharply.

'Leave her Miss Julie. She's one simple woman.'

'She understands no-thing.'

The women laughed. They showed each other their progress, and laughed again over the wonky hems and the corners that would not lie down. They clustered round Julie as she demonstrated fixing the thread to the fabric, and how to make neat little hemming stitches that were invisible on the other side. The women nodded and praised her work, and threaded needles of their own. Two left to feed their babies. Rifkatu asked if she could use a machine, and Sara went to fetch the iron. The strange woman sat at the end of the table, watching them all in silence.

At the end of the afternoon there was a small pile of hemmed squares, and Julie had demonstrated how to thread the machines. The women had talked and laughed and mostly followed her instructions. She had broken Fran's dreary school-room atmosphere.

She asked Yewande about the silent one. 'Mathenneh. The hospital sent her. She doesn't speak Hausa so we don't know the full story. All we can do really is make her feel safe.' Yewande told Julie that fewer than half of the women spoke English. 'Most of them can speak Hausa. But their first languages – their tribal languages – well, at the moment we have Duguza, Tarok, Izere, Yoruba, and Berom speakers. Berom is the main one locally. I think Mathenneh must come from quite far north.'

The sewing class became a great success. The women learned to use the sewing machines; they chattered non-stop. Sara and Hanatu sat by Julie and translated the jokes and scandals that set the others off. When Mathenneh wandered in, the chorus of voices fell to a low mutter, then silence. She turned to leave without even sitting down, and a couple of women called out after her. There was an explosion of laughter. 'What did they say?' Julie asked.

'Nothing,' Sara told her. 'These women like to talk nonsense.' Sara was in her thirties, a big woman with a droll way of rolling her eyes when Fran was holding forth. Hanatu was younger, around Julie's age, with a three month old daughter. She radiated gentle kindness like a pilot light. Her husband beat her regularly, Sara told Julie, but last time he did it they had to take her to hospital otherwise the baby would have died. After that Hanatu didn't go back to her home. The two of them constructed elaborate futures for themselves, in which they would move to Lagos and have well-paid city jobs. They delighted in the copies of *Vogue* and *Elle* which Julie had brought, and Sara made withering comments about the skinny, ill-clad models. Everyone in sewing laughed a lot. Alright, one or two things went missing. The number of scissors declined to five, and the pinking shears seemed to come and go. It was worth losing a few bits and bobs, not to have to do that primary teacher thing of counting at the end of class.

Soon all the patches were machined, then sewn together in strips, and finally the strips were joined, with half-patches as fillers where measurements had been a little out. There were three bright bedspreads. Fran decreed that they would go on the beds of the three newest arrivals, passing on to each newcomer in turn. Those women who could have the bedspreads first were Mathenneh, Rifkatu, and Catherine. This was received in silence. Julie emailed to Elspeth, 'Fran takes the joy out of everything.'

Yewande said Mathenneh was a Muslim, and maybe that was why the others avoided her.

'But you have other Muslim women here? Kubra wears hijab.'

'Kubra was born in Jos, she went to school here. It's different. Mathenneh comes from one of the herding tribes in the north. You know it was herders who committed the atrocities in March?'

All Julie knew about the atrocities was that Muslims had killed Christians in villages south of Jos. It had been on the news. By stressing the religious nature of the conflict, and its distance from Jos, she had calmed her mother and boxed it for herself. Yewande, in her gentle husky voice, explained as they shared morning coffee in a corner of the courtyard. 'Those herders rode into Dogo Na Hawa at 3am and fired their guns to frighten the villagers out of their huts. Then they hacked them to pieces with machetes – men, women and children – and burned their huts. Over three hundred died. All the women here know someone who knows someone who died.'

'But *why?*'

Yewande shrugged. 'Reprisals for Christians burning mosques and killing Jasawa, back in January? Anger because the settled farmers have more rights? I don't know, it's mad. Christians and Muslims live side by side here in town, they even intermarry – and then you get these explosions of violence. The killings are always revenge. And then revenge for the revenge.'

Fran appeared in the doorway of the office, blinking against the light. She made her way across to them. 'I was looking for you,' she said to Yewande.

'Sorry, I'm coming.' Yewande got to her feet. 'These women have so much to deal with,' she told Julie. 'All the personal shit, and then tribal and religious conflict too. We have to keep them safe.'

Watching them return to the office Julie wondered if Fran was jealous. Yewande nearly always sat and chatted with Julie, at morning coffee. 'Wish I *was* a lesbian,' Julie emailed to Elspeth, 'I haven't met a single man, apart from the security guards who're scared of me. Beware nymphomaniac when I get home!!'

After four weeks Julie was an old hand. The sewing class had made multi-coloured dressing gowns from remnants for their children. Fran's old school provided a bolt of cheap undyed cotton and they sewed pinnies for the pupils. Julie took pictures of the women at their machines, and of the cute grinning children in their pinnies, and emailed them to *So Sew Right*.

Then there was no more fabric, and no money to buy any. Julie went to the market with Sara. They combed the fabric stalls: 'Very fine quality, Madam, newest Paris fashion!' 'No fading, no shrink, will last you a lifetime Madam.' There were golden anchors on a strident blue background; green palms and purple coconuts on white. Julie finally bought a regal red-purple batik in overlapping circles. She described her plan to Sara. She had designed a simple garment; a kaftan-style shirt with wide sleeves and a v-neck, loose enough to pull over the head. She would make a prototype and persuade Fran and Yewande to cough up some money. With a small injection of capital, the sewing class could buy a range of these eye-catching fabrics, make kaftan shirts and sell them to tourists. They were perfect souvenirs: ethnic, unisex, and cooler than a t-shirt. The women could quickly make enough to repay their loan and to pay themselves. Julie explained the term 'no-brainer' to Sara and they laughed all the way home.

Fran and Yewande were hesitant. Julie had known they would be but it was still exasperating. They argued that the refuge was a charity not a business; they were not allowed to make a profit. Also, what about health and safety? And who would sell the shirts? Who would decide the price, and what proportion of the profits should go to whom?

In her email to Elspeth Julie described Fran and Yewande as 'the kind of people who wouldn't strike a match in case it caused a forest fire. Aaaargh! I want to put a bomb under them.'

Fran finally decreed that the refuge would pay for the fabric and the shirts would be sold at school and church fundraising events. Profits could finance improvements to the refuge, such as the installation of a new shower unit.

'You can make them to sell for yourselves when you leave here,' Julie pointed out to Sara. 'You and Hanatu can set up business.'

'There is the small matter of a sewing machine.'

'I don't see why I can't give you one of these. After all, I brought them here.' She felt awkward about suggesting this to Fran and Yewande, but in reality, weren't they hers to give?

Soon, each of the sewing women had completed her first shirt and there was a race on to see who could make the most. At mealtimes Julie sat with them; she felt awkward with the other women, who didn't speak English, or whose lives were so crisis-ridden that sewing was an irrelevance. She regretted the absence of Mathenneh, though. Yewande speculated that she might be an elective mute: the Fula translator had not been able to get a word out of her, and now Yewande was trying to get her to draw pictures. 'She's traumatised. God knows what she's seen. She needs a psychiatrist, but who's going to pay for that?'

The Fulani woman no longer wandered into sewing at all; she hovered at the edge of the courtyard, or squatted in her room, which was three down from Julie's, watching the children playing through her open door. Once Julie heard Rifkatu hissing at her, 'Keep your eyes off my boy, ghost woman!' But Mathenneh couldn't speak English, so she wouldn't have understood. When no one was looking, Julie paused to speak to her. 'Why don't you come back to sewing with me?' She pointed towards the sewing room and mimed the needle dipping in and out of the cloth. Mathenneh's big sad eyes were fixed on hers, but when Julie extended her hand Mathenneh shrank back. It was then that Julie noticed a pair of her scissors, lying on the table. Mathenneh must have seen the look because she snatched them up and hid them behind her back.

'You've got my scissors,' Julie said.

Mathenneh held her position and Julie laughed. After a moment a ghost of a smile seemed to flicker across Mathenneh's face. How young she was! Slowly she brought the scissors from behind her back and replaced them on the table.

'Can I have them?'

Mathenneh laid her fingers protectively over the scissors.

'That's a no, then.'

They watched each other.

'You'll come to sewing one day, Mathenneh? Bring the scissors and come to sewing?'

Mathenneh tightened her hold on the scissors, and Julie went to sewing feeling rather flattered. Perhaps the scissors reminded Mathenneh of a time when her own life was normal, before whatever happened to her had happened. The scissors showed that she valued something Julie had brought. Perhaps she really would come back to sewing.

On the second Saturday in June there was a Gala Fête Day at Fran's old school. Julie and Sara were going to take the first batch of thirty kaftans to sell. Julie managed to persuade Hanatu, who was afraid of leaving the refuge, to go with them. That same day Fran and Yewande were driving over to Abuja for Yewande's mother's sixtieth. 'We'll have to leave at midday but everything will be fine, as long as you're back to do security sign-in at three,' said Fran.

'Look I'll probably be back before you even go. I just want to help them set up the stall. A couple of hours will do me.' It was rare for Fran and Yewande to be away; Julie looked forward to the different dynamic of the evening meal. It seemed to her that Fran cast a bit of a pall.

Julie didn't think the fête would be up to much. A pitch on the street near the museum or in the market would attract more tourists. But when they arrived to set up their stall, there was already a festive crowd at the gates. Children gleamed in their uniforms, women were resplendent in bright new wrappas or western clothes with gorgeous hats and turbans; there was a party of Americans with cameras and bulging money belts. The Local Government Area Minister for Education stood on a specially constructed stage in the schoolyard and thanked the Head, the governors, the teachers, and the parent association president and treasurer. He thanked the Governor of Plateau State, and his gracious wife, and a string of other officials each more remotely connected with the occasion than the last. Sara rolled her eyes and Julie giggled. Hanatu, her scarf over her head, slipped away to feed her baby. Prizes were awarded; the school choir massed onstage and sang; the Head made a speech of thanks for the thanks, and a band of older children played recorders. Fried snacks, coffee, cola, cakes and slices of fruit appeared from the kitchens, and people clustered to the tables set out under the shady trees in the carpark, which had been closed to cars for the occasion.

When the stalls opened at noon they were besieged, and at the women's refuge stall the shirts were a sensation. One American woman bought six. 'That's my bible group catered for!' she told Julie happily. By 2.30pm they had sold out. There was so much cash it wouldn't all fit in Julie's little red satchel, and they had to stow it in a shopping basket. Julie couldn't stop grinning – they could buy rolls of new fabric. Rolls and rolls. Women could set up in business, their lives would be transformed!

They wandered round the other stalls; most of the good stuff had gone but there was a second-hand clothes stall Julie wanted to go through. Then at 3.30pm a group took the stage with acoustic guitars and tambourines. It was impossible not to dance; Julie lost herself in the heat and rhythm of the crowd, until Hanatu gently touched her arm and said, 'It is late.'

Walking back, they agreed that Fran and Yewande would have to rethink their attitude to the kaftans now. Suddenly Julie remembered. 'They're in Abuja! The security–'

'They handover three times each day, you know,' said Sara. 'Maybe these men have got the hang of it by now?'

'Fran likes to keep us safe,' said Hanatu, pulling her scarf over her face. 'But it will be fine, nobody will tell her.'

Sara laughed. 'Wait till they see how we are rich!'

But when they got to the compound, there was no guard on duty. Julie pushed the gate. It swung open. She realised there was no sound from the courtyard. No rhythmic thud of the children's football, no chanting or laughing, no babbling radio. Silence. Treading carefully as if their footfalls might rouse something terrible, they entered the empty courtyard. All the doors were closed.

'Something's happened. Something's –'

'Maybe Maria have her baby,' whispered Hanatu.

But Julie knew that was wrong. Even if Maria had to go to hospital, it was 6pm, there should be preparations for the evening meal. She walked to the first door and knocked. No reply. She tried the handle; locked. 'Rifkatu? Rifkatu?' She spoke softly, leaning in to the wood, her heart thudding out of time.

There was movement behind the door. Then Rifkatu's voice. 'Miss Julie?'

'Yes. Rifkatu, open the door.'

Slowly the lock was turned, slowly the door pulled back. Rifkatu's two children sat on the bed behind her. Their faces were grey.

'What's happened? Where is everybody?'

'Everybody in her room,' said Rifkatu. 'We heard trouble.'

'What kind of trouble?'

'Trouble,' said Rifkatu heavily.

'What?'

Rifkatu shook her head.

'What did you hear?'

'Nothing.'

Sara tutted. 'I will try Maria.' After a moment the door opened a crack. Maria was there, she was fine. The sounds of their voices must have been audible in the other rooms, because gradually, one after another, around the courtyard doors were opened. Unsmiling, the women glanced out. No one spoke.

'What's the matter?' asked Julie. 'What happened?'

Four doors remained closed. Sara's, Hanatu's, Julie's own, and the third room down from Julie's. As she crossed to Mathenneh's door she felt, rather than saw or heard, the other women closing their doors again. 'Mathenneh? Mathenneh? It's Julie.' She touched the handle and the door swung open.

Red. Red enters the eye more quickly than any other colour. On the wall, across the bright bedspread, on the floor, splattered across the ceiling. Blood red. As the red entered Julie's eye the smell of it hit her throat. The bundle on the floor was red, red and soaking wet, with crimson pooled on the floor around it. The red kept entering Julie's eye. It wouldn't stop. And then the scissors. They were sticking out of Mathenneh's cheek.

Even when Julie got on her plane home, she still didn't know what had happened. Only rumours. Obi had not turned up to relieve Simon. Simon told them he had waited 35 minutes past his time and then left because he had to take his wife to visit her sister's new baby. Simon wept. Obi claimed that he had been held up by the theft of his bicycle and then the friend who had promised him a lift let him down and it is a long way from his quarter to the refuge. He claimed he arrived only 45 minutes late but when he came there the gate was open and no one was about. It gave him a bad feeling so he left again. He may or may not have been telling the truth. The gun, which should have been passed from one guard to the next, was found propped unused in the corner of their shelter.

All the women said they knew nothing. They heard a scream, they said. Around about 4pm. They heard a scream and they thought someone dangerous was there, so they locked themselves and their children in their rooms, as Fran and Yewande had advised them.

'Her bad husband come to find her,' pronounced Rifkatu. 'Track her down like a beast.'

But the murder weapon was scissors. There were so many stabs, so many wounds – could they all have been made with one pair of scissors?

Fran and Yewande barely spoke to Julie. They dealt quietly and matter-of-factly with the police and the coroner. They spoke to all the women and staff who had been in the compound at the time of the attack. Julie went to tell them, in tears, that Mathenneh had kept a pair of the dressmaking scissors lying on her table in full sight. 'I didn't collect them in. I don't know why. I'm so sorry.'

Next morning Fran came to Julie's room and told her she must leave. 'You are not a suspect. It was nothing to do with you. You should go home.'

'I'm so sorry – Fran, I'm so sorry, I should have come back on time, I should have counted all the –'

'Use the phone in the office, get yourself onto the soonest flight.'

'But – isn't there anything I can –?'

Fran turned to go.

'Was it her husband?'

Fran stopped in the doorway. Her face was in shadow. 'If it was, he knew just which half hour the gate would be unguarded.'

'Maybe he lost his temper and grabbed the scissors –'

Fran did not reply.

'What's going to happen?'

'I've told you, go home. The refuge will be closing.'

'For a while? Temporarily, while it's sorted out?'

'If we can't keep women safe then we are failing.'

'But it's not your fault. It's not your fault! I'm the one who –'

Fran made a strange sound, like suppressed laughter. 'It *is* my fault. I would have kept a closer eye on you. But because Yewande... I didn't want Yewande to think I was...'

'I'm sorry,' Julie whispered again.

Fran snorted. 'I asked her, I said, What do you two talk

about? *We've been talking about Dogo Na Hawa,* she said. *Now Julie understands the tensions here. She cares about these women.*'

'Fran, I don't understand.'

Fran spoke flatly. 'A Fulani woman has been killed here, amongst Christians. What don't you understand? We have to send these women away. We cannot protect them.'

Julie didn't go to dinner that night but Sara came to her room and whispered that all the women's rooms were being searched by police.

'What are they looking for?' asked Julie. But she knew. 'Even if they find them it doesn't prove – well, they *will* find them, because seven lots of scissors are missing. It doesn't prove –'

'No,' said Sara. 'It doesn't prove. But they are scared.'

On the plane home Julie remembered the bag of money from the fête. She hoped Sara and Hanatu still had it. She wondered where everyone would go, and what Fran and Yewande would do. She thought about them in their room full of masks and dolls. When she remembered their dull and careful rules her stomach turned over and over as if she had been pitched head first down a steep flight of stairs.

So she stared out of the window at the stupidly blue sky and the golden-white clouds below, forcing her eyes to stay open. Every time she closed them, red entered in.

Conception

MY DAUGHTER ASKED me where she was conceived. We were slicing runner beans. The allotment had gone mad and we couldn't eat them all at once. We were going to freeze them in old ice cream containers, we were housewifely and companionable.

Still, I was surprised she asked. I wondered if she had been trying to imagine a time when her father and I got on, in prehistory, before the rows which were all she ever really saw. But when I stopped to think, of course her question was about herself, as it should be: she was interested in the place her own life had begun, not in the messy intricacies of ours. 'Derbyshire,' I said. 'In a beautiful village in the White Peaks.'

'Why were you in Derbyshire?'

'We went away for the weekend, we stayed in a B&B. Hillcrest Cottage.'

'You're sure it happened then?'

'Yes. That's when we decided to have children.'

'Look how stringy this one is! The big ones are really old.'

'Chuck the old ones,' I said. The juicy tang of cut beans filled the kitchen. 'There's plenty more.'

'And you got pregnant the minute you decided?'

'Yes. Astonishingly.'

'How d'you know?'

'I just knew. And the date you were born proved it.'

She laughed. 'So, it was a romantic spot?'

'Not really. It wasn't what I was expecting when I booked it.'

'Why?'

'For a start it wasn't a cottage. It was an Edwardian semi. And it wasn't on the crest of a hill, it was more in the depths of a valley.'

Lizzy laughed. I thought about the weekend, and wondered how much I might tell her, and whether knowing it would make her happy or sad.

The man who answered Hillcrest Cottage doorbell was slight and sandy-coloured, fast moving, eagerly smiling. He was glad we were early because he had to go out; he'd just show us the room then leave us to it. We must help ourselves to tea and drink it in the conservatory at the back, where we could watch dusk fall. In the hall lay a defeated-looking black Labrador. It raised its head to stare mournfully at us then got up and slunk into the kitchen. The hall was tiled, with one wall covered by a mirror. The mirror reflected us back to ourselves surrounded by cardboard boxes piled almost to ceiling height. To get to the stairs I had to push a child's scooter out of the way with my foot.

Our room looked out over the garden. There were twin beds although we'd asked for a double, so we grimaced at each other. There was a cheap white wardrobe full of extra pillows and blankets, and a skirted dressing table with assorted soaps. There was a neatly handwritten breakfast menu on flowered notepaper.

'Everything alright then?' he asked hurriedly. 'I'll leave you the key. I'm – I'm visiting someone in hospital so I'm not sure when I'll be back.'

'We'll be going out to the pub to eat,' said Mark. 'Should we –?'

'Yes, please lock it, no one else is staying. And can you lock up when you go to bed? What time would you like breakfast?'

'Eight-thirty? Nine?'

'Shall we say nine? I may not be back tonight. There's towels in the bathroom.' He was already fleeing down the stairs. A minute later the door banged. We stood listening, heard the dog's nails clicking on the tiled floor as he circled the hall then flopped down again. We were all alone. We laughed.

'He couldn't wait to get away!'

'Where d'you think he's going?'

'I don't care. Want to test the bed?'

'Let's have a bath. If there's really no one here...' We were giggly like kids left home alone. It was a nice bathroom, big and square with a huge frosted window and a claw-footed iron bath. There was a thick powder-blue carpet. We ran a foamy bath and frolicked in it. A couple of times we stopped and held our breath in case someone had come in – but the house was empty, all ours. Mark wrapped me in a towel and dried me tenderly. We didn't make love and I remember the flutter of excitement in my stomach, because we wanted to but we were both waiting until something had been decided. And neither of us said a word about it.

We put our clothes on and went down in search of tea. The dog barely lifted his head to glance at us; a thoroughly disgruntled dog. The kitchen was big and well-appointed, a rayburn and a gas cooker, plenty of cupboards and work-tops, everything you'd need to run a B&B. There was a plastic box of kids' toys in the corner, and a miniature cooking stove, with dolls' size cups and saucepans balanced on it. Mark put the kettle on and I looked in the fridge for milk. There were two fresh pints, a packet of bacon, six eggs, four tomatoes and a tub of margarine. Nothing else at all.

'Look. D'you think he even lives here? He's just bought this stuff for our breakfast.'

'There are all these toys. Where are the kids?' We looked at each other and laughed at the strangeness of it. When we'd made our tea we went through the breakfast room and into

19

the conservatory, where two budgies in a cage greeted us excitedly and a bored marmalade cat stretched and tested its claws on the sofa. There was a scrabbling sound in the corner; a hamster running on his wheel. 'How many pets have they got?' There were children's colouring books and chewed felt pens piled on the coffee table.

'Big garden. Shall we take a look?' Darkness was already falling, but a sensor light switched on as we stepped out onto a paved area which ran down to a lawn. A table tennis table stood on the patio. Two big rabbits hopped heavily to the front of their cage as we passed them. Over the other side of the lawn were dense shrubs and a dark area that gleamed faintly with reflected light. A pond.

'Probably an alligator in there,' said Mark. 'Eaten the children.'

In the darkness it seemed almost plausible. 'The rabbits think we've come to feed them – look. I bet he hasn't fed any of these pets for the night.'

'If you want to start feeding pets, I'll meet you in the pub.'

'No. No. Of course not.' We turned to go back into the warmth. There were two children's bikes leaning against the wall. I wanted us in agreement again. 'It's like the Marie Celeste. He's seeing someone in hospital – but he seemed so cheery –' Suddenly and very loudly the phone rang. It switched to answerphone after four rings, and we could hear it whirring to itself over its message.

'I don't think he's visiting hospital.'

'Well where are they all? D'you think the wife's taken them on holiday?'

Mark shrugged. There was a TV in the breakfast room. He turned it on to watch the news and I hurried upstairs to get ready to go out. All the bedroom doors were closed but I couldn't resist looking inside a couple. One was a boxroom, very pink and girly, with china and plastic horses on the windowsill, and fluffy toys on the neatly made bed. The next was untidy and anonymous, its single beds strewn with heaps of clothes.

At the pub that evening we looked at maps and planned our next day's walk. We were both drinking quite a lot. I remember thinking the important conversation was waiting to happen: the conversation we had come away to have, the conversation about children. I couldn't raise it. It would have to not be me nagging him or pressurising him, it would have to come from Mark. I imagined him suddenly cracking a grin and going, 'Well, me dear, shall we take the plunge?' I had been wanting to get pregnant for a long time, and for a long time he had reacted with exasperation, as if the idiocy of it should have been obvious to me. But now he had proposed this weekend. He was ready to talk about it.

We didn't, though. Instead we talked about our landlord. We speculated about what he did: administration of some sort, in a college or hospital? But he could equally well be something exotic, racing driver or airline pilot. Or architect, possibly. He was hard to place. We remembered the cardboard boxes in the hall and wondered if he ran his own business, by post. Model trains, I suggested. Sex aids, said Mark. We argued about his age. I thought he was early thirties, maybe a couple of years older than us, but Mark insisted he was forty at least. The man was so boyish and eager and smiling I couldn't see that. There was still something undefined about him. And the house – a big rambling house, it must have been expensive, but it was not expensively furnished. I thought of the incongruous mirror-wall in the hall, the chipboard wardrobe in our room, the battered sofa in the conservatory.

'His wife's probably away visiting her mother with the children. Or staying with her sister while her sister has a baby.'

'OK. And he's arranged to spend the night with his mistress while they're away.'

That made sense but I didn't like it at all. His unseemly haste to get away when we arrived; his doubtfulness about

returning before morning. It did make sense. 'But he seems so...
decent!'

Mark laughed at me.

We floated further explanations; one of the children gravely
ill, the wife staying in hospital with it, the others farmed out to
friends during the crisis. But then why hadn't he told us so we
could sympathise and help by feeding the animals? Why had he
been so cheery and so secretive?

With increasing hilarity we discussed his clothes, his
income, what his wife might look like and whether she had a
job, how many children there were ('a dozen at least!') and what
all their names might be. It was nearly 11 o'clock. I remember
thinking this is displacement behaviour, he doesn't want to talk
about a baby. I remember making a decision not to raise it now,
because it was too late and we'd drunk too much. I was afraid of
another argument. Better leave it to the morning.

We walked back along the dimly lit village street and not a
single car passed us. Hillcrest Cottage was dark. The light and
laughter of the pub slipped away.

'He's not back.'

'No.'

We let ourselves into the empty house. The dog opened an
eye but never even lifted his head off the ground. There was a
rattling, whirring noise, which we realised must be the hamster
on his wheel. We crept upstairs as if we were intruders, and lay
like spoons in one of the single beds.

'It's making me feel sad,' I whispered to Mark. 'All these
toys and animals – it feels so... disrupted. So abandoned.'

'Don't be sad,' he said. He started to stroke my back.

When I turned to face him I said, 'I don't want to have a
house like this. Ever.'

'We won't,' he whispered in my ear. 'We won't, we won't.'
When I reached out to get my cap from the bag on the bedside
table he put his hand on my arm. 'Leave it,' he said.

'Leave it?'

And that's when our daughter was conceived.

I've thought about it since in different ways. Mostly I think we were just young and shiny and invulnerable. But on bad days I see the whole thing was fraudulent: we didn't plan a future, we didn't even dare discuss our motives. We used Hillcrest Cottage to make ourselves feel better, revelling in our superiority to the cluttered, broken household where we found ourselves. We created a child in order to prove we were not like that. And in doing so proved, of course, how exactly like that we were. The flavour of that house returned to haunt me in the dark days of our break-up. The beds strewn with clothes; the disconsolate dog; the dementedly whirring hamster.

Sure enough in the morning we found out the story. When he had served us our meticulously cooked bacon, egg and tomato, none of them touching each other on the plate, and brought in a second rack of fresh white toast, he hovered and asked if everything was OK.

'Fine,' we assured him.

'Good. It's the first time I've ever done a breakfast, you see. It's usually my wife, she does the B&B.' His wife, it transpired, had left him. For a riding school instructor. All he had ever wanted was for her to be happy. The house here in the countryside, the children, the pets, had all been his wife's idea. He worked in the city. She'd wanted to be a real mum, she'd stayed at home to look after them, and earned a bit by the B&B.

'She hardly ever left the house,' he said, smiling at us eagerly. 'She loved it. The kids, their pets, making the rooms nice, cooking breakfast. She loved every minute of it. But then in the summer she said she wanted riding lessons. She thought she could go riding with our daughters.'

'What happened?' asked Mark.

'She told me last week, she's in love. It came out of the blue. She told me she was leaving then she went.'

'She took the children!' I exclaimed.

23

'Yes. She's the one who looks after them. I have to go to work.'

We stared at him in silence.

'She was happy,' he insisted. 'We had it all planned out. We did everything she wanted. She wanted them to have all these pets and now –'

'What are you going to do?' I asked.

He shook his head, he seemed puzzled more than anything. 'They're going to move to Essex. He's bought a riding stables down there. I don't know about the animals.'

There wasn't much we could say. We packed up and paid him and wished him luck. I felt close to tears. Partly, I was sorry for him. He seemed not really to have taken it in, the way something that was humming along so happily could fall apart in a day. Also I was emotional about what Mark and I had done. I felt tremulous but satisfied, as if I had known all along it would work out as I hoped. But Mark said, 'I'm not convinced.'

'That his wife has left him?'

'Oh yes, I believe that. But that he's only known for a week.'

'That's why he didn't cancel us. It was too short notice, he didn't know what to do.'

'Think about the dog. A dog doesn't get like that in a week.'

I thought about the dog. After I'd thought about the dog, I thought about the fridge, and imagined him going through it chucking out all the half-eaten pots of yoghurt and the bendy carrot sticks and sweet sticky childish drinks, binning the opened jars and packets, wiping out the food history of his family. And I thought, you wouldn't do that if you hoped they'd come back. I had the edge of a nervous feeling about what Mark and I had done, as if I was getting my way by sleight of hand, as if I was trying to take what could never belong to me.

I thought how happy his wife was supposed to have

been. I tried to imagine the house ringing with childish laughter, the pets frisky, a song on the radio in the kitchen. Instead I saw her stripping the beds after the paying guests had left, and the washing machine churning, and limp sheets on the line every afternoon. Her in rubber gloves, cleaning out the hamster and the rabbits. I thought no wonder she's riding off into the blue. I felt sad for them, but still more than anything I was glad. Glad, glad, glad about my baby.

Which was really, I decided, the only part of all this that was worth telling to my daughter. If I told Lizzy the truth of it, wouldn't she find herself thinking of her own existence as somehow provisional? Might she imagine herself to be the result of a domestic crisis amongst strangers? I wanted her to believe her conception was four-square and planned for, the product of the sort of thing other people construct their lives on; commitment, vision, love. 'We were happy there,' I said. 'The owners had two toddlers and a beautiful baby, and a whole menagerie of pets. The place was full of life. It clinched something – we both knew we really wanted you.'

Lizzy flushed and smiled at me. 'That makes me so glad – to know it was a happy start.' Her face was like a flower.

'Me too,' I said.

Morphogenesis

HE IS TEN years old, hot, with itchy grass seed sticking through his socks. The glittering loch lies behind him; up here he's surrounded by a sea of purple heather. He's come to a standstill by the bothy, which is at the intersection of 52 bee flight paths and now his body is pinging his still-computing brain with messages: lungs gasping for oxygen, left heel sore where the new shoe rubs; ears tuning in to the intensifying buzz; eyes – scanning... yes! Fix on the crack beside the corner post where bees are alighting, crawling in, crawling out, taking flight. It's at shoulder height. He can get the honey, easy. As he watches their angular dances, the thudding of his heart recedes and his bladder gives a plaintive twinge. Unbuttoning his flies with his right hand and grasping his penis with his left, he aims at the base of the corner post, drilling a hole in the dust with his pee, splashing darkly up the wood. The hot ammonia smell rises intensely for a moment then mingles with the heather and dust, dilutes, diffuses, fades into the summer air. When the pee has evaporated, it will leave that little ridged circle in the dust which it has turned to mud. Like a volcano crater. It was part of him, that pee. Cells from inside him will be left there in the mud. And when it dries completely, and the dust gets blown by the wind, and a speck of the dust falls to the ground by this heather plant, and the heather drops a seed which sprouts from that dust which was partly made by his pee, will the heather have his cells in it? Will the honey, made by the bee who collects the pollen from the flower that has grown from the pee-dust? And if he came back and ate that honey,

27

would a bit of it recognise it had come home?

He buttons himself up and crouches to look at the shape of the pee-crater; now the heather is at eye level and he notices a white flower. Five petals, veined and tender as eyelids: fairy flax. A white star against the dark peat. He stares at its perfect shape. Five petals equally spaced around the yellow centre; how does it *know*? How does it know to grow like that? And not dark and knobbly-secret like the heather? How does it know to grow its simple open face; how, when it is nothing but green mush in the stem, does it know to unfold in the same perfectly recognisable pattern, every time? A human being, with all the cleverness in the world, couldn't make a thing that grew to that shape. Unless he planted a seed. Alan laughs. So the seed knows all that. In code, probably. He recites to himself from his new book, *Natural Wonders Every Child Should Know*. It is the best book he has ever read, but the things it doesn't know are the things that echo for the longest. 'We are made of little living bricks. When we grow it is because these living bricks divide into half bricks, and then grow into whole ones again. But how they find out when and where to grow fast, and when and where to grow slowly, and when and where not to grow at all, is precisely what no one has yet made the smallest beginning at finding out.'

Yet. He scrambles up. Now he will get the honey.

*

He's sixteen. Sitting at the far end of the library, at the one table which can't be seen from the librarian's desk; screened by Reference. Their table, his and Chris's. He's tearing through a Latin translation with the wretched pen splattering and blotching all over the page as per usual, and focusing on precisely how many things the Stanster got wrong in Maths, and the door's swung open twice now but it's not Chris yet. His knee's jiggling and stomach a bit fluttery but under control, he will be able to tell when Chris opens the door without looking up, he'll sense him. Compluribus expugnatis oppidis Caesar: Caesar, having captured many of their towns, perceiving that injury could not be done to them, determined to wait for his fleet. He needn't have bothered, it would have happened anyway, whatever was going to happen. The idea that Caesar could have changed it is impossible, he was only programmed to do exactly as he did – but is Alan? Only programmed to sit here waiting for Chris hardly daring to breathe because he's not here yet? And why is he so agonisingly jumpy when whatever happens was always going to happen anyway?

Every embryo develops from two cells into a precisely ordained human shape: history is no more than the unrolling of a prefigured series of events. The illusion of choice is simply ignorance. Thinking only happens through not-knowing. Yesterday evening, he and Chris sat here doing prep together and he put his fingertips (right hand, index and middle fingers) onto Chris's naked wrist to draw his attention to a diagram, and Chris glanced up and smiled into his eyes. So that if he wanted Alan could have slipped his fingers right around the marble-cool wrist and encircled it so that both of them really knew and didn't have to be breathless with panic anymore. But he didn't. Because he's so pathetically afraid of Chris jumping away in disgust. And because he's afraid, he never *will* touch Chris like that, and nothing will ever happen, because his destiny is in his cells as much as his hair growing back the same sandy colour each time one falls out. The thinking happens now because his brain still pretends there are choices. That he still might manage to plan to touch Chris and not bottle at the last moment. That he might do it. And if he does, then the history will be different. Which, therefore, it was always going to be. He can't read his own writing. Although turrets were built, yet the height of the stems of the barbarian ships exceeded these … stems? Puppium, *sterns*, idiot.

Chris is here. Alan can feel him. A moving cohort of

29

intensely dense matter, drawing in all around it through its gravitational pull. His own head, without his volition, tilts up like a puppet's to greet Chris. Who nods curtly and slips into the seat beside Alan, leading every cell in the right side of Alan's body to yearn towards his radiance, a field of sunflowers turning their faces to the sun. 'Stanster!' Chris mutters in disgust, and they both laugh.

'You know the Fibonacci numbers?' Alan spills it out before there's time for him to seize up. '1, 1, 2, 3, 5, 8, 13 – you know?'

'Each one's the sum of the previous two?'

'Yes. They're replicated in fir cones. Look.' His fingers close around the cone in his pocket. It has half opened in the warmth. He sets it on the desk between them. This was this fir cone's destiny. Not only to grow its spiral patterning in exact Fibonacci sequence, but to be delivered as an offering unto the young god Chris, to sit upon this library desk alone of all its species, exemplar.

'Look, start at the bottom.' He turns the fir cone, counting, demonstrates. Chris takes it from him, holding it with his long cool fingers, turning it delicately as he inspects. Alan imagines Chris's long cool fingers touching him – there – no, no! Blocking it blocking it desperately blocking it and edging his chair closer under the table to hide himself.

He has control. But something has shifted in his head. Something has shifted into its rightful place. Knowledge. Recognition of the inevitable, bringing joy. He won't be afraid any more. Because it will happen. As surely as that fir cone grew into a fir cone. This is what he, Alan Turing, is.

*

He is seventeen. One week ago, on Thursday February 13th 1930, Chris Morcom aged eighteen died of bovine tuberculosis. Now it is 3am.

Alan kneels by the dormitory window, balancing his

telescope on the window sill. Behind him the syncopated breaths of the sleeping boys rise and fall. The sky is clear, stars pulsing. Alan puts his right eye to the eyepiece and has the swimmy sensation of falling out through the black cylinder into space, as a star looms towards him. Which is it? He can't remember, the vast unknowability of the heavens lurches at him sickeningly. Raising his face he looks again with the naked eye and the stars settle into the names and patterns Chris has taught him: Cassiopeia, Perseus, Ursa Major, Ursa Minor, Polaris – the Pole Star. He feels Chris's confident presence at his shoulder. 'There, Turing. Work from left to right. Use the church spire as your direction finder. Slow down, you are always in such a tearing hurry, you mad oaf.'

Chris is here; Alan's brain reports that as objectively as it notes the sharp brilliance of the stars and the grainy chill of the dormitory floorboards impressing their patterns on his knees through his old pyjamas. It is fact enough for him to assert it both to his own mother, and to Chris's; and for it to drive him, in a few weeks' time, to a written explanation: 'As regards the actual connection between spirit and body I consider that the body by reason of being a living body can 'attract' and hold onto a 'spirit'; whilst the two are alive and awake the two are firmly connected. When the body is asleep I cannot guess what happens but when the body dies the 'mechanism' of the body, holding the spirit is gone and the spirit finds a new body sooner or later perhaps immediately.' In Chris's case the spirit is attracted – by reason of their similarity – to Alan's. 'I feel sure that I shall meet Morcom again somewhere and that there will be some work for us to do together, as I believed there was for us to do here. Now that I am left to do it alone I must not let him down.'

But a spirit is not a body. Kneeling stiffly on the cold floorboards Alan feels as ancient and distant as the stars he is watching. He must hold his course and shine, even though there is nothing around him but cold black void. He must do his best to shine. Because what else is life for?

31

★

He's thirty-eight. This is the idea that has been coming – moving towards him through the mists of unknowing – all his life. It follows a pattern; as all ideas must. Since it is a theory, in which that which we term real (by the evidence of our senses, which are themselves a system of invisible electro-chemical reactions) is represented by mathematical formulae, it is capable of proof. Here is a shell, brown and creamy white, striated in wave patterns of deeper and paler colour. He cups it in his hand, then touches its cool curve to his cheek. Passes it under his nostrils and takes in the faintest breath of the sea. Sight, touch, smell: three of his senses bear witness. His theory explains the mechanism by which the striations occur. And in grasping this, he sees, he has grasped the mechanism which gives shape to all living things.

It is not a discovery: it is not new. But to give it a mathematical proof will be new, and will create a space for other thinkers, chemists and biologists who do not like to mingle, to explore in search of physical proofs. They can devise experiments to provide all the evidence the literal-minded need.

He does not think it is *his* idea. Well, it is not an idea, but part of the truth lying out there waiting to be uncovered. If it is anyone's maybe it is Eddington's. And Chris has been at his side in this, this is what Chris would have discovered: no, through the agency of Turing, *has* discovered. Though Alan no longer fully believes in the inevitable – as was, perhaps, inevitable.

He read Eddington a long time ago – when Chris was still alive. *Science and the Unseen World* – they sparred at it together, unwilling to be convinced by Eddington's religiosity. There are sentences he absorbed; words and images laid down in his memory, in chemical sequences in the grey tissue inside his skull, buried treasure uncalled-upon for twenty-odd years, and now resurfacing in his conscious mind: Eddington's description of the formation of the universe.

'The void is sparsely broken by tiny electric particles, the germs of things that are to be … The years roll by, million after million. Slight aggregations occurring casually in one place and another drew to themselves more and more particles, until the matter was collected round centres of condensation leaving vast empty spaces from which it had ebbed away. Thus gravitation slowly parted the primeval chaos.' From homogeneity to shape and not-shape. From diffusion to concentration. From smooth to lumpy. From chaos to pattern.

And the Earth was without form, and void; and darkness was upon the face of the deep. And the spirit of God moved upon the face of the waters; And God said, Let there be light.

It is a metaphor which has been used before. And will be reused again when he is gone. But Alan is here in this moment in time and able to formulate it in this precise way. Which is a raid on the unknown. He has turned the opening sentences of his paper in his mind for days. The claim is so large the language must be modest: 'The purpose of this paper is to discuss a possible mechanism by which the genes of a zygote may determine the anatomical structure of the resulting organism.' A chemical and mathematical explanation of the *mechanism* which permits a bundle of tissue to develop in this direction, and that, and that, and that, forming the buds of four distinct limbs: and not to develop (in the case of a human being) four more; but only to do that in the case of an octopus.

'We are made of little living bricks. When we grow it is because these living bricks divide into half bricks, and then grow into whole ones again. But how they find out when and where to grow fast, and when and where to grow slowly, and when and where not to grow at all, is precisely what no one has yet made the smallest beginning at finding out.'

But now he has. And he's right. He knows it in every

living brick of his body. Which, like every other living form, has obediently grown into its correct predestined shape thanks to the controlling genius of the reaction and diffusion of morphogens, as he has named them; those chemicals which inhibit growth here, foster it there, by switching on or off the potentialities within each individual cell.

'Each morphogen moves from regions of greater to regions of less concentration, at a rate proportional to the gradient of concentration, and also proportional to the diffusability of the substance.' Because nothing is perfectly homogenous. And the slightest disequilibrium, the slightest imbalance or intrusion of an external factor – heat, gravity, motion, anything – generates an appropriate instability, enabling diffusion and reaction, triggering that slow and never-ending process, the tendency of all living matter to shape and form, the tendency of chaos to become order.

Morphogenesis. The budding and flowering of a shape from an indistinguishable mass of cells. Not by the hand of God, but by the simple, mechanical reaction and diffusion of chemicals. Moving into the cells, flicking switches, as a man might enter his house and turn on the lights.

*

He's thirty-nine. He's brought Arthur back to his room and now there's the tremendous awkwardness, as ever, of how to proceed. Arthur's a good-looking chap but now he seems disgruntled, peering into the jars and bottles on the shelves, fingering shells and cones from the mantelpiece as if he expects them to be something more than they are. Sniffing. It does smell, even Alan can detect that. The gas. But also ammonia, formaldehyde, cyanide, iodine, there's a lot of admixture in the air he breathes. The thought of it in Arthur's lungs makes his own breath quicken.

'What's this?'

'A mixture of chemicals. I'm waiting for them to react

– they react very slowly – to form a pattern.'

'Why?' asks Arthur.

Is he interested? Playing for time? Does he want to be here, or is it just the thought of the money? He's got the kind of looks women go for too.

'I'm not stupid you know,' says Arthur in an aggrieved tone. 'You can explain it to me.'

'Alright, I will.' Kneeling, Alan puts a match to the fire Mrs Clayton has laid. The flame nibbles at a corner of newspaper, leaps forward into the nest of dry twigs, and begins to crackle through them. He picks up a shiny lump of coal and sets it in the centre of the blaze, relishing the wash of heat over his bare hand. 'I've written a paper on morphogenesis. Which means, how things get their shape.'

'I know what it means,' says Arthur sulkily, and Alan wants to laugh. Laugh and put his arms around the boy. No one knows what it means. Only him.

'Well then. If you take an egg – a human egg – that's just been fertilised, it grows into a sphere. The cells multiply and they grow into a sphere.'

'Right.'

'But when you are born – when one is born, one is not spherical.'

'Bleedin' obvious.' He's turned away from the jars and is moving towards Alan and the fire. The firelight makes his handsome face glow.

'So the question I wanted to solve was, what makes the sphere grow into a different shape?'

'What does?'

Alan hasn't been expecting another question. Nor that Arthur will fling himself into the armchair to ask it, rather than continuing his advance upon Alan, who has held his position, weak with desire, on the hearth rug. 'Do you really want to know?'

'Yeah.' There is something in his tone of frank acknowledgement, almost surprised acknowledgement, and

35

gruffness at himself for acknowledging it, and within that gruffness a gentleness of concession to Alan, so that the 'yeah' has a wondering as well as a rude 'it's obvious' quality: so many slender and contradictory threads of meaning intertwined in the utterance that Alan quite loses his heart.

'Well then. There are chemicals – I call them morphogens – within the cells. They diffuse through the cell walls and react with one another. The reactions cause some of them to intensify, others to diminish. This affects the genetic content of the cells, so that some develop and multiply and others are inhibited. Does that make sense to you?'

'Yeah.' A single note to this one. Defiance. Which means he probably doesn't understand. Alan puts more coal on the fire.

'Do you know what gastrulation is?'

'No.'

'Within the sphere, the first development of the zygote – the tiny tiny baby – is that a groove develops. There's a perfect sphere, then a groove. The groove determines which end the head is. It's not a sphere, it's not even symmetrical, so what makes that happen? What makes a sphere change shape? The individual motion of molecules, caused by the triggering of the morphogens: all those cells in the sphere were the same, but now they're changing, some are replicating and some are not, they've been given their instructions – chemically.'

'Right you are.' Now he sounds unconcerned. Alan wonders if it's enough. The fire is beginning to make heat. He allows himself to topple onto all fours and crawls to Arthur's chair.

'Lesson over?' he says.

After a tiny pause, Arthur smiles. He puts his Judas hand on Alan's head.

★

36

He's forty-one. If he is meant to die he will be dead. The illusion of choice is simply lack of knowledge. Living cells at death transform into another state. Christopher has been in that state for 24 years, and has remained a constant companion. There is nothing shameful in joining him now. There is nothing shameful in staying alive but he'll never be able to pick up another Arthur, now Her Majesty's Government are so interested in his private life. At death his body will degrade and metamorphose into a range of other useful substances. The knowledge generated by his brain will continue to diffuse through the lectures, papers and computing machines he has authored. Diffusion continues long after the agent has ceased. The diffusion is complex, containing many elements of other men's thinking (Eddington, Chris, all those living and dead with whom his brain has engaged and reacted) and the diffusion will – in the nature of diffusion – continue to spread and be altered by the reactions of other men, until it is so dilute as to be scarcely recognisable as anything of his. One cell in a pot of honey. He smiles. There will be a meteorologist called Edward Lorenz who will discover that the tiniest alteration in initial conditions can drastically change the long term behaviour of a system, who will ask, 'Does the flap of a butterfly's wings in Brazil set off a tornado in Texas?' knowing consciously – or maybe not knowing, except by background diffusion – Alan's vision of appropriate instability. And after Lorenz there will be all the exponents of Chaos Theory, and after them another wave of seekers after truth, and the waves will lap on and out in regular irregularity through time towards an end he cannot fathom. His own physical part in this pantomime is done. The law will not allow him to be the man his own cells tell him he is, so now he will offer those rebel cells the chance of escape, which they will probably prefer, to the chemical restraints recently imposed upon them by HMG. He will try the effects of cyanide upon his system.

A radical alteration occurs when, through reaction and

diffusion, a tipping point is reached, and the changes which have been occurring one light switch at a time, one room at a time, in one single street, are multiplied across cities, countries, a continent, as a million million lights go on and in one mighty flash, blow the grid, and fade to black.

Where are You, Stevie?

AMANDA

I ALLOWED MYSELF to hope the switch-on might not be till December the third, with Christmas being on a Tuesday. But it's in tonight's paper; Monday, in four days. I shall go mad. I need to try a different tack with the council – pretend to be someone else. That would lend me more weight. I mean, lend weight to my original letters, the letters I wrote from me.

> *Dear Sir or Madam,*
>
> *It has come to my attention that the Christmas music will be switched on in The Planets shopping centre on Monday 26 November. As a regular customer I should like to point out that the loop of Christmas jingles is highly repetitive and plays at a distressingly loud volume. This is off-putting for the public and must surely have a deleterious effect on the health and tempers of shop workers. In particular I have noticed the speakers positioned at first floor level, under the windows of the offices of Grotton and Smallwood estate agents, and I imagine the volume in that office must be really quite intolerable, even to the point of affecting the mental health of employees. Surely this contravenes legislation on noise pollution?*

Right. As if they give a toss. Rehearsal at 7.30. I need to get going. *You-will-get-a-sentimental-feeling-when-you-hear-Christmas-time-so-let's-be-jolly-Deck-the-halls-with-* Oh for heaven's sake stop: if you're like this *before* November 26th, how are you going to be afterwards? How will you be at, 'Yes, a lovely little cottage-style home with newly fitted kitchen, laminate floors throughout, gas CH and *Here-comes-Santa-Claus*?' It's still looping round my head from last year. Blot it out. Blot, Amanda, blot. What am I taking to the rehearsal? Script, glasses, pencil. Some decent biscuits, and rooibos tea bags. What else? *Have-yourself-a-merry-little-Xmas-Let-your-heart-be-light-* What *else*?

Focus. Focus. Think about the rehearsal. That's right. The set; those ridiculous yellow painted curtains with folds like iron bars. Trying to mimic drapes. That strange youth who's painting them, Steve. Who clearly should be behind bars himself.

Did Harriet really imagine that a few evenings set-painting while a bunch of middle-class thespians made a spectacle of themselves, would repair sixteen years of social and financial deprivation? Does she think her virtue is contagious? 'We'll be giving Stevie a chance to prove himself, to achieve something positive and gain some self respect.' Here we are, rolling up in our cars, griping about our jobs – why on earth does she imagine he started thieving in the first place? She comes to rehearsal with chicken kiev in her belly, with pasta carbonara. Then she offers him stewed tea and a digestive. Why couldn't she leave him in peace in the life he's used to? *Let-the-bells-ring-out-for-Christmas-Here-comes-Santa-Claus-here-*

I'm not going to sleep on Sunday night. I won't be able to go in to work on Monday morning. Eight hours of *Rockin-around-the-Christmas-tree* and then sixteen hours at home with it clanging madly in my head…

I didn't tell her I'd caught him red-handed. Any fool could've seen it coming. Any fool but Harriet. I nipped back to the green room for my inhaler during the second scene. Everyone else was onstage or watching. And there was Steve, with my bag in his hands. 'I was putting it back,' says he. 'Sorry, I knocked it off the chair.'

'Leave it alone,' I said. 'If you've taken anything I'm calling the police.' He left in a hurry. Yes, I thought to myself,

I bet it's burning a hole in your pocket. I went through my bag and when I opened my wallet £20 was missing. I'd taken £50 out of the cash machine at lunchtime and I hadn't done any shopping. But there was only one £10 note and one £20 left. Other people's bags were dumped on the table or by the wall – if he'd lifted £20 from each he'd have made a good haul. I just hope he took plenty from Harriet, since she's responsible for him.

Nobody mentioned they were short. Maybe mine was the first, maybe I interrupted his little spree. I wasn't going to say anything: not for £20, not when I couldn't prove it. Not when the boy should never have been there in the first place, with temptation put under his nose. He knew. He knew I knew. I suppose that's why he's not been back, dripping yellow paint all over the floor. Harriet worked herself up into a fine old lather last night but frankly I'm glad to see the back of him. I don't want to have to make a fool of myself going whining to the police about £20. He knew I'd got my eye on him, so he moved on. He's heading for jail whichever way he goes. *Here's-to-you-raise-a-glass-for-everyone-*

I should take bras. Harriet's asking for old bras for her Soroptimists club. There are some I haven't worn for years. But the way she chirrups, 'Ladies, this really super charity is collecting old bras. Sorry to disappoint, kind gentlemens, nothing to do with you!' If I could have cringed and curled up any tighter I'd have burst my own skin and turned back into an egg. 'Of all the charities I support, this is the bestest.' And lo, Saint Harriet saves the planet, with a triple whammy charity. For every kilo of old bras they give a pound to breast cancer research; they send the bras that aren't totally worn out to Africa, for 'poor women who, you know, never get a chance to have a decent bra'. Pity they don't get a chance to pelt do-gooders with their old knickers. And the really clapped-out bras get taken to pieces and all the parts recycled! Saving us all from drowning in a tidal wave of old bras. How can I resist?

Here goes. Triumph sports; yellow-grey, gone. Gossard

41

with blue lace, lumpy under a jumper, gone. Wonderbra, what was I thinking of? Gone. See-through Chantelle for a special occasion – who are you kidding Amanda?

But what if she looks? Imagine, after the rehearsal, her and Paul delving into the box: 'Oh let's see what poor old Amanda brought. My god, she fancies herself doesn't she? Reckon she's got a secret life? Hah hah hah!' No, that's uncharitable, Harriet wouldn't do that.

Alright, how will the Chantelle save the world? It weighs about as much as a feather. It's hardly the sort of garment that'll recommend itself to an impoverished drooping-boobed African woman. Unless she's a prostitute. Which if she's poverty-stricken she may well be, her life may depend on it. Do I want my bra to support African prostitution? On the other hand, how can you recycle something totally synthetic? Maybe if you melted it down you could make a blob of plasticky stuff. Binliner.

Shut up, Amanda, just shut up. This is how lives are wasted. *Have-a-holly-jolly-Christmas, It's-the-best-time-of-the-year-* Right. The bra rant provided all of three minutes off. This is why the play's a good idea. And dress rehearsal all Sunday. It may be a stupid waste of time but at least it gives me something else to worry about.

White noise. So now I'm forced to create it for myself? That's what the drama group is, white noise. Harriet rattling on like a collecting tin, filling the silence. Everyone spouting lines. And musak, jabber; earphones in, iPods on. Any sound, no matter how moronic, is better than silence. To them silence is never golden, it's black, a great black hole. *Have-a-holly-jolly-Christmas-It's-the-best-time-of-the-year-I-don't-know-if-there'll-be-snow-But-have-a-cup-of-cheer-Have-a-holly-jolly-* Dear Lord. My brain's polluted. I spend my time trying to drown out one kind of interference with another.

Imagine just sitting here. Imagine sitting here alone in the middle of the carpet, cross-legged, spine straight, body balanced and relaxed; emptying your head. And listening to the silence, with nothing breaking in. *Let-the-bells-ring-out-for-Christmas-* There you are. I'm better off rehearsing with that lot, than sitting alone in my blizzard of jingles just waiting for Monday morning. *Here's-to-you-raise-a-glass-for-everyone-Here's-to-them-underneath-that-burning-sun-Do-they-know-?* Stop it. Now, right now. OK.

I wish I hadn't told Harriet about the jingles. I keep myself to myself. I don't go around blabbing, interfering in people's lives, making white noise of myself hither and yon. I don't know why I allowed her to winkle it out of me. Why can't she leave people in peace when she sees they're troubled?

In the car going down to rehearsal it's not just one after another but one on top of another, over and over, a stampede of hooves pounding my soft grey brain. *Frosty-the-snowman-was-a-jolly-happy-soul-Here-comes-Santa-Claus-Here-comes-Santa-Claus-Right-down-It's-the-most-wonderful-time-of-the-year-There'll-be-much-mistletoeing-And-Hearts-will-be-glowing-Last-Christmas-I-gave-you-my-heart-But-the-very-next-day-* Could I get a doctor's note? You can't take three weeks off sick in December! But I just want to lock myself away. Lock myself away and hide. Surely my last letter to the council will have some effect?

Don't delude yourself. You're nothing but a crank, to them – some sort of hilarious Scrooge figure, probably an office joke. 'Hey, we've got another letter from the old bat who works in the estate agents in the precinct – you know, the saddo who doesn't like Christmas music?'

We're all in the same boat. But no one else at work seems to mind. Why am I the one who lies awake all night worrying and dreading, with these awful jingles pounding in my head? Every word of every ditty is engraved on my memory. Why must it be me who's so wretchedly sensitive she can't block it out? And why have I demeaned myself by babbling to Harriet? How can I retain a shred of self respect?

When I sidle into the rehearsal room she's waiting for me; sitting at her director's desk with a big silly smile on her face. 'Ah Amanda, well done, you're the first.'

Does she think I'm a child? That I want a pat on the back for being on time?

'Got any goodies for me?' She taps the cardboard bra box beside her table.

'I'll have a look tomorrow.'

'Super. Oh, that reminds me, I've got something for you.'

'For me?'

'Yes, here.' She ferrets in her handbag and passes me a tiny packet. 'They're awfully good, my son sends me them from the US of A. I've not seen them in the shops here.'

A little polythene bag with two crocus-yellow thimble-shaped objects inside.

'It's a kind of high-density sponge, it moulds itself to the shape of your eary-wig.'

I stare at her.

'For you to take to work. To block out that dreadful music.'

'Thank you.'

'I know what it's like. Malc snores like a lion. I'd go mad without my eary-plugs.'

'But don't you need them yourself?'

'Pauly sent me a new pack of six. Try them – go on!'

I unseal the little bag and press one squashy plug into each ear. Harriet smiles and nods. I see her lips are moving, but I don't hear her. I am cocooned from the sound. I am encased in a golden casket of silence. 'They work,' I say, and my voice booms hollowly inside my head. 'Oh Harriet, thank you! They work!' I take them out and she's saying:

'(I knew) you'd like them. They're more comfy than any others I've tried – and I've tried them all, I tellee true.'

'But it's so kind of you!' I have quite a lump in my throat.

I'm crossing the stage to put my bag away when she calls me back. 'Amanda? I've got some very sad news. About Stevie. Well, maybe best wait till everyone is here, then I can tell you all together –'

'In trouble with the law?'

She purses her lips. 'I only wish he was.'

'What then?'

'He's – the poor boy's passed away.'

'What d'you mean?'

She doesn't seem able to reply.

'He's had an accident?'

She nods and turns her head as Gerry bobs in the door.

I fumble my way into the green room and switch on the lights. They are too bright. Harriet has been very kind. I can't seem to see very well; my eyes are stinging. The boy Steve is dead? I have to sit down. What on Earth is wrong with me? Who are these tears for?

Have-yourself-a-merry-little-Xmas-Let-your-heart-be-light-

I seem – I seem to have forgotten what kindness is.

MAGGIE

I GIVE HIM the choice. I said, you can come and live with me, Stevie. But I'm not having her. I'm not having your mother and her sneaking and thieving and caterwauling, not under my roof. Never again. I've got your grandpa to consider. D'you not think he deserves a bit of peace and quiet at his age? It was nowt when we wed, me being ten years younger, but he's an old man now – eighty-seven. I've got to think for both of us. D'you not think she hasn't broken his heart?

She were the apple of his eye when she were young, and she knew it. On a summer's day he'd take her out walking, with a picnic and dog, and I'd not see hide nor hair of them till gone six. What've you been playing at? I asked when they came for their teas. Paddling in the beck, building a dam, playing hide and seek. What about them walls? I said. Aye, that too, he says, tha's helped me build a wall missy, hasn't tha?

I thought as I should have another lad. A lad to help him in his old age. Not that a lass couldn't – but not our lass. I wanted a lad, to make up for the one I'd lost. A lad for me, a lass for Jed. If she were Daddy's girl, what's left for Mummy? I wanted a lad because lads are straight and girls are crooked. I know – I know, because I've been one. But never such as one as her we've been saddled with.

Last time she were here – a couple of year ago now – she sat on that sofa and never stirred all day. 'Can you not lift a finger to help?' I said. 'What do you want me to do, Mother?' like I was asking for the moon. 'Anything you like, Julie, there's always work on a farm. Your father's struggling with his veg right now, his back's too stiff for weeding, you could give him a hand in garden.' 'I don't know which are weeds and which are plants, I'd pull up all the wrong ones.'

She sat and she sat and it were only in the afternoon I realised she were sipping her way through his brandy and slipping the bottle behind sofa cushions when I went in. I said have you no shame? Look what your father's done for you: out in all weathers, up half the night with lambing, soaking in filthy sheep-dip, hefting stones into walls – look out the window, I said – I grabbed her and made her look. Look at that hillside my lady – barn, ditches, walls, gates, sheep, he's made all that with his bare hands, and what have you got to show for yourself?

'Lucky, isn't he?' says she. 'To have made all that. Only thing I'm good at is drinking.'

It's not the ingratitude, it's the waste, that's what gets me. She's not stupid; she *was* pretty, still could be if she tried. She could've done owt. But from the minute she started at that school it were nowt but lies and messing about with lads, and slyness and secrets. Staying over with her mates in Uppermill and Dobcross! And me too wet behind the ears to twig what she were up to, until it were too late.

I went to her room that morning. I'll never forget it. Sunday morning, the sun were already up over the hill, slanting in through the windows. She were seventeen. One year older than I were when. It were a rare treat to see her home at weekend, and I took her a mug of tea in bed. She was as white as her pillow. 'What's up?' I asked her. And she jumps out of bed and runs to bathroom. I heard her retching. I sat on th'end of her bed with sunlight sharp in my eyes, and I listened. Pitched me back forty years, like you'd slip down a well. Nausea rising in my throat, terror stopping me windpipe. But *my* mam knew afore I did: 'I know what ails you, my girl. I'll ask you no questions, you tell me no lies.' She knew full well. His bony hand over my mouth, his harsh breathing in my ear. *You tell anyone, I'll kill you girl.*

When Julie come creeping back she crawled into bed and I passed her her tea. When I could draw breath I asked her, 'Who?'

'Who what?'

'Don't mess with me, lady. Who?' I knew it weren't Jed. I knew it weren't. He weren't that type of man. That's why I married him.

'John.'

'John who?'

'John Hadfield.'

'Mike Hadfield's lad? As is engaged to Melanie?'

'Yes.'

Lightning don't strike twice. My heart leapt in my chest, so I slapped her. 'Well you filthy little slut.'

Her tea sloped onto the sheet and she began to cry. I hauled her up and stripped the bed afore it soaked through and stained mattress, and she stood there snivelling in the cold in her pyjamas. What did she have to cry for? Nowt. Nowt compared to what I went through. I took her to the doctor, he arranged the lot. I drove her to the clinic and I sat and waited while she had it done. In and out in under an hour.

Mam's taxi service both ways. She started snivelling in the car on the way home and I nearly said to her, 'You don't know you're born my girl. You don't know the half of it, you mucky little tramp.' Maybe I should've told her. Maybe I should've told her about being in labour for twelve hours with never a kind word, and about that first cry that brands your heart like Jed brands ewes with the red hot iron. Maybe I should have told her I asked if I could see babby and they said, *No you can't see him*, and so I knew it were a boy, when some of the girls in there never even knew what they'd had. Maybe if I'd told her she wouldn't have felt so sorry for herself, and she might've thought about someone else for once in her life, and mended her ways.

Once a slut always a slut. She got rid of two more to my knowledge, before she had Stevie. But she sorted them herself, I'd washed my hands of her by then.

My lad. My lad would've been like Stevie. I know it in my gut. First time she brung him home I knew he were spit of the lad they took off me. He smiled and summat flared up inside me. She were a crap mother. I'm not saying as you should treat a babby like it's made of glass. But she was that careless with him, it's a wonder he survived at all. I said, 'You can get cream for cradle cap.' She said, 'Go ahead.' I said, 'You're wasting a fortune on them disposable nappies.' She laughed. She kept him up till all hours. I said, 'If you don't get him into a routine now there'll be hell to pay later.' She said, 'Like you paid with me?' When she went out I bathed him and changed him and washed his mucky clothes, and he was the sweetest natured baby you ever saw, laughing at the whole world. I took him out and showed him the fields and lambs and sky and told him it was all for him. I said to her, 'You don't know you're born.' And she gave that nasty grin of hers and said 'Nor does Stevie, do you babes?' and I thought there's no justice on this earth, why has she got him?

He come to us for holidays, right up to his fifteenth birthday. When she was bad I went and picked him up; I saw the state. Bottles. Cans. Filth. I said to her, you're not fit to bring up a child. Like a pig in muck. She said go on then, I dare you, call the social. They'll put him in care in no time. *You* won't get him, you interfering old bag.

When he were here, he were the lad we should've had, Jed and me. Up on barn roof helping replace that rotten beam: out with dog rounding up ewes for tuppin; he helped Jed asphalt the yard so's the truck could come down to the pens; he'd turn his hand to owt around the house. He liked to sit on the back step at night, watching the sky, waiting for a shooting star. Jed taught him names of the constellations, as he'd learned when he were a lad. When it come time for me to take him back to her he were quiet. I said, 'Would you like to stay, Stevie?' and he shook his head. But he sat in front of fire with his arms round dog, like someone was trying to part him from his best friend in all the world. I said, 'I can ring your Mam, Stevie, and ask for you to stay another week.'

'No.' He were afraid. Afraid of what'd happen to her if he left her too long on her own.

One time I went there and she were sober, leafing through paper for a job. I said, 'Run out of booze have you?' She called me a bitch. I said 'I'll have Stevie for you if you want. You can get any job then – move away if you have to.'

'Oh that would suit you fine wouldn't it? For your daughter to vanish and your grandson to move in. You should be so lucky!'

I never have been lucky.

I knew she were getting worse because she started asking me for money again. Phoning up asking for money and swearing at me. In the summer I said to Stevie, 'You've done your best, son. She'll never change. You want to get your exams and go to college, you'd be better off moving up here with Granddad and me. I don't mind running you down to bus stop.'

'Can Mum come too?'

'No.'

Next thing I hear, he's in juvenile court for theft. Car

radios. I know what they thought. His mother's a bad lot, so he's a bad lot. But it wasn't so. It wouldn't surprise me if he weren't stealing for her: she never could manage money, God knows what they lived on half the time. When the lad came to us he looked as if he hadn't had a square meal in months. I used to cook and cook for him, Jed'd rag him and say, 'You better come more often, lad, grub's better when you visit!' He got off with probation – I tried again to get him to come to us, and he said only if I'd take Julie back. 'She's ill. She can't be left on her own,' he said. 'I can't leave her on her own.' Well, he's left her now alright.

I'm shedding no more tears. I broke my heart over my own lad. His cry still wakes me in the dead of night, when all the world's asleep. I take myself off downstairs and warm a cup of milk, and my ears hunt his cry to cradle it, soft. To catch it and cradle it in.

Jed's a good man. I were cracked and cold inside but he give me time. Then Stevie lit that little pilot light in my heart again, and I had a lad to love. I couldn't do what he wanted when he was here so I've got to do it now. I reckon Stevie knew that, I reckon when she drove him to the limit, he knew that. She's up in her old room; been there all week. She's quiet now, after all that roaring and carrying on last night. Well, I gave her the sherry. She asks for him. I tell her I don't know where he is. That's all I need to say. It's the truth.

LISA

I DON'T KNOW what to say. I mean, I'm grief stricken and all that – look, I am, right? We'd been going together for two months and I'm sorry he's dead. But how'm I supposed to behave? It's not like we were married. Everyone's going *You must be heartbroken*.

They tip-toe round you like you were made of ice and if they so much as breathed near you you'd crack and melt into a waterfall of tiny tears. Which even if you were ice, you wouldn't. The crying thing… I don't – I don't understand it. When Jenny rang me *she* was crying and I started blubbing before she even told me, out of sheer fright, and when I found out what it was – I just dried up. Like he wasn't worth my tears.

Hahaha. Right, I'm heartless. Just totally without human emotions, I'm a cyborg or something, I don't care what happens to anyone, OK? Bring it on, doom, disaster, death! You won't squeeze one tear out of me.

I think I should be thinking about him and remembering him and stuff. But a million other things just keep popping into my head. I can't – I mean, just now, for example, when I said about being made of ice, I was thinking about those ice sculptures Dad took me to in Canada, on Lake Louise. Carved out of huge chunks of ice solid as rock, set out for a competition on the frozen lake. There was a Sleeping Beauty in a four poster bed – life size, a girl like me – and you could see every detail – no, really, like her fingernails, her eyelashes, like you really could touch her and she'd wake up – and the curtains on the bed, drapes they call them in Canada, the drapes were so soft you couldn't believe they'd been chiselled out of ice. I'd show you, but the light was too bright for my cheapo camera.

But why am I even talking about that? You see, it's ridiculous. I'm just a totally trivial person. I'm going to think about Stevie. Right. The day I met him. At college, first week of term, and that headbanging cafeteria where you have to scan five hundred tables of yada yada to see if there's a single face you recognise, and the longer you stand there scanning the more it looks like you're Johnny No-Mates, and if you spot someone vaguely familiar who might have been in one of your classes and you head for them, they'll know you're a social misfit. I *was* looking for Ali, but standing there was totally embarrassing and I just had to make myself march up to some random table and bang my tray down and ask this

51

lad if the seat by him was taken. And he goes, 'All yours.' That was Steve. I didn't fancy him or anything, I didn't even look at him, I just wanted to sit down and melt into the crowd. All I noticed was his hands, they were spattered in yellow paint. Then the other kids got up and there was only me and him left at the table. And when he'd hoovered up all his chips and practically scraped the glaze off his plate he said 'You new too?' So we had that boring *what school did you go to blah* conversation. Not exactly romance of the year! In fact apart from the paint, which was slightly interesting because he said he got it painting scenery, the main reason I remembered him was totally skank. I'd got cheese and onion pasty and salad and I left half the pasty and he went, 'If you don't want that can I have it?' so I went *right*, and he goes 'I'm saving the planet. I'm a food recycling centre.' So I go, 'What are you recycling it into?' and he looks quite surprised and goes, 'What d'you think? Poo.' Haha. It wasn't even funny.

I don't *know* anyone who's dead. I've never been to a funeral. I don't know how you make yourself believe someone's dead. Maybe when you see a coffin – but they won't, well – they're doing a thing, autopsy, to confirm cause of death, so I don't know when the funeral will be. I don't want to go to it anyway, it'll be awful. I've seen in films, the coffin starts sliding along on its own like your shopping going towards the checkout at Tesco's. It goes through these red curtains and vanishes. Checkout without passing the till. See? I'll giggle, I'll be so embarrassed I'll snort with laughter and everyone will hate me.

The thing I don't get is, *anyone* can go away. For a weekend, on holiday, move house, they can emigrate to a whole different country if they want, can't they? And then you don't see them. And it's just the same as if they were dead. I mean, they might send the odd email or Christmas card, OK, which you wouldn't get if they were dead – but you know what I mean. So how d'you convince your brain that you're never going to see a dead person again? That it's not just that you *can't* see them, but that they don't exist? It's like when you're a kid playing at hiding and you think if you cover up your own eyes, no one else can see you. Stevie has covered up his own eyes and it really does mean no one else *can* see him. Oh I wish I would just stop *thinking*.

There's something I... look. I don't believe in ghosts. This morning Mum said 'Lise I've got to go to work, why don't you try going in to college?' I don't want to go to college. Everyone staring and pointing, and going *That's his girlfriend*? Or waiting to see if I'm going to start skriking, or carefully asking if I'm alright, or walking round me like I'm a road accident? I don't ever want to go to college again. And then she said she'd ask Jenny to come round so I said, 'I'm fine Mum, I'd rather be on my own.' When she left I just had this feeling... it wasn't, how can I describe it? I really wanted to *know*. Because I thought, if I can believe it's real, I'll react properly. Instead of acting like I'm in a film of someone else's life. So I turned off the radio.

It's a bit mental, but after the radio I turned off the DVD player, because it was buzzing, and the central heating because of that churning noise. I put the washing machine on *pause* before the spin cycle, I went round the house like some kind of obsessive/compulsive freak, tightening the taps so they didn't drip and switching off the whining fluorescent in the kitchen and even unplugging the fridge when it started juddering. And then I stood in the front room and tried to think to him: like, Where *are* you, Stevie? Really, *where*? He can't have got that far away yet, he can't have gone beyond Earth's atmosphere. Only there's this continual hum from outside, you know? Traffic, planes, other people's music, birds singing dogs barking cows farting, this constant background grumble, the whole world's grumbling, and you're thinking just stop for one minute – if you'll only stop for *one minute* so I can hear him –

Well. You must think I'm a right nutter. I am. An idiot. No, worse, actually. Worse than an idiot. More like a murderer. He asked me to go with him on Saturday night, and I said no. If I hadn't said no he'd probably be alive right now. So, if you really want to know, it's my fault.

And why did I say no? I'll tell you now, it's not a good reason.

It was our first row. Friday night; we'd got a bottle of cider (which I paid for) and we'd walked halfway round the reservoir, looking at the stars and all those electronic winking things, satellites, radars, space probes. He's into all that. He was. He was talking about all the messages bouncing around up there, weather reports and top secret military stuff and plane guidance systems and everyone's texts and phone calls and scientific data and radio waves and how amazing it is none of it gets mixed up. He said, each message finds its home. It was good but I was freezing. As we were walking back he said *Tomorrow night let's go round to John's.* I said *Why can't we go clubbing?* and he said, *You know I haven't got any money* and I said *You can never afford to go anywhere proper* and he said *But my Mum* – and I said *I'm sick of your Mum.* I told him I was cold so I was getting the bus. I knew he didn't have his busfare and I just got on the bus and left him behind. Then on Saturday night I went to Sarah's. Her mum'd had a clear out and there was this heap of vintage clothes. So that's what I was doing, I was with Sarah, trying on her mum's old jackets and skirts, while Steve was – doing that. And now I've got a Biba top and a long skirt cut on the cross, black and grey panels, flared.

Instead of Stevie. A skirt instead of a boyfriend.

It's not funny. And he didn't kill himself. It was an accident. Accidental overdose. But what if it wasn't? What if they find out it couldn't have been an accident; am I the one they'll question? We've only been going out two months! I didn't say we should split up or anything, I texted him from Sarah's while I was wearing that skirt. 'Soz' and a smiley, and 'C u 2moz xoxo'. But I don't know if he got it. I don't know what time he –

He didn't *do* drugs. So – it happened because of me. Whatever the weather. Because if I'd been at John's with him, he wouldn't have. See? It's down to me.

Right. And if a kid gets run over in the street is it my fault, because I should have been standing outside school making sure no one ever runs into the road? *Hi, I'm Lisa, I'm responsible for everyone's health and safety!*? No *way* is it my fault. No way. I don't even know if he really liked me. He probably went out with me because he couldn't get anyone better.

I was in a bad mood with him on Friday because I was cold. Now he's dead because I was cold. He's stone cold. How on Earth can someone who was alive be dead? I tried again, this afternoon, listening. I can't even remember what he looks like and I only saw him on Friday. I have to look on my phone to even remember his face. I tried to reach out in my mind like a laser probing the atmosphere to locate some trace of him, even just one word. Instead of this demented traffic jam that's doing my head in.

He's in it, isn't he? Stands to reason. He's got to be somewhere. Nothing vanishes: he's up there with all of that stuff he likes, the radio waves and phone signals and satellites. I'm not a kid, it's not like I think he's got to be in the sky, like souls go to heaven kind of thing; but if a bit of you flies out of your body, the life-bit, the energy – it's got to go somewhere and since it can travel for free it might as well go to its favourite place. Favourite time and place. I mean, I might go to that lake in Canada where everything was so bright and perfect and Dad was in a good mood and never asked about Mum once, I might go and be there in that day forever. I'd love it! What's to be afraid of? And Stevie, he could go up among all those winking lights, and wave bands, noseying round their signals, working out what's what, it'd keep him happy for ages. Forever.

You know what? I'm going to send him a message. I mean, why am I sitting here with everything switched off trying to listen for something when I've never even asked him a question? I'll text him. Why not? It's got to make more sense than asking some freak with a crystal ball. A text goes right up there and bounces off a satellite. He can answer. Surely he can.

Where's my mobile? OK. Stevie.

Y are u ded? XXX Lisa.

Look, I don't mind waiting for an answer. I'm not daft. I'm not expecting a ghost to pop up. I'll just hang on till I hear from him. Just one reply from Stevie, that's all. It's cool – and then I'll know.

KATRINA

I SAW THE old lady in Stevie's yard this morning. I was at my open bedroom window, the December air was damp but less flatly cold than it had been. It tasted different, something in it was more rounded, softer, stirring with life beyond winter. The old lady was piling stuff into their bin. She looked over the fence into my yard then up at the house. When she saw me she raised her arm, half-beckoning, and shuffled back indoors.

I went down to open the front door. Close up, her eyes were puffy and her nose a chapped pink. She spoke using her facial muscles like her features were too stiff to move. 'When you put out your bin – would you mind –?'

I nodded. She was staring at me. She smelt cloyingly of being unwashed, of staying in bed to sweat out sickness. Plus something animal, maybe sheep droppings. The air around her was dark and terrible. 'Have they gone away?'

'An accident. Stevie – my grandson. He's dead.'

My throat sounded but it wasn't a word. She startled. I concentrated on forming my words with precision. 'I'm very sorry.'

'I've come to get my daughter's things. She's staying with us.'

I couldn't form more words, nor did she. If anything should have happened to anyone it should have been to Stevie's mother. I went back into my house. The centrally heated air made it like walking into an oven. My throat spasmed and choked. I wish I had managed to ask what happened to him.

I'd been planning to visit my parents tonight. I can't put off telling them much longer. But I find I am not going to my course today. I don't go for the train. It is dark and airless downstairs, so I take my mug of tea up to the bedroom where the window is still open and the low winter's sunlight has barely reached the sill. I am afraid. There's a flood of egotistical thoughts like, *Is this a sign? Would it be better if I didn't go ahead?* Only the greatest selfishness could imagine any scheme of things where one person's tragedy happens in order to forewarn another. It makes me hate myself, but I'm paralysed. I can't shake it off.

I sit in the little basket chair and stare at my room. Everything is as it always is. Nothing has changed. The chest of drawers is hunched in shadow like a crouching bear. My stones and shells on the table are rounded and shadowed, hollowed and polished by gleams of light, their whites and creams and greys and rosy pinks shyly rejoicing in the light, releasing deepening colour like a scent. Each holds its own cool smooth form for me to lift and cradle in the palm of my hand. Why would I want to change? If you change one thing, everything changes, things beyond your control. What might I lose?

I think of Stevie. It could have been something small – trivial, almost unnoticeable – that happened. That went wrong. But he has been changed from living to dead. A great block of darkness I bump against. You can't go through it or round it, you can't see into it. Solid darkness. It sits there bunging up the world.

Light through tears swells then melts. My whole room ripples and shimmers, until the hot ache at the top of my nose makes me squeeze my eyes shut, and the trickle down my cheeks releases me.

I met him on my fourth day here. The front doors are only feet apart along this terrace. He was coming out at the same time as me. You should be on good terms with your neighbours. I said hello. He looked up and nodded, fiddling with the lock. I could see he was irritated and impatient but I had the sounds lined up ready and they came out. 'I'm Katrina. I've just moved in.'

He said something I didn't catch, turning his face to the street. Then walked quickly past me. I smelt stale alcohol. He was dressed in jeans, scruffy, younger than me. I thought he was a student too. He turned the corner and went down towards the station. I hung back a moment but I needed to catch the train too so I had to follow him. It was easy to avoid him in the crowd at the station.

Next time it was the same routine coming out of the house. I didn't look but I felt the thud of his door closing and his body blocking the light to my left. The dark bulk of him came towards me and stopped, so I had to look up and he was talking. He looked nervous.

'I'm sorry?'

'At night. It's not what you think,' he said.

'I don't understand.'

'The noise.'

'But I don't hear any noise.'

He made the face of a laugh. 'Really.'

'Really. I'm deaf.'

We started to walk up to the corner and down to the station. I felt him glancing at me. 'How d'you hear me talking?'

'I lip-read.' His skin was pale, with an angry red spot by his nose.

'Can't you hear anything?'

58

'I can feel vibrations, the train coming, something like that.'

'But not shouting. Or music.'

I shook my head. I could smell alcohol again. He laughed.

'What a great neighbour!'

I didn't understand so I didn't reply.

'So how d'you learn to talk? If you can't hear the words?'

'I went to deaf school. They taught us to make the shapes in our throats, and push the air through them. And signing, of course.'

'You can do signing? Like on TV?'

I signed back to him, 'Yes, I'm not an idiot you know.'

'What was that?'

I shook my head.

'No, what did you just say? It was more than yes.'

I said nothing.

'Tell me – please?'

I told him, and he grinned.

He caught my train twice a week. He was at college part time, taking physics A level. He never spoke about his mother. I saw that she didn't use the front door, only the back. She would slip out in all weathers without coat or umbrella and return minutes later with heavy plastic bags from the off-licence. The alcohol that I smelt was not on his breath but in his clothes. I paid attention at night for the noise he mentioned; once or twice there was the thud of an impact, maybe something heavy falling or being thrown. The windows in their house were not opened, the curtains remained closed. It was a house in hiding, its paintwork neglected, its yard piled with stuff under plastic sheets.

One night he came to the door holding his right arm up in the air. 'Can you do me a favour? Can you put a plaster on this for me?' So his mother was out of the frame for applying plasters. Blood ran from the base of his thumb, down his arm. I asked what he'd cut it on. 'Broken bottle.' I made him hold it under the cold tap then dried it with a clean tea towel and put on two big plasters, one criss-crossed over the other. His nails were bitten to the quick. He smelled of turps.

'If it still comes through you should get stitches.'

'It'll be fine.'

'D'you want a cup of tea?'

He pulled a face.

'Coffee? Orange?'

'Orange is good thanks.' He was still a kid. My art folder was open on the table, I'd been working on a life drawing we'd started in class. He asked if he could look, and sat down and leafed through the pictures slowly, stopping to take them in. He came to the small paintings of stars.

'I like these.'

'They're copies really. I've been studying Van Gogh's stars.'

'I like the way you can see the light coming off them. Like they're jiggling with it. You can practically see the waves.'

I asked him about his course. He was into space, and waves that can travel through space. Electromagnetic radiation, radio waves, microwaves, infra red and visible light, can all be used for communication, he said.

'There's not much communication in a microwave,' I quipped.

'Microwaves are how mobile phones work, they're how you communicate with satellites.'

'But a microwave is heat, surely.'

He shook his head. 'These electromagnetic waves move energy from one place to another. OK. A star. They carry its light to your eyes. But within the same spectrum are radio waves. Which can carry sound. The wavelengths are different, the frequency is different, but otherwise they're the same. They travel at the same speed through space.' I'd left a packet of biscuits on the table and as we talked he ate them all. I put out some crisps and he ate them too.

'I can't hear but even I know that sound travels slower than light.'

'I didn't say sound. Sound can't travel through space at all. I said radio waves, waves that can be translated into the sounds that come out of a radio. Or microwaves, the voices out of your mobile phone.' He looked at me. 'Sorry, I didn't mean *your* mobile.'

'Obviously. If their waves are the same as light it almost seems as if –'

'Not the *same*. Sounds in radio and mobile phones come from waves that are within the same spectrum as light. That's all I'm saying.'

'I wonder if people could listen to stars.'

He stared at me. 'Can't you get some kind of transmitter implanted? Isn't there an operation for deaf people?'

The room felt dim and I switched on the lights over the cooker and work surface. Another body in the room was absorbing light and making the dimensions different. No one else had come into my house since my mum and dad helped me move. I liked it, that it was my space, and that each of the four rooms had its own particular scents and air currents which only I disturbed. But now he was making my kitchen unfamiliar, with the turps, and sweat, and another warm body smell which somehow unbalanced me, so I was like a landlubber walking on a rolling deck. 'Yes. It's called a cochlear implant.'

'Don't you want one?'

'Why? I can lip-read and talk, I can do everything I want, deafness won't stop me being an artist.' I opened a packet of almonds and offered them to him, he took a handful. 'Anyway, implants work best if you have them really young. It's hard to adjust when you're older, you hear noises all jumbled together, close up and far away.'

'Why didn't your parents have it done when you were little?'

'Because they're both deaf and they're perfectly happy.'

He shook his head. 'That's crazy. Isn't it against the law? To force you to be handicapped?'

'I'm not handicapped!'

'You're missing a basic human experience.'

I went for a walk with Mum on Sunday and the sunlight was pale and weak as water shimmering over the frozen fields. We laughed together we could feel the earth locked in a perfect spell of winter, the ground iron underfoot, frost crystals sparkling on the bare hedges, the air so purely cold it skewered your throat then sat like solid ice in your lungs. The world hung still in space, suspended, waiting for the season to turn. We were the only things that moved. I knew the cold with every bit of me, there was none left over for knowing more. For hearing. How can you experience more than you experience? Someone who could hear whatever there is to hear on such a day – wind? birds? – would know less. There is a balance between loss and gain, and gain is found in loss.

In reply to Stevie, I laughed. 'I'm happy. Why would I want to change?'

He shrugged. 'I just think you'd enjoy it. Music. Having the choice – hearing words.'

'But I've learned to see sounds. I mean, that's how I learned to talk. Different sounds –' I touched my throat to show him, 'have different shapes and colours.'

'Colours?'

'Col-ours. That word is round and yellow, holding the throat open.'

'You've learned more than a normal person already. I

don't think the cochlear thing would confuse you. You'd pick it up quickly, the range of distance, stereo. You'd like it.'

'So what is this night time noise I'm missing?'

He laughed. 'Ha ha.' He cocked his head then got up. 'Deafness is great.' He went towards the door, waving his bandaged hand at me. 'Gotta go. Thanks.'

When I went for my check up I asked Mr Godley's opinion, just in passing. 'I'd be cautiously optimistic,' he said. 'I'd say one of the new generation implants would give a 70% chance of significant gain in hearing. But you know the downside.' I nodded. 'Over to you,' he said. Over and out.

I saw Stevie at odd times in the yard, shifting stuff around. Slates, bits of pipe, builders' materials. Once a van came round the back and Stevie and the driver loaded it up.

I asked him; 'You work for a builder?'

He grinned. 'You could say that.'

'What if you get caught?'

'Who's going to rat on me?'

'Don't think your secrets are safe with me. You know the story of Midas' wife?'

He didn't, so I told him how she couldn't keep her secret, and told it to the reeds because they were dumb. 'The King has ass's ears.' And the reeds whispered it all across the land.

'Well stay away from reeds.'

'Why don't you get a proper job?'

'My mum needs me at odd times. I've got one, anyway, I do part-time at the off licence.'

He wanted to know about my student loan; how much it was, how I had got it and when I would have to pay it back.

'You going to carry on with physics then?' I asked.

63

'Yeah. I'll go to Manchester.'

'Is that the best place?'

He shrugged. 'Can't leave her, can I?'

'Couldn't she have treatment?'

He laughed.

'You think *I* should have treatment, why not your mother?'

'You can listen,' he said, then pulled a face at himself. 'I mean, you can *learn*.'

One time on the train he asked if I could help him with some art. 'You can do perspective, can't you?'

'I suppose.'

'I've got to do this scenery, for a play. Windows and curtains. They want it to look like a bay window. Can you draw that?'

'On a flat backdrop?'

'Yup.'

I sketched a bay window for him on my pad. 'If you told me the size I could do you a proper drawing on graph paper and you could scale it up.'

'Thanks.'

'What's the play?'

'Something about an inspector calling. It's boring.'

'How come you're doing the scenery?'

'Community service.' He shrugged. 'Car radio. Stupid.'

My mother knows. Not consciously, but she knows. Why else would she have suddenly said, 'A handicap is a barrier to doing what other people do. But a barrier doesn't just hold you *out* of a place. It can also hold you *inside* a place where you might be safe and happy.' I thought about waking up after the operation. The noise would already be there, going on unavoidably, like daylight seeping through your eyelids before you open them. And you can't close your ears, remember. You can close your eyes to keep out sights, but not your ears: the sounds invade your head. Noise. I don't know what it might be. People talking. TV and radio, music? Objects, what noises do objects make – trolleys, beds, monitors? They say all the things around us make a noise; lighting, water, heating, traffic, even the air. I wouldn't know what was what, as if all the bright colours of the rainbow were splodged on top of each other and mixed into one great dirty brown. How would I learn to untangle, to clearly see each sound?

I am trying to think about Stevie, the last time I saw him. He missed the train twice so when I saw him in the yard I went out and asked if he was OK. It was getting dark, the light from my kitchen made a yellow oblong outside.

'Yeah.'

'You missed college. I thought you might be ill.'

'No. Just skint.' It was hard to see him clearly, I didn't catch what he said and he had to repeat. 'I walked.'

'Oh. How long does it take?'

'Hour, hour and a half.'

'I can lend you some money, if you like.'

He shook his head. He was transferring slates from a rucksack into what looked like an old filing cabinet drawer. 'If I haven't got it, she can't spend it.'

'Well I could just buy your train ticket.'

He replied quickly, his face was angry, all I got was the last two words: '– leave it!' It was too dark for me to talk. I waited a moment then I turned and headed for my house. When I reached the back door something hard tapped me on my shoulder. He was leaning over the fence holding an old clothes-prop. 'Sorry! Sorry! I called but you didn't hear me –'

'If I can't see your face –'

'I know. Sorry. Sorry I snapped at you.'

'OK.'

He laughed. 'See, if you had that cochlear thing, you'd get this all the time – people apologising, calling out hello, running after you to say nice things.'

I nodded.

'So will you?'

'I'll think about it.'

I'm hungry now. There you are. I said I was paralysed, but my living body continues to pump blood and suck in oxygen, to use its fuel and demand more. Life goes on without a second's pause. The damp air and feeble sun has turned to drizzle, running down my window, darkening the room.

If I go to tell my parents, I know exactly what will happen. First, from the end of the lane, I will see the beautiful Christmas tree in their window. Its reds and purples and blues and golds will be pulsing in the dark with all the happiness of my childhood. My mother will say, deafness is a blessing. My father will wag his head from side to side, so-so, 'It's a blessing if you think it is, Katrina. When it's not a blessing it's a royal pain in the arse!' He'll tell the story of the cyclist yet again. The cyclist who ran him down when he was a boy, out with his brother in the lane. The cyclist who, when he picked himself up and examined his grazes, did not apologise for having nearly broken my father's back, but who screamed at him in rage, 'What's wrong with you? I rang my bell, I yelled watch out! Are you fucking deaf?' He always tells this story against himself when people want encouraging. 'You see how stubborn I am,' he says. 'Even though the bastard nearly killed me, I still believed it was better to be deaf.' My father will tell me he's sorry they didn't agree to it when I was young. He'll understand. My mother won't. She'll argue, she'll tell me I'll regret it, she'll tell me I will never be the same again.

Well I won't. To be alive is to change. Don't all your

cells renew themselves every seven years? In seven years no bit of me will be the same as it is now, whether I want it to change or not.

Only the dead can't change. That's what I must tell them.

The Tale of a Naked Man

WHEN GRACE ONYANGO's husband came home at 4am, she was in no mood for foolish tall stories. She had been wide awake since midnight. She heard the bush taxi approaching their huts, and saw the light from its headlamps bouncing along the wall, so she laid down the baby and got up from her bed to peer out of the window. The vehicle was dark inside, but when the passenger door slid open a light came on. And in that light she saw two large enormous naked breasts, practically rammed against the windscreen. Then the door slammed shut and she could make out, scuttling towards her hut, the skinny figure of a man. He turned the door handle gently, so it wouldn't click; he pushed it open just a sliver, and he sidled in without a sound. In the glow of her little night-light she saw her husband was as naked as the day he was born.

'Oh you wretch!' she cried.

Her husband ignored her. He grabbed his work trousers and scrambled into them, then he lifted the tea-tin from its shelf, took out a handful of notes, and darted back out to the waiting taxi. He passed the cash through the driver's window and the taxi pulled away. When he came back into the house Grace ran at him and began to beat her fists against his chest. The wicked man tried to put his arm around her. She ducked. She would take the baby and run away to her mother's. But her husband blocked the door.

'Hush woman! This night I nearly died.'

The baby began to cry. If she woke the other children there would be pandemonium. Grace put her to the breast.

'You are a liar,' she hissed. 'A liar and a cheat!'

Her husband shrugged and sat down. 'If I had been up to no good, do you think I would come home like this, naked as a plucked chicken?'

'Where are your clothes?' she whispered ferociously. 'Did your whore steal them?'

Her husband laughed. 'Look here,' he said, 'I am very hungry. Do you have something for me?'

'Ask your girlfriend to cook for you!'

He closed his eyes and rolled his head back against the wall. 'I can tell you what happened. It is a most incredible story.'

'Why should I listen to a liar and a cheat?'

He opened one eye. 'You want to hear the story?'

Grace was stuck. She could hardly run through the night while her baby suckled. 'You have five minutes,' she said.

This is the story he told her.

He caught a bush taxi leaving Kampala around 5pm. There were some important-looking passengers inside; two men and a woman in business clothes with laptops, and their suitcases strapped to the roof. There were a couple of teenage boys who had been to see the football, and had drunk too much beer; they were already snoring. There was an old woman with a hen in her basket, and a bearded tourist with a rucksack. The driver was morose, not speaking even when you paid him. They drove out of Kampala and the only sound was the muffled fuzz of the radio, and a low discussion between the business types. Thomas learned that they had been attending a top-level meeting with investors. Darkness fell; fewer vehicles on the road now. They approached Mabira Forest.

The black trees either side of the road blotted out the evening sky. Thomas was sitting behind the driver, watching the wedge of light from their headlamps being pushed across roadside, ditch and tree trunks. The jolting and swaying of the vehicle on the unrepaired road must have made him drowsy because his eyes began to close.

All of a sudden the driver swore. He stamped on the brakes and they were all pitched forward in their seats. One of the boys fell onto the floor.

'What is this?' shouted the older business man angrily. His laptop had slipped off his knees and his paunch was so big he couldn't bend over to pick it up. Thomas could see there was a tree trunk across the road.

His wife puffed out air between her lips. 'Road block? You expect me to believe this? Robbers steal your clothes then drive you home? Hah!'

The driver glanced wildly over his shoulder and began reversing. But there was already a dark shape at his window, there was already somebody yanking open the door at the other side, and a third party bashing on the back. The passengers began to shout until the man at the side door, who had a scarf tied across the lower half of his face, leant in and waved a gun at them. The robber at the driver's side had a black hood over his head, with roughly cut holes for his eyes and mouth. When he moved back from the light you could think he was headless, until you caught the gleam of his eyes.

'Mobiles!' he bellowed into the sudden silence. 'Pass them forward!' The gun gleamed under the taxi's interior light, swinging slowly round to point at each of them in turn, as a cobra sways before it strikes. Thomas gave his phone to the hand at the driver's window. The boys behind him passed theirs forward. The phones crunched as the man stamped on them. The paunch said he did not have a phone. The gun swung round to point at him.

'Give.' The gunman flexed his fingers then re-curled them tight around the trigger. The paunch surrendered his phone.

'Now get out. Leave bags. Leave everything.' The gun indicated the way. Thomas stumbled out of the van into the stink of the gunman's sweat.

'Kneel down. Kneel!'

Thomas fell to his knees.

'I landed on a rock. Look.' He rolled up his trouser leg to show his wife. His kneecap was crusted with dried blood.

'Any fool can bang his knee,' she retorted, shifting the baby to the other side.

Old paunch started up again. 'This is dirt! You think I want to ruin my suit?' The man with the gun prodded him and he sprawled backwards into the ditch, yelping.

'Now lie down,' said the hooded man, and all of them did except the old woman with the hen in her basket, who had already begun to walk slowly away down the road, as if this was her stop and she was going home.

'You! Old mother! Halt!' shouted the hooded man in Luganda. But she didn't. Even though she walked slowly, shuffling her feet, she was already becoming indistinct in the dark. Thomas, who had turned his head sideways on the prickly roadside weeds to watch her go, looked up to see that the gun was being aimed at her back.

'Shut your eyes! Lie still!' shrieked the hooded man. 'Any moves and you are dead.' Thomas shut his eyes. The gun was not fired.

Thomas could hear vigorous pushing and scuffling sounds, and he realised that the third man was rolling the tree trunk aside. Behind Thomas' eyelids the darkness intensified and he knew they had switched off the vehicle lights.

'Now listen,' said the hooded man in English. 'You will stand up, one by one, and hold hands in a line. I lead you into the forest. My friend with the gun comes behind.'

Everyone did exactly as he said. Holding hands like little schoolchildren they stumbled into the dark forest, with undergrowth scratching at their legs. Then the hooded man and the other accomplice flicked on two powerful torches, shining them at the passengers who stood, blinded and foolish, in a small space between trees.

'Take off your clothes,' ordered the hooded man.

'Are you going to kill us?' asked one of the boys. His friend was crying.

Grace tutted. 'Poor child. Surely they do not need to take the clothes.'

'Valuables in the pockets,' said Thomas.

She shook her head angrily. 'How many times am I hearing your stories!'

'Shut up,' said the robber. 'Take off your clothes.' The gun jerked.

So Thomas took off his t-shirt and trainers and jeans, and the boys and tourist did likewise, and the business types peeled off their jackets and shirts. When the garments were all on the ground, the hooded man gestured to the third to collect them, and he took out wallets and a camera and other goods. The paunch began to put his shoes back on.

'Who tell you do that?' screamed the hooded one.

'Something is pricking my feet,' explained the man, and the hooded one ran at him, slamming him against a tree. Thomas considered that there were three robbers and seven passengers – eight if you included the driver. It should be possible to overcome the robbers. But the gun was a problem. It might be real.

'Take off the rest of your clothes! Now! Take them all off!' The hooded one's voice was becoming hoarse.

The business woman began to cry. She also was very large, and the rolls of her naked flesh gleamed in the light. This was the most shameful moment, Thomas told his wife, because the robbers shone their torches on each person's privates. Robber Three collected shoes and underwear and staggered back to the taxi with his arms full.

'You – driver! Go with him,' ordered the hooded man. 'The rest of you lie down and close your eyes.' His voice cracked. 'Now! Or we shoot!'

Everyone tried to lie down, though there was barely space between the tree trunks and bushes and dead branches poking into them. There was the sound of running feet crashing through the forest – of an engine starting – of slamming doors – of the taxi accelerating away. Thomas opened his eyes. The torchlight was gone. There was nothing but the black outline of the trees against the deep blue sky. He got painfully to his feet.

'Have they gone?' the woman asked, and one of the boys, hobbling in the direction of the road, peered round a tree and called back, 'Yes!'

'The driver was in on it,' announced the paunch. 'The bastard, he drove us into a trap!'

The younger business man spoke. 'If we flag down the next car we can be on their tail in no time –'

'Would you give a lift to naked persons?' scoffed the woman. 'Or would you think you had seen zombies in this bad place?'

The boys began to giggle.

'Show some respect!' she shouted, 'or you will end up behind bars also.'

There was the sound of a car approaching. The tourist staggered through the trees to the roadside. Everyone else crept quietly after him, as if afraid of scaring off some rare beast. The car came closer, bumping slowly over the potholes. Its lights flickered through the trees. The tourist called out, then the note of the engine changed. With a roar of acceleration it vroomed past, leaving darkness behind.

'You should go,' the young man told the woman. 'A woman is less alarming.'

'You think I am a whore?' she cried. 'You think I can stand naked at the roadside calling to cars?'

'Mmm-hmm,' said Grace. 'She is right. No decent woman could do that.' Thomas smiled and squeezed her knee. Grace froze. She stared coldly at his hand until he felt obliged to remove it. 'You take me for a fool?' she asked.

So all seven of them went together to the side of the road. Two cars came past after nearly an hour's wait. But how can you stand in full view as the light draws nearer? You try to hide behind the others. You are trying to cover yourself, you have no spare hand to wave. Everything is sharp or prickly underfoot, you are unbalanced, mosquitoes are hovering around your face. How can you look normal? Both cars speeded up as they drove past. The boys reminded everyone that there are baboons in Mabira Forest, known for attacking people.

All they could do was wait for day. In daylight they would be even more ashamed, but there would be more cars, and with luck a policeman. There came the sound of another car approaching, and miserably they huddled onto the verge again, trying to wave and smile and not look like naked evil ghosts, as the glow of the headlamps came nearer. The driver slowed. The scuffle to hide behind one another intensified: each person was trying to shove someone else in front, into the glare of the lights. The boys lost their nerve and ran away into the trees. What kind of pervert stops to pick up seven naked people? Thomas decided a night of thorns and wild beasts was surely preferable, and he joined the scramble for cover. Then the driver's door opened and a voice called out to them, 'I have come back to fetch you.'

'Is it the driver?' asked the woman. 'Is it the same man?'

'The barefaced cheek!' shouted the paunch. The tourist made for the taxi first. The boys followed, then Thomas. They were all in the vehicle by the time the business people came.

'Make a space further back,' demanded the woman. 'I can't sit up front.'

'You double-dealing devil,' the paunch shouted at the driver. 'Where are our things? Why didn't you fetch the police?'

'Those bandits made me drive them to a dark shack. They unloaded your goods then told me clear off. Should I drive all the way to Jinja looking for police, or come back for you?'

'Thank you,' the younger one said. 'Thank you for rescuing us.'

'Ask him how he got his clothes back,' muttered the paunch.

'Any of you can go in the front,' said the woman. 'A man's chest is acceptable. Do you think I want to expose my breasts to the world?'

The boys began to giggle again. No one moved. Thomas didn't want to because the woman was rude, and he didn't like exposing his nakedness anymore than she did. At last she had to heave her bulk in beside the driver, and they set off.

Only now did they realise their misery was not yet over. The foreigner was worst off, Thomas reasoned, because he had lost his passport. He would not even be able to go to the police or buy new clothes, because he had neither clothes nor cards nor money, nor any way of getting those things.

'You will have to take us to our homes,' the younger business man said to the driver.

'I would like payment,' he replied. 'My fares were stolen. I agree to take you to the door if you fetch me out some shillings.'

'You won't get a penny off me,' said the paunch. 'How many times a week do you play this trick?'

'Then I shall drop you by the market,' the driver said simply.

After much discussion, the places where, and the order in which he would drop them were agreed. The foreigner gave the name of an hotel. Thomas decided that if the hotel rejected a naked guest, he would invite the man to his own home and lend him clothes.

Grace snorted. 'I am not having naked foreigners. You ask me before you invite them.'

'OK woman,' said her husband, stroking her arm. 'I did not invite him. You will see.'

When they came to the hotel the driver went in and spoke to the night guard, and came out after a long time with a white towelling robe which he passed to the tourist.

'Bring one for me,' the woman demanded. The driver

ignored her and drove on to drop off the two boys. Thomas was next. The business types were still complaining as he got out. He was very glad to be home.

'Now do you believe me?' he asked his wife, flashing his teeth in a smile.

'Well... everyone knows there are robbers in that forest.'

'True.'

'But to strip you naked! That was very bad.' Gently, she laid down the sleeping baby.

Thomas leant over to kiss her. 'I am very hungry, wife.'

'You are always hungry.'

'It's true.'

Grace gave a little smile. She took meal from the sack and began to make him posho. 'And you have lost your mobile, and your wallet?'

He nodded.

'Will the driver report it? You will all go to the police together?'

'We didn't really discuss that.'

'How could you not discuss it? It is four hours drive from Mabira Forest to here. You had all the time in the world.'

'Remember, we had been threatened with a gun.' Thomas crept up behind her as she stirred the pan. He placed his hands gently on her hips. 'To be naked in the night-time forest, to be exposing yourself to cars – it's no joke! I was even thinking the driver's return was another trap, maybe he planned to hold us to ransom.'

'Did you say this?'

'No. We had to contain our fears. We were powerless.' He leant forward and breathed into her ear. 'We were stark naked. Imagine – we had nothing but our wits.'

Grace turned to face him. 'You drove in silence all that way?'

77

He grinned, pulling her close. 'No. We told stories. To calm our nerves. To take our minds off the stress we had endured.'

'Uh-huh? Uh-huh? What story did you tell?'

'Mmnnn, mmnn, my sweet wife.' He wriggled himself against her. 'You know how it began?'

'No.'

'You cannot even guess.'

'You are teasing me again,' she said calmly, turning back to her cooking.

He laughed. 'When Grace Onyango's husband came home at 4am, she was in no mood for foolish tall stories...'

My Mother and her Sister

MY AUNT LUCY was married for forty-nine years, until her husband died. They had five children. Sometimes my mother laughed about her and said we'd have been better off with Lucy for a mother, we'd have had hand-knitted cardigans and a daddy who came home from work. We used to yell 'No! No! No!' and pretend to pummel our mother. She'd laugh and push our flailing hands away, and gasp 'Darned socks! Homemade jam!' Giddy with happiness, Tim and I tried to pull her over or climb up her body. No! No! No! A mother like Aunt Lucy must be pathetic.

When I strain now to see Lucy as I saw her then, it is as a picture in a child's book: a Beatrix Potter bunny-mummy, in a safely rounded patch of colour in the centre of the clean white page; up to her elbow-paws in floury dough, with a cheerful fire blazing in the hearth, and a clutch of little bunnikins merrily playing hide-and-seek behind the comfy arm chairs.

We learned from our mother that nothing is more important than your freedom, and that familiarity breeds contempt. We knew that no one wants to be taken for granted. When her boyfriends came round we made ourselves scarce. I liked it when she had a new one, she'd put the radio on loud and let us bounce on her bed while she danced in her underwear in front of the mirror, and tried on clothes. She worked in a travel agents', and in school holidays we went to stay with Aunt Lucy because she was always at home. We played with our stolid, large-faced cousins and ate Aunt Lucy's sponge layer cakes which she glued together with butter-cream, and we waited for our mum to phone us.

Now Aunt Lucy is seventy-five. She's been staying with me since Mum's funeral; my cousin Alexander brought her, in his car full of hot sticky children, and on Sunday I shall drive her home. Uncle Bill used to drive – Aunt Lucy never learned.

I haven't cried at all, I don't know why. When I tell myself she's dead I can't think anything. I seem to be quite hollow, to have gaps in my head. You think you need to talk to someone but what is there to say. Nothing.

It's rained since Lucy came. My house is terribly quiet. She sits near the TV with the sound turned down, knitting. She knits endlessly for her grandchildren. My mother doesn't have any grandchildren. Didn't have. Outside the rain makes a hiss like we're caught in a radio frequency where nothing is being broadcast, the persistent pressure of the sound makes my head ache. Why did I ask Lucy to stay? Because I don't go back to work till the end of the month, and it seemed the right thing to do. She's on her own now in that big shabby house, and I never visited after Uncle Bill died. I owe her. Gratitude or something, for all those summer holidays. Recognition. I thought we might talk; my mother, her sister – there must be something to say. I thought she'd know how to behave, that grief would rub off on me.

But Aunt Lucy is difficult company. She doesn't like the rain and refuses to go out, even to the shops. She seems mildly surprised when I try to talk to her. I always thought of her as an easy, chatty woman, good at small talk and making you feel at home. But she's self-contained and silent, she's composed. Her routine is inflexible; she goes to bed at nine, gets up at half past eight, rests in her room from two till four each afternoon. It occurs to me that she may be ill. She doesn't look like I think she used to look, she's not large or comfortably rounded, but short and angular, the sort of old lady who shrinks right down to the bone. In fact she looks very like my mother, although I swear she never used to. She has a rather sharp, intelligent face, and a habit of making a longish pause before she replies to things, giving considered weight to what she says. She makes me feel like a gabbler. I ask about her children, their careers, marriages, divorces, children; and she speaks of them in a rather distant, disinterested way. When, out of politeness, I watch *Coronation Street* with her, she's more animated bringing me up to date on its plot than she is describing her own children's lives.

And then there's the problem of food. All those meals she cooked for me and Tim, all that good healthy fare; roast lamb with brussels and carrots from the garden, and gravy; shepherds pie; fresh cod coated in crushed cornflakes; apple turnovers with baked custard. She made everything. Pastry, bread, jam, the curtains, the tea cosy and my cousins' clothes. So I forsake the freezer and microwave, and buy fresh chicken breasts and lamb chops. I visit the funny little greengrocer on the corner and buy real potatoes, green beans, a brown paper bag of carrots. I consult recipe books about gravy, but gravy is beyond me. I spend the long afternoon while Aunt Lucy is resting, trying to prepare a simple tea that will look as if I know how to cook. The potatoes remain hard – almost crisp – at the centre, but disintegrate on the outside, into a floury mush. I make strong tea to drink with the meal, that's what she used to have. When I place the food on the table she takes a child's portion and leaves half of it. My house smells like someone else's, the fatty stink of grilled chops, the steam of boiled vegetables. I can't bring myself to want to eat it either.

At night I lie awake and listen to the rain. I think perhaps I don't believe my mother is dead. I am a hot dry island in my bed and I wonder what Lucy is thinking.

On Thursday the rain stopped and I went for a walk while she rested. Everything was sodden, and all along the hedges huge, perfect cobwebs were festooned with silver drips. It reminded me of walking to primary school with Tim. Of the walk and what we saw being vivid, insistent; of seeing things without the layers of crackling cellophane or whatever it is that holds me separate and hot and dry in the space behind my eyes.

I didn't think about her tea. At 6.30 I put a frozen biryani and a lasagne in the micro, and opened up some wine. I'd refrained all week because I kept forgetting to buy the sweet white muck I thought she'd like, and it seemed rude to drink what she couldn't enjoy. Wrong again. She drank the rough red with gusto, and shot my last stupid assumption down in flames by choosing the Indian rather than the Italian, and eating the whole serve.

'This is what I usually eat,' I said.

She nodded. 'The food they have these days is marvellous.' The bottle was empty. I opened another.

'You used to cook such lovely food. I think Tim and I survived the rest of the year on what you fed us in holidays.'

'Your mother wasn't a cook.'

'No.' She was looking at the table with a little frown on her face; it was the first time we'd mentioned Mum.

'I think sometimes she envied you,' I said. 'Your settled life. Being happily married like that.' I don't know why I said it because I'd never thought it before, never dreamt of it. Lucy glanced at me and I felt embarrassed.

'I don't think so. She was always more hopeful than me. Eternal optimist, Dorothy.'

When I visited her in hospital she had the shrunken childish puzzled face of a monkey. She couldn't believe it; that life was going to kill her. Why is she dead? Why? I made myself focus on Lucy. 'Hopeful – how do you mean?'

'She was an optimist. She kept looking forward. Thinking she would find real happiness. Love. Something like that. With all her boyfriends.' She took a sip of wine. 'Being married a long time makes you see things differently.'

'You mean you don't think about happiness any more.' My voice sounded harsher than I intended.

She began to trace an invisible pattern on the table-top with her thick, yellow old-woman's fingernail. 'William and I – I wouldn't call us happy. But we had an understanding.'

Understanding? Not Aunt Lucy and Uncle Bill. An *understanding*, concerning *working late* and unmentioned blonde hairs on his jacket?

She continued in her deliberate way. 'We understood one another. We had the children and we loved them. When you live with someone all those years; working for the same things, knowing the same people; knowing each other, warts and all – you don't make each other happy. Any more than the worms make the earth happy, or the earth makes the worms happy. That's just the way it is.'

I was relieved about the understanding.

'You *think* about being happy,' she said. 'But your mother never *learnt*.'

'Learnt what?'

'That you can't have it. That the thing you want – when you get it, it's spoiled.'

'But Lucy –' Suddenly I can talk to her, we are leaning over the table and we are here and now. 'Lucy how can you say that? It's horrible, it's Victorian. *Practise self-denial. Don't dare to want –*?'

'No,' she says patiently. 'Listen. The wanting – is everything.' She looks up through the kitchen window at the darkening autumn evening. Heavy clouds are backlit by a sinking sun. I see her lips move as if she is testing out what she will say. 'I was in love.'

'With Uncle Bill.'

'Oh no. Well, maybe, once, but too much happened. No, I fell in love later. He had black hair.'

I try to remember Uncle Bill's hair. Nondescript. Maybe bald.

'It was – as if I'd been reborn. As if I'd stumbled out of years of fog, where nothing had come close to me, into a brilliant sharp new world. It was so – vivid.'

I don't know what to say. She drinks her wine and looks at me.

'I met him in the library. I used to go there after shopping, if I was early for meeting the children from school.' Aunt Lucy with her shopping bag full of sponge-cake ingredients and soap. A man in a library with black hair.

'What did you do?'

'He asked me to his house. For tea. At two o'clock.'

'Did you go?'

'I went to the house. Number 32. I went to the gate and I stopped then I unlatched it and went down the path. And he opened the door before I knocked because he'd been waiting, listening for the gate. I knew that. I knew he would be.' She suddenly smiles at me and raises her eyebrows, and I see that her pale old eyes are absolutely swimming with tears.

'I put my hand on the doorframe,' she says. 'Just – you know – to steady myself.' She raises her arthritic claw, to demonstrate. 'And he did the same, his fingers just brushed mine... We were both – shaking –' She closes her eyes.

'You didn't go in.'

'Oh no. Of course not. I didn't go to the library again either.'

'Because of Uncle Bill and the children,' I say stupidly.

'No. No.' She looks at me and sees that I am lost. 'He would have become a man – like your mother's. I've kept that afternoon, all these years. It's the most real thing that ever happened.'

We sit in silence, the kitchen window is black now, and the room feels cold. I get up to draw the blind.

'Your mother was like a child. She never learnt to stop hoping. She thought she could have happiness.'

There is the sudden piercing pressure of tears beneath my eyes. Lucy leans across the table and covers my hand with hers.

'She shouldn't have died,' she says. 'It wasn't right for her to die.'

I cry. For my mother, who wanted happiness. For her sister who knows it is impossible. For myself, for what I couldn't see, and for what I cannot understand.

Saved

WHEN ALICE LIFTED a corner of the tarpaulin, a cidery whiff of rotting apples escaped. Leaning closer in the failing light she saw that the trailer was full of them. Excellent. Had she not clearly explained to Head that she needed the trailer to move her grandma's bed?

'I haven't had time to get rid of them,' he told her.

'Don't you want them?'

'Couldn't sell 'em. There's a glut.' He was called Head because he was always off it, according to her brother Nick: Nick who was skulking in Oxford like the idle toad he was, pretending his term hadn't finished yet.

'They would have kept better if you hadn't left them in plastic bags.' She glanced around his so-called garden which was piled with rusty old bits of farm equipment and random builders' supplies, and saw there was nowhere to put them.

'Dump 'em. Take 'em to the tip.' He turned towards his peeling front door. 'I need the trailer Sunday, OK?'

Quite a few of the apples in the first bag were alright, as far as she could see. A bit wormy, and the odd brown patch, but plenty of them could be saved. How could he throw away perfectly good food? 'Trash the planet why don't you?' she muttered to his closing door. She backed up the car and attached the trailer to the rear bumper, winding the rope around both ends so the weight was evenly distributed. It would be fine over a short journey. If her parents had had a better car it would have had a tow bar. Well, if they'd had a better *bigger* car, there would've been room in it for the bed.

She turned cautiously out of his gateway and eased the car up through the gears, watching the trailer in her mirror.

It was fine until she pulled out onto the main road. There she got stuck behind a car which had tinsel wound round its aerial and a diamond shaped sign dangling in its back window, bearing the legend *Fab Mum on Board!* The Fab Mum stopped at every junction, major and minor, and allowed all the traffic waiting there to file out in front of her. Each time Alice had to stop, no matter how gently, the trailer jolted the car. By the time she got home her teeth were on edge.

She began to unload the bags of apples into the hall. They were heavy so it wasn't safe to use the handles; she clutched the plastic bags to her chest and realised, too late, that festering juice was smearing all over her leather jacket. The bags pretty much blocked the hall. She might as well sort them immediately for the full joyful Friday night experience. Vince would probably be getting ready to go out partying, hunting for some new female. Well hey, why should Alice care? This was so much more fun. Close inspection revealed that each bag contained soft brown putrefying apples mixed in with the green. Swiftly she filled the kitchen bin with rotten apples and the washing up bowl and clothes-basket with half-bad ones. It was strange the way they went; you'd pick one up that was green but then its underside was brown, with a kind of raised dottiness where the two colours met. When you cut it in two, the decay inside went right up the core to the top. All you could save was the top sliver of the apple's cheeks. She imagined slicing Vince out of her system like this, like a surgeon removing a tumour. Even the white, fresh-looking slices still seemed to have an aftertaste of rot. She sprinkled them lavishly with cinnamon and cloves. Then her mother came home from hospital visiting and put her hand on a sleepy wasp on the doorknob.

Once things had quietened down, they took a bottle of red into the sitting room, where the box of Christmas decorations sat accusingly on the sofa.

'If I'd known you'd have to go to all this trouble –' her mother said.

The wine at home wasn't as sour as the wine Vince

chose in York. 'When are you getting the tree? Did you tell Dad why I couldn't visit?'

'I haven't got *time* to get a tree! All he talks about is Grandma's. I could understand it if he'd been there even *once.*'

Grandma had died in the spring leaving her house full of dirty old junk to Dad. Now suddenly there was a buyer who wanted to move in before Christmas. Alice watched her mother drinking. Her face was puffy, she seemed to have aged disproportionately since Alice started university.

'He's alright, Dad? I mean a hip replacement's routine, isn't it?'

'Yep. They'll get him up on his feet tomorrow, the nurse told me. Two to three days and I'll have him on my hands here needing waiting on.'

'I'll visit tomorrow after I've moved the bed.'

'He wants *me* to go and look through Grandma's stuff – I'm at the library till five tomorrow, I've told him –'

'Mum there's no point.'

'Her knick knacks, her photos, he says there are things of sentimental –'

'No there aren't. And where would you put them anyway? This house is completely stuffed.' Alice's university possessions were heaped in a pathetic mound on the landing, since her mother had filled Alice's room with a rowing machine and bags of remnants to make a quilt.

'Alice, I don't see why the clearance people can't drop the bed off.'

'The man told me he'd need another van for the bed. Look, you want it don't you? I'm happy to fetch it.'

'*I* don't want it. It's your father who wants it. He claims it's some kind of antique.'

'Well I'm not saving it if you're not going to use it, Mum.'

'Oh we'll use it! It's not as if our bed's anything to write home about.'

'OK then.'

'I can't understand why Nick's not back for Christmas. He could have given you a hand.'

'Mum, I can manage.'

'The whole thing's ridiculous. We'll end up paying the clearance people more than the stuff is worth.' Her mother took a bottle from the sideboard, poured a mouthful into her wine glass and swirled it round, then drained the pink results. 'Would you like some whisky?' she said, pouring it into the rinsed glass. 'Sorry, I can't be bothered with getting more glasses.'

You come home from university with issues – real issues: like deciding to drop out of your course, and splitting up with Vince, and having paid six months rent in advance when now you can't go on living in the same house as him: you come home and your parents have turned into an alcoholic and an invalid, and *you* have to help *them*.

It would be alright. She would be helpful now, and tell them about leaving York after Christmas. It would soften the blow. She took a sip of the fiery whisky. 'What's your badge, Mum?'

'Oh – it's supposed to be an angel, I think. You press it and it flashes.' She demonstrated. 'They were giving them out at work.'

'Cool! Can I see?'

Her mother passed her the little pink and white plastic angel, the tips of her wings were flashing yellow. Alice laughed.

'Keep it if you like,' her mother said. 'They've got all sorts. I'll bring you a reindeer to go with it.' Alice pinned the angel to her jumper. 'Come here and give us a hug,' said her mother, smiling at last. 'It's good to have you home.'

By midnight her mother, sedated with Famous Grouse, had gone to bed, and Alice had filled another binliner with peel, core and bad bits. Vince had not texted her. Four saucepans of apples were stewing on the four cooker rings and the air was thick with steam and wasps. Other forms of

88

wildlife, slugs and maggoty things, had been revived enough by the warmth to start crawling up the walls. Excellent, she had saved a whole eco-system. Alice turned everything off and went to bed, hoping Vince was so drunk that he would suffer humiliating erectile dysfunction. Assuming he was with someone else. Which she might as well assume.

She was awake at 6 so she got up and dealt with the rest of the apples. Then she sat on the doorstep to have her breakfast cigarette, and worried about money. Maybe she should offer to clear Grandma's whole house and sell the stuff on eBay. But it'd have to go into storage and that would cost. The clearance people were charging the earth for storage. She should go online and check prices. All of it was rubbish but things like the Formica kitchen table and red plastic chairs, they were probably retro by now, probably collectors' items.

The post came; a card from Nick in Oxford. It showed two shrunken heads from the Pitt Rivers Museum, against a queasy green and yellow background. On the back he had scrawled, *Pater and Mater, Yo! Giving Xmas a miss this year END CAPITALISM NOW! X.*

Excellent.

Her mother was getting ready for work and fussing about the apples. She didn't have enough freezer boxes for them. She didn't want Alice to put the rotten ones in the compost. 'It'll be full, I won't be able to use it all winter.'

Alice explained patiently that it would be full of decaying vegetable matter which is what compost bins are for. But her mother was surprisingly assertive. Alice ended up reloading bags of slimy remains into the trailer and getting stung in the process. The pain was a welcome distraction from the larger pain of the entire world's idiocy. She drove carefully through the suburban streets to Grandma's. The bay window was empty and dark: Grandma always used to put the same old moulting Christmas tree in the window, festooned with two sets of lights, tie-on chocolates that she called 'fancies', and crowned with an angel. The ends of the branches were bald from when Alice and Nick were little and had tugged the chocolates off and stripped the soft plastic needles with them. When Mum offered to buy her a new tree Grandma had said, 'It'll see me out,' and Alice had been glad. She wondered what had happened to the angel – a proper little doll with a steady smile and white gauze wings, who lived the rest of the year in a twist of yellowed newspaper in the shoe box that held the lights. Alice had always felt sorry for her: how could one month of glory on the tree make up for eleven months in that dark box?

She carried the apple mush round the back and emptied it out near the hedge, where it could rot down in peace and put some goodness back into the soil. At least something would come from it; unlike her relationship with Vince. Nothing was going to come from that. Why couldn't she just have the strength of mind to turn her stupid phone off?

When Alice finally unlocked the back door and stepped into Grandma's silent house, it wasn't possible to keep going. The atmosphere in the house had set; the mingled smells of chip fat and disinfectant and Vick had congealed in the cold, into a medium it was barely possible to push your way through. Alice leant over the sink and forced the window open, then sat at the kitchen table. She stared down at her feet and saw there was a sticky teaspoon lying on the floor. Her Dad hadn't been here once. That was her mum's complaint: his own parents' house and he hadn't even been once in six months. She remembered coming here when she was little, how the warm air smelt of baking and her grandma was flicking the cat off the table with a tea towel, while the radio chattered and Grandpa was playing the piano and singing *Old Man River* in the front room and Grandma was rolling her eyes and saying 'You can't hear yourself think!' and Alice was begging 'Can I help you ice the cake? Please? Please?' and Grandma was laughing and lifting her onto the chair for a cuddle.

Hot tears sprang to Alice's eyes. Of course Dad hadn't been here. How could he bear it? Alice glimpsed down a tunnel in her head, herself, twenty-five years on, forcing her way into Mum and Dad's empty house. Facing the mess, having to sort it.

Why would you go there? What could you possibly hope to find?

The lives that had been lived here at Grandma's, they'd had their moments. There were smiles in the photos, music sheets in the piano stool, once-brilliant daubs of hers and Nick's magneted to the fridge door. There were ingredients for Grandma's fantastic almond cakes in the kitchen cupboards; now stale, sour, grey. Crawling with silverfish. The good things were already gone. Nothing could be saved. Her father must have known this.

She could see that you would be ashamed. But it would be like being ashamed of wetting your pants. Ashamed that you couldn't help it. Ashamed that it had come to this, to old age and dirt; ashamed that you hadn't been here every day, washing things; ashamed that Grandma wouldn't let you buy her anything new; ashamed that she had refused a cleaner and sacked the home help and told the community health nurse to fuck off, and that you had been powerless to stop her, and that everything was broken and dirty; ashamed that nothing you had done had stemmed the rising tide of decay.

Alice imagined seeing her dad (who was in hospital, who she hadn't even visited yet, for God's sake) and liking and understanding him. Instead of being impatient with the irritating old buffer of her mother's complaints. She blew her nose and gathered herself and went slowly up to the bedroom. The bed looked OK. Not all that old, really – a bit Charles Rennie Mackintosh-ish. Quite designer-y. She dragged the stained mattress to the floor, where it blocked the door and she had to battle on all fours to roll it over onto itself. The sour stench and floppy dead weight of it were almost welcome. All those tiny flakes of sloughed skin; she was practically rolling up her grandparents' bodies. It was the least she could do. She wedged it by the chest of drawers and fetched a knife from the kitchen drawer to unscrew the bedframe. But the screws were stuck fast, the blade broke before a single one had loosened.

The bedhead was weirdly sticky to touch; from medicine, Alice supposed, or from honey and lemon drinks, or breakfasts in bed. Or even, a million years ago, her grandparents' sexual secretions? She tried to unthink the thought. Abandoning her broken knife she searched under the stairs for a toolbox, then went out into the sweet fresh air to the DIY on the corner. There was a product you could use for loosening stuff; Vince had sprayed it on her bike lock when it had jammed. It was true, he used to be kind. When was the last time he was kind? She fought back tears.

The balding man in the DIY refused to understand what she wanted. 'In a can – you spray it on, it loosens things –'

'Lubricant, you mean?'

'Yes, for screws.'

'Lubricant for screws.'

To Alice's humiliation, a spurt of laughter escaped her.

'WD40,' said the man. 'Here. What kind of a screwdriver are you using?'

'A normal one.' How could he know about the knife?

'What you want is one of these. Best screwdriver a girl could have.' He wiggled his toilet-brush eyebrows and handed her a heavy metal-handled tool with a price sticker that said £22.50.

'I – why is it better?'

'Does all the work for you. All you need's apply a little pressure. See?' He demonstrated a little switch in the handle. 'Up for screwing. Down for unscrewing. Turns itself around, see?'

She didn't see but it was pretty obvious she needed the best tool for the job, since the bed probably hadn't been taken to bits for fifty years. And the sooner she got out of this lecher's shop the better. She crossed her fingers and gave him her Visa card.

Having duly sprayed all the screws she tried to use the screwdriver. But when she leant on it, as Mr Lech had demonstrated, the handle twizzled round uselessly while the head remained motionless. The only way to make it work was to put the little switch in the central position, which turned it into an ordinary screwdriver. But it was big and clumsy to hold and all her force could not budge a single screw.

Alice fell back against the folded mattress. Something, one single thing, surely, had to go right this weekend. Dispassionately she wondered what it would be. She pressed her Christmas angel badge and watched it flashing for a while. Such daylight as there was had almost drained from the sky and she got up and switched on the lights. She was starving. What were the options? Mum would be going straight from the library to hospital because Alice had the car. Who could she ask to help her? There was no one. Head wanted the trailer back tomorrow. If she hadn't had to deal with his wretched apples she'd have finished hours ago. To have done all this and still no bed – it was beyond enduring.

In a rage she snatched up the screwdriver and attacked the screws again – heaving, twisting – and was at last rewarded by an infinitesimal give, then movement. Slowly, grudgingly, the screws at the top end began to yield. She loosened them all then moved on to the foot. The problem would come in removing them; the whole frame would collapse, probably onto her. It was already listing drunkenly to one side. Her phone went and she crawled to her bag to get it. Not Vince. Of course not: wrong ring tone. Mum, from the bus, wanting to know if she could pick her up from the hospital at eight-thirty. 'Probably Mum, but I'm just in the middle of this. I'll text you, OK?' Her mother wondered plaintively what they could eat. 'Applesauce,' she said meanly and hung up. Vince would be cooking his disgusting onion-and-baked-bean omelette which he made whenever she asked him to cook so she wouldn't ask him again. She thought bitterly of the delicious things she'd cooked for him from her Jamie Oliver book. He said they'd got boring. It was him that was boring. Not her. *Him*. She had a brainwave. The frame could be balanced on kitchen chairs, one each side. The seats were too high but when she laid them on their backs it was just possible to slide them under so the frame rested on their legs. She fetched a cup to put the screws in.

Piece by piece she carried the frame downstairs. The bedhead was unwieldy; it caught a couple of the pictures above the stairs as she tried to angle it round the top banister. Tough. Nobody would miss them. The glass crunched into the carpet as she trudged up and down the stairs. At last all the pieces of the bed were in the hall. She emptied the screws into the glove compartment and began loading the bed into the trailer. Header. Footer. Side frame. Side frame. Top frame. Bottom frame. Slats. The wood was dense and heavy, probably some precious, endangered-species, non-renewable hardwood.

She slumped into the driver's seat, trembling with hunger and fatigue. As she pulled away from the kerb she heard the wood slither and rattle into position. She should have brought something to pad it where it leant against the sides of the trailer. Well there was plenty of cloth in Grandma's house – old sheets, towels? No. She couldn't bear to stop. It would be alright. She was driving so slowly and carefully that it would hardly shift at all, there probably wouldn't be a scratch on it. She made herself keep her eyes on the speedometer – don't go above 20.

Then her phone started up. *Sweet Gene Vincent.* He had selected the ringtone for her. Well, tough. It was too late. She didn't want to speak to him. She glanced at the speedometer, 20mph. She didn't allow her eyes even a flicker towards the phone. She looked straight back to the road. There was an angel.

An angel. Life size. White in her headlights. She hit the brake.

A lot of things happened at once, and it was only

possible to itemise them afterwards. The angel stretched out her white wings as if she would fly. Alice's seat belt ripped into her neck and shoulder like a bear-claw, while the car tried to pitch her through the windscreen then jerked madly backwards. There was a long noise, shockingly loud, of crashing and splintering. A man running to the flight-poised angel. Then pounding silence, expanding like a mushroom cloud in her head.

The man's face loomed at Alice's window. The silence popped. 'Are you alright? Please – let me –' He opened the door. 'Can you get out? You – you stopped – like that!'

Alice fumbled at her seat belt and slithered out of the car. She saw that the trailer was on its side in the road and that pieces of bed were scattered everywhere.

'Here,' said the man. 'You've had a shock. Come and sit down.' He led her into a lit doorway and spoke a different language to some other people who went outside and began to move the trailer. He sat her and the angel on a sofa and went into the kitchen to make a cup of tea.

Alice could see now that it was a child, not an angel. She had on a white dress, intricately embroidered at neck and hem. Her brown face was solemn and her black eyes examined Alice minutely. She looked about four years old. After a moment she slid off the sofa and picked up a bowl of sweets from the table. She carried it carefully to Alice, and offered it to her. Alice took a gold-wrapped toffee.

The man came back with two mugs of tea. 'I'm so sorry. It's her birthday. She was dancing when her cousins left, I forgot to lock the door –'

The little girl stretched out her arms again as if she would do a twirl, then noticed Alice watching her and concentrated very hard on choosing a sweet from the bowl.

'Her mother –' the man said quietly, 'she runs out looking for her mother.'

'Her mother?'

He brushed his hand across his eyes. 'She's not here.' Alice saw him gather himself into politeness. 'I am so sorry.

I'll pay for your trailer, your firewood. I don't know how to thank you. You saved her life.'

The man's face was beautiful. The child's face was beautiful.

'It wasn't firewood. It was a bed.'

'Ah. I will pay for a new bed. Of course.'

The child, whom she had thought was an angel, was alive and gravely unpeeling a mini Mars bar. Slowly, with the tinny taste of the tea, feeling began to creep back into Alice's numbed body and soul. She had not killed the child. She had saved the child. The beautiful man was smiling at her.

The feeling that was creeping through her was happiness.

'That bed was a lost cause,' she said. 'I'm glad your little girl is safe.'

The Ghost in the Corner

THERE WAS A ghost in the corner of the room. Well you know how busy I am. We had a client meeting for a mill conversion that Friday, and I was still working. I was trying to come up with something for the roof, which was flat and had been used for water storage. It was a 1924 brick thing, ugly as you please but solid, and they wanted it for a retail outlet.

I don't know when he turned up. The ghost. Like I said, I was busy. It seems to me that by the time I got round to speaking to him, he'd already been there a few days. I must have ignored him for a while, or avoided looking at him, naturally hoping he'd go away. Usually when you ignore men, they do. Our firm had been renting that suite of offices for five months, and the other possibility was that he had always been there, but for some reason invisible to me, up till that time. I was busy; I was tired. He wasn't intrusive. He just sat there on the floor, hugging his knees, staring vacantly at my office.

It was irritation, in the end, that drove me to speak to him. He was ruining my concentration. I asked him what he wanted. He turned his slow gaze on me and opened his mouth but no sound came out.

'Can't you speak?' I snapped. 'Can't you speak English?'

'I can Madam,' he replied in a surprisingly deep voice.

'What are you doing in my office?'

'Sorry, I do not know.'

This made me even angrier; his subservience was infuriating. 'Well you can't stay here, you're interrupting my work. And I need that corner for storage.' I glanced away from the screen to see him looking up at me mildly.

'I think I do not take up any space. I am a ghost, you know.'

I saved my work and turned to face him properly. It was true, I could see the skirting board behind him, through his abdomen. He was wearing a red t-shirt advertising Tusker beer, but I could see through the t-shirt as well. 'But this is no place for you,' I said. 'Where's your home?'

'Mbale, Madam.'

'Marble? What country?'

'Uganda.'

'Well why don't you go there? There must be nicer corners there, near your friends – your family.'

He shrugged. 'I do not know.'

'How did you get here?'

He shook his head.

I glanced at my screen. I had placed a restaurant on the roof of the mill, semi-glazed, with an outdoor terrace for fine weather. I had added potted palms and parasols in the atrium, but not outside because of the wind. There were Health and Safety features I needed to consider. 'You must know why you're here,' I said. 'Surely.'

'I am not knowing.'

He didn't look unhealthy. His black skin was lustrous, his shoulders broad and strong. I put his age at maybe eighteen. 'How did you die?'

'Range Rover Sport SE, 3.0 litre advanced sequential turbo diesel,' he replied.

'What?'

'Metallic blue. Very nice car,' he said. 'Top of the range.'

'You were in a car crash?'

'Hit and run, Madam.'

'They hit you and they didn't stop?'

'Oh no Madam. The car hire companies advise, never to stop, when a car is colliding with a pedestrian.'

'And why's that?'

'Everyone will be angry. If they see that driver, all the

relatives of the injured party will chase after him with their machetes. They will quickly chop him up.'

'Oh.' He didn't seem to blame the driver. It wasn't clear whose fault it was. 'Did you die straight away?'

'I am not remembering. I saw my father running, I heard my grandmother cry. Now I am here.'

'You're very far from home.'

'Where is it here?'

'England. Manchester.'

'Manchester United?'

'Exactly.'

He peered around the office as if expecting to see a football team materialise.

'Well you can't stay here,' I said firmly.

'OK.' At least he was biddable.

'Can you move?'

He unclasped his knees and rose to his feet, right hand on the wall for support. His injuries were not evident, for which I was grateful. 'Where to?' he asked.

I indicated that he should come out of his corner and he walked to the middle of the room, but then retreated to his original position.

'No,' I said. 'I meant, you should leave this building. Go back to your own country.'

'But how, Madam? I think it is very far.'

'Did you travel to England before, you know, before this happened?'

He shook his head. It was Thursday evening, nearly 8pm. My meeting was at 10 the next morning.

'Look,' I said to him, 'this really is nothing to do with me. Nothing at all. It's my office, and I have some very urgent work.'

He watched me carefully, as if I were dangerous.

'I don't see how I can help you,' I said. I spoke slowly and clearly, enunciating every word. Maybe he didn't understand me. 'There's nothing I can do.' It wasn't just fine details of my design that needed sorting; I hadn't found a space for any toilet facilities. I needed to present drawings that at least seemed plausible, and the restaurant was missing a kitchen.

He didn't reply and he didn't move.

'Look,' I said to him, 'it's obvious you can't stay here, and ghosts don't book seats on planes. Try thinking about your home. Maybe you can shift yourself back by an effort of will.'

He squatted down in the corner and I resumed my work.

By midnight I was ready to print off my drawings. I was ravenous. There was a carton of orange and some cheese in the fridge, and I had my Ryvita in the desk drawer. I glanced up to see him watching me mournfully. 'Want some?'

He nodded.

I walked over to him with a biscuit in my hand but when he tried to grasp it his fingers went through it and he groaned. I retreated to my chair. 'D'you *feel* hunger?'

He nodded.

Rather embarrassed in front of him, I ate my cheese and crackers and drained the juice. The plotter whirring into life was a welcome distraction. 'Pictures of what I've been drawing,' I explained. 'My work.'

He looked confused.

'Here, come and see.' I beckoned to him and he crept out of his corner to stare at my screen, and then I held the first printed sheet in front of him. He glanced from screen to page and grinned.

'I have never used computer,' he told me.

It occurred to me that now he never would. 'You can sit on the other chair, if you like.'

'The corner is best.' He resumed his squatting position.

Let's be clear. I pay a monthly standing order to *Save the Children*. I have never been behind the wheel of a Range

Rover Sport. I have never even been to Uganda. And I have certainly never injured a pedestrian. His death could not be laid at my door. I gathered up my printouts, switched off the plotter, and closed down the computer. I took my coat from its peg.

'You are going?'

'Well yes, I'm going home to sleep.' I switched off my desk lamp.

'I will be alone.'

'This is all a big mistake. You shouldn't even be here.'

'I am scared.'

'Aren't there other ghosts – other ghosts to keep you company? Can't you see anyone else lurking in corners?'

'Only you.'

Only me.

I gave up, and sat down again. Something shifted. Slowly, like a sleepwalker coming to, I formulated the sentence: 'Tell me, how can I help you?'

He looked at his hands. They were large, capable, wide-palmed hands, they looked strong enough for any work. I unclenched my own fingers and toes. A flicker of impatience rose again in me, and I made myself watch it, waiting for it to subside. We sat in silence.

'How you can help me,' he said slowly. 'How you can help me.'

I waited, not knowing what he would say. I felt as if I was floating in warm, still water.

'I have died.'

'Yes,' I said, 'I'm sorry but you have.'

'You listen me. I have died.'

'Yes. I'm sorry.'

He looked at me and I looked at him: we looked at each other, in the strangely deep silence unique to a city centre architect's office at twenty to one in the morning.

'You have seen me,' he said at last.

101

'I have seen you.'

'Alright.'

I was staring at him but he was gone. The corner by the filing cabinet was empty, I even walked over to it and passed my hand through the vacant air. I couldn't see him any more. He was gone. I wanted to call out to him, I wanted to tell him – what it was, I don't know. I felt ashamed.

I sat in my chair again, then I turned off the light. I waited, alone in the dark, in case he would come back. But he didn't. So after a while I left and went home to my bed.

Sports Leader

THE WINDOW CLEANER took on his new boy as a favour to Gary, who was after the boy's foster mum. It was almost November. The boy was sixteen and he hadn't passed any exams so they wouldn't let him go on to college to do his Sports Leadership. He had his head in the clouds. That's what his foster mum said. He'd spent September and October trailing about not finding a job, and Eileen was sick of him parked in front of the telly. She didn't want him thinking the world owed him a living.

The boy was surprised not to be going to college. The other kids were all going, he saw them waiting for the Huddersfield bus. Still, sooner he started work the sooner he'd be earning. Eileen told him he needed to stand on his own two feet. He'd be in a place of his own in eighteen months. And it wasn't bad work, like she said, at least he was out in fresh air; at least there'd be tips, come Christmas.

And he might get an eyeful. 'Sometimes you get an eyeful,' the window cleaner told him. 'Boobies, fannies, shagging, I've seen the lot.' It was the best bit, when you got to the top of the ladder and leant forward to look in the bedroom window. The boy didn't get an eyeful; mostly people were out, but he still liked looking in. You could see rooms where people lived – kids, mums and dads – you could see all their stuff. Their beds with the duvets thrown back, toys and clothes on the floor, drinks on the bedside table. It was better than telly. Sometimes there'd be a person doing something normal like tying their trainers or vacuuming and they'd hurry out of the room when they noticed him. They all had their own special life and family. And stuff that belonged to them. Their rooms were a secret part of their life.

'Come on you dozy bugger. Stand up there much longer yer'll freeze ter't winder.'

Downstairs there were rooms people had dashed out of to go to work, leaving a half-full mug on the windowsill, paper spread wide on the table, cat stretched out under the radiator. Sometimes the lamp was left on like in a film when a person's going to walk in any minute. Or the TV flickering with no one to watch it. The rooms held out their arms, waiting for their people to come back.

He knew none of the houses he looked in were as good as his mum and dad's. Theirs was like one of them stately homes on TV. Long shiny floors and lights like diamonds, and proper framed pictures on the walls. And a white sofa. Two white sofas. The smell when you opened the door, that would be the best. His mum's cooking could beat all them TV chefs.

'Get a move on you dozy twat!' Phil shook the ladder. 'Are you off on one again, you?'

He was alright, the window cleaner. They'd always stop at 11 and have a hot cuppa out the Thermos. Phil bought a union jack mug off the market for him. On Fridays they did the Bennet Road chippy and stopped there for chips after. Phil paid for them and everything. The place was toasty warm, it used to make his cheeks burn.

In Phil's opinion the new boy was not a lot of use. He was that slow, he was doing one house to Phil's five. But it was never easy getting a decent boy in winter. And he was reliable. Every morning, come rain come shine, he was waiting by Phil's garage when Phil came out the house. No sense no feeling. And he didn't mind collecting the money.

'He's honest enough,' Eileen told Phil. 'I've drummed that into him. You won't catch him thieving. He's not a bad lad.'

Privately Phil thought the boy was too thick to half-inch. But that was good news, because he could be sent out on his own collecting on a Thursday night, which was the worst part of the window cleaner's job bar none. In his black account book Phil wrote the number of each house and the amount owed, and gave the boy a bag to sling across his chest, with a tenner in change. The boy pitched up next morning with a heavy bag of cash and a careful 'O' pencilled next to the addresses that hadn't answered. It took him hours, but as Eileen said, it wasn't as if he had owt else to do. Spent every night in front of the telly; do him good to get out and socialise a bit.

The boy liked collecting. He liked being on his own, without the window cleaner's chivvying. He liked pressing the bell, or knocking, or flicking the letterbox and waiting with nothing in his head, for the door to open. He liked the interrupted faces people had when they saw him, and the music and chat and smells of food leaking out their houses. He liked standing in the warm light that fell on him out of their doorways.

Mostly they didn't have the money on them. They turned back into the brightness yelling for other people. If they tried chequebooks or cards he had to say no. Quite a few told him to come again next week. Some of them made cracks about how cold or wet or late it was. Once a man gave him a toffee. He had to take his time over the change because his maths wasn't great, and sometimes they snapped at him. But it was Phil's money after all, and if he came back short Phil'd dock him.

After he'd done the last one he walked back the way he'd come past all the closed curtains where people were having their private lives. But when he got home and went upstairs to his own room (quietly, because Eileen was knackered, she had two babies to look after now) and drew his own curtain and turned the light on, his room looked empty. There was stuff there alright; TV, bed, chair, wardrobe, everything you'd need. His computer off Children's Care was on the table, with a Harry Potter book even though he wasn't one for reading. And a jar for the pens and pencils he'd had at school. There was his deodorant and the birthday card with a train on he'd got from his mum, and the Walkman Eileen gave him. In the summer he had a nest he'd found on the pavement, a ball of twigs like a scribble, with a little hollow scooped out one side where the bird would lay her eggs. Smooth as your bum cheek. Eileen asked him to get rid of it because black bits dropped off it also birds have fleas which is a little-known fact.

Maybe it was just because he knew the room too well. He wished he could stand on the ladder and look in through his own window. So he could see if it looked like the others from the outside. See if it looked like it had secrets. But he wasn't that bothered. It felt great taking his boots off. He couldn't put his telly on because of the noise, but he liked lying watching the car headlights flash on his curtain as they went past. He needed to get some tunes on that Walkman. That'd be great. Then he could listen when he got in late. Eileen said he was music mad. He liked collecting from houses where there was music – anything with a bit of a beat to it. Sometimes people'd smile when they came back with the money. 'Jacko fan, are you?' Or Cheryl Cole, or Sugababes, or Black Eyed Peas – it didn't matter, he liked them all. The best thing ever was the school Christmas disco. He went last year, swinging his arms and stamping his feet, making the other kids laugh. *You are The Dancing Queen,* that was the best. *You are the night and the music.* He danced till he was drenched in sweat, until he didn't know which way was up. Miss Archer said 'Whew! You've danced them all off the floor!'

There were places in town, clubs, where you could dance all night. But Eileen said not while she was responsible. There'd be lads who'd had a skinful, with knives, drugs, God knows what. He was too young. He was better off at home with a DVD. One day he'd go somewhere you could dance, maybe on a holiday. If there was a competition he'd be bound to win.

Twice when he was with the window cleaner he saw lads from school. They weren't his mates or anything. Well, he didn't really have mates. He was more of a loner. He called out 'Hiya!' but they didn't reply. Maybe they didn't recognise him, all bundled up. Eileen told him about layers. She got him some charity shop jumpers, nowt wrong with them after a good wash, he wore them one on top of the other.

One wet Thursday night when he was collecting on Mill Street, Martin Hadfield from school opened the door. He yelled, 'Winder cleaner!' to his mum then did a double take.

'Hiya Martin,' said the boy, wiping the drips off his nose.

'You callin' at every house?' asked Martin.

'I do this end of round one week, an –'

'How much you got, then?'

'How much?'

'In t'bag, thicko.'

The boy began to add it up in his head. He'd done High Moor and Stamford and most of Mill, he still had to do...

'Fucks sake.' Martin's mother was behind him. 'By end of night, how much?'

The boy could answer that. 'Two hundred quid, near enough. Depends how many's out.'

'Collectin' on yer own?' asked Martin.

'Yup.' The boy could see he was impressed.

'Out of road,' said Martin's mother, pushing him aside and handing a tenner to the boy. 'I want some change for that, lad.'

'See ya!' called Martin from behind her back.

The rain never let up that night. It got down his collar front and back, he could feel the damp chill of it spreading across his chest and between his shoulder blades. He was looking forward to sitting with his back against the radiator in his room. He put his hands deep in his pockets and felt the gloves. The window cleaner'd given him them cos they were waterproof. They were great but the first time he wore them his hand slipped on the ladder. Lucky he was near the bottom. After that he kept them in his pocket just in case. The sides of his nails bled. Eileen said they were hangnails and he shouldn't bite them so much. She gave him hand lotion but it stung and the window cleaner called him a poof, so he stopped using it. The skin on his fingers was that rough his socks snagged on it when he tried to turn them right side out. But he was pretty tough anyway, his hands didn't bother him much.

He came to his favourite house on Manchester Road. The bedroom was full of sports gear. Rowing machine, treadmill, weights bench, the lot. That's what he was going to save up for. He was going to get back to being fit like when he lived with his mum and dad. Fastest runner in his class, he was, in Juniors. When he got the money he was going to join the gym at the Rec. He could do weights, cycling, pushups, and the ones where you open your arms wide and push the levers back. Then he could take his Sports Leadership. Once he got his qualification he'd be training athletes. Olympic, probably.

The bloke wasn't answering the door. The boy could see the light on upstairs. He must be doing his weights. The boy pencilled a wobbly O onto the damp page and moved on. As he was walking back down Mill Street Martin Hadfield showed up. 'Goin' home now?'

The boy nodded.

'Wanter give us yer cash?'

The boy laughed and shook his head.

'Yeah.'

'No.'

'Yeah.'

'No.'

'I mean it.' Martin grabbed the boy's arm and the boy shook him off and made a run for it. But he wasn't as fit as he was when he used to live with his Mum and Dad, when he was the best runner in the school. He couldn't get his breath. Martin caught him. 'Give me the money you fat fuck.'

'No.'

'I've got a knife.'

It was hard to see in the dark. The rain was streaming down the boy's face, he could see glints of light from the street lamp reflecting here and there in the blackness. Reflecting on the wet. On a blade?

'Hand it over, or else.'

Slowly the boy lifted the strap of his bag over his head. Martin snatched it and was gone.

The boy stood patiently in the rain, like a bullock, waiting for what would come next. Rain appeared out of the blackness, streaking past the streetlight like bright glass needles. After a while the boy went home to the quiet house and took off his wet things and went to bed.

In the morning he was waiting by Phil's garage when Phil came out.

'Where's bag?' asked Phil. The boy explained.

'And you just let him tek it? You bloody thick oaf. Where's he live? Mill Street?'

They went in Phil's van to Martin Hadfield's house. His mother answered the door in her dressing gown. 'What sort of time d'you call this?'

Phil told her the boy's story and she shook her head. 'No way. Martin were in watching telly with me all night. He never stirred out. That lad of yours isn't the full ticket.'

'He's not a liar,' said Phil.

'Nor's my Martin.'

'Let me talk to him.'

'He's in bed.'

'I don't give a toss.'

'It's bloody ridiculous, this.' She shut the door on them and they stood staring at the closed door with the rain trickling down their faces, until at last it opened again and there was Martin standing next to his mother.

'Where's my bag?' asked the boy.

'How should I know you fat poof.'

'Did you steal anything from this lad?' Martin's mother asked him.

'No.'

'Right. Satisfied?'

'No I'm not,' said Phil. 'I'll get the police onto you.'

'You'll be bloody sorry if you do.' Martin's mother slammed the door.

Phil was in a filthy mood. He looked in Martin's wheelie bin and gave it a shove so it fell across the pavement. He shouted at the boy to get to fucking work because he had some bloody making up to do.

When they got to the Bennet Road chippy he told the boy to sit near the window. The boy stared at the beautiful girl on the magazine left lying on the table. She had green eyes and blonde hair, big tits, and a look on her face like she was smiling right at you. He'd marry a girl like that, one day. Probably meet her in the gym when he was training. Chat to her, ask her her favourite colour, girls like to talk about stuff like that. Maybe they'd go dancing. Maybe they'd have children. He could hear Phil talking to Dan behind the counter.

'There's not a mark on him cos the other lad had a knife.'

'If you believe that you'll believe anything.'

'I don't think he's a liar.'

'Makes no odds, does it? If other kids know they can get money off him that easy, you can't send him collecting again.'

'Why should that thieving little bastard get away with it?'

'Forget him. You've no proof. And there's plenty of folk to say that lad of yours is odd.'

'Odd?'

'You know. Pervy.'

'What d'you mean?'

'Well you've bloody seen him as much as I have. Standing there with his nose pressed ter glass, starin inter people's houses.'

'He's just slow.'

'I wouldn't want him being slow near my house. Near my wife and kids.'

'He don't mean owt.'

'Right.'

At the end of the afternoon the boy didn't get any pay because, as Phil said, he had nothing to pay him with. And Phil told him not to come back Monday morning. He was trying to unlock his garage as he said it, so he didn't really look at the boy. Just said, 'See ya then.'

'See ya,' said the boy. 'D'you want the gloves back?'

'Keep em,' said Phil, disappearing into his garage.

Walking home the boy wondered if Eileen would let him watch daytime TV on Monday. When he was a Sports Leader, he'd watch it whenever he liked.

Kiss and Tell

I MET THE great man's wife at the Sunday dinner. She had flown in that afternoon. She was not a trophy: only five years younger, the mother of his children, and with a self-deprecating husky voice. She carried off peacock blue silk with aplomb; she brought glamour and style to our dowdy writers' gathering. She had all-American confidence. He was holding forth at his end of the table, and she sat some distance from him, but their eyes still met from time to time. They were a couple. I thought about what I could tell her.

★

On the day your husband arrived he was purely obnoxious. The silence of the writers' retreat was shattered. The whole place was thrown into a flutter by him. He thundered up and down the stairs demanding bottled water, internet, a better desk-lamp, coffee. We had been told he was there to finish his memoir; it was implicit that we were privileged to be in his company. But please consider: does the world need another politician's memoir? Is it likely that a motley selection of little-known writers and poets would rally to feed such a man's ego?

We lingered stubbornly in our rooms, pretending to redraft, ears attuned to his every move. He played Beethoven's 7th (for goodness' sake); he ran an endless bath; he talked importantly on his mobile, which house rules state must remain switched off at all times. It was clear he wasn't writing for a minute. He was on the floor below our garrets, in a proper ensuite double room. But he invaded our headspace. We were filled with unspoken resentment.

Of one telepathic accord, we skipped the pre-dinner drinking hour, and sidled down to the dining room only when we knew food was about to be served. Imagine our disappointment then at finding the great man was not there to be snubbed: he had been invited out to dinner. Of course. We ate meagrely and retired early to our monk-like cells, irritated by ourselves and each other.

The next day his radio went on at 6. I wasted half an hour second-guessing when he would go to breakfast, so I could avoid him. He played Beethoven all day and when I complained to the administrator I was told he couldn't write without music, and that he was playing it softly especially to accommodate the other writers. I asked if he had heard of headphones but I am not sure the message was passed on.

He finally made his appearance when the rest of us were already at the dinner table that night. He nodded briskly and set two bottles of wine on the table, announcing that the wine here was piss. The administrator introduced us all and your husband gave us each a curt nod. There was a pile of lamb chops on the big serving dish, and when it was passed to him he took four. He declined all vegetables with an impatient wave, and when everyone had helped themselves to a single chop, he took the remaining three, and set about eating all seven with focused intensity. Someone muttered that the Atkins diet had been discredited but he affected not to hear. A desultory conversation about what to do with a jammed printer continued on one side of the table; the rest of us kept our eyes on our plates and ate in silence. He drank off a glass of wine like orange juice, then asked us to excuse him as he had work to do. Beethoven (the First, for the second time) was still playing at 11pm when I turned out my light.

On Friday night we had planned to go out to the pub. It would be the sociable highlight of our week. We were dismayed when the administrator told us the great man would like to read a chapter to us, after dinner. 'But it's Friday night,' we objected. 'Readings happen on the last night.'

'It's *his* last night, for reading,' the administrator replied.

Your husband was giving an after-dinner speech at a charity do on Saturday, and then you were arriving on Sunday prior to your departure together on Monday morning. Clearly the GM knows better than to read in front of you.

After Friday dinner we lounged like recalcitrant teenagers on the sofas and armchairs that were all slightly too far from the fire. It was bitterly cold: draughts rattled the single glazing and sliced in under the hems of shrunken velvet curtains. The great man positioned himself with his back to the fire, effectively blocking it from the rest of us. He gave us a big warm public smile, arranged his typescript and launched into a self-serving rendition of his rebellious but politically-aware teenage years. He read for twenty-five minutes which is a long time when you're cold.

At the end he flourished the pages and bowed, which obliged us to give him a thin spatter of clapping. Maria, who is young and enthusiastic, but who I had assumed knew better, asked him a sycophantic question. He produced a bottle of scotch from his briefcase, poured himself a good slug and sent the bottle off around the room, then answered her at length – mellow, smiling and relaxed. He was the nicest man in the world. Barmy Chris and poet Steve ventured nervous contributions, and he expanded, embracing us all in the warm glow of his switched-on personality. To them he is a celebrity. They grew up seeing his face on TV, reading his views in the papers. I thought of him as a chancer who must, by definition, be fraudulent and unscrupulous to have reached so elevated a position. As an American you are probably more generous. When the first small silence offered itself, I chipped in, 'Are we going to the pub, then?'

The great man stood up, rubbing his hands. 'An excellent suggestion, yes. You people must be demob happy, after a week cooped up in here.' People scattered to find coats and boots, taxis were phoned, and when I went out of the front door he was standing there with his head tilted back and clouds of steam rising from his nostrils. 'Wonderful stars up here.'

'Yes. We're not cooped up, actually, we can always go for a walk. There are some beautiful walks along the river.'

'Is that what you writers do for inspiration?' He made it sound rather pathetic.

'For exercise. For the joy of it.'

'I like walking,' he said. 'How far's the pub, Lily?'

I was surprised he remembered my name. 'Not that far. But there are no street lights. It's very dark.'

'I'm game. Are you?'

It was anger as much as anything that made me agree to walk with him while the others rode off in warm lit vehicles. And it was certainly anger that helped me set our pace, while he talked about his travels, namedropping world leaders and celebrities, then about his good fortune in having a beautiful and witty wife (he can't praise you enough) and two high-achieving children. He boasted simply and enthusiastically, like a child. There was no moon. As we moved away from the lights of the big house, the stars shone more and more brightly, and there were answering sparkles from frost on the grass. The air was so cold it numbed my face and felt solid as ice cream in my lungs.

He began to boast about his very expensive hat, which has special thermal properties and was purchased at a ski resort in Canada. I laughed. There was a short silence then he asked me what I wrote.

'Novels.'

'Best selling?'

'No.'

'Here,' he said. I made out a glinting in the solid darkness that was him, and he passed it to me – the whisky bottle. I uncorked it and glugged; it lit a line like the trace of a sparkler, from my mouth to my belly. 'So why d'you do it?'

It was hard to maintain my policy of monosyllabic answers, and by the time we got to the pub the whisky and exercise had thawed me out. He questioned everything I said, as if he knew better, and it ignited a flame of indignant volubility in me. Both of us had raised voices – we were talking over each other as

116

much as listening; in the pub hallway I felt my cheeks flare red with the sudden heat, and saw his face crimson too. We looked at each other and burst out laughing.

'More of the same?' he asked, and eased his way through to the bar. The pub was packed; I saw a few people glance at him then stare – perhaps wondering if they really did recognise him. He looked more ordinary than he does on TV. I could see some of my fellow writers squeezed into the corner by the slot machine – two of them were leaning against the wall, there were no spare seats.

I made for a bench under the window, and asked the girl sitting at the end to squeeze up a bit. I was peering about for another seat when the GM appeared, bearing double whiskeys in one hand and a stool in the other. He installed himself at the corner of the table and we launched into another fierce debate, until a general shushing made it possible to hear the sweet lamenting voice of a young female singer, accompanied by two wild-looking men on guitar and bass.

Time passed quickly, as it does when measured in double shots and music and laughter. When I glanced at my watch it was nearly midnight. The heat in the place was incredible, I felt the bright red flush on my cheeks spreading through my whole body until I was radiating heat like a glowing coal. I pulled my jumper over my head; I was wearing my blue v-necked t-shirt, the one that only gets worn under a jumper because it's too revealing. I saw GM note the cleavage and I laughed. He looked straight up into my face, grinning, caught in the act. 'Let's get outta here!' The grin and the look were unmistakeable.

'What?' I pretended I hadn't heard.

He leant right forward and breathed his hot words into my ear, cupping his hand around my neck to draw me near. 'Let's get outta here. There's more whisky in my room, Lily-gal.'

Your husband was propositioning me.

I laughed again. 'It's probably not a good idea,' I said.

He raised his eyebrows, as if he expected me to explain why. The evening was punctured. His hand had gone from my neck but I could still feel his touch. 'I think I'd better go,' I said lamely. He swigged from his glass then nodded at me with a half smile. He turned his head to the girl who had squeezed up for me. She was twenty years my junior, with smooth olive shoulders and a black fringe over her eyes. He jacked the smile up to full radiance again.

'And where have you sprung from? You live here?'

When I'd hauled on my big coat in the lobby, I went out into the icy night. Glancing back through the window I saw their heads bent close together over their drinks, then the girl throw back her head in joyous laughter. She would be sharing the bedroom whisky then. Easy come easy go.

There was a taxi waiting and I climbed into it and rode back to the writers' retreat feeling bereft. I like sex. Your husband was sexy and he was funny. I didn't particularly like him (the shit – do you?) but he did make me laugh. Fancy the GM fancying me!

Have a bit more self-respect, I told myself.

Oh stop being such a prude, I replied.

Why encourage him to think he's God's bloody gift?

Sweetie he won't even have noticed you turned him down.

This pointless schizophrenic squabble dragged on through the night; together with my determination not to hear any sounds from another room, it kept me well and truly awake.

I got up at six, since I was there, after all, to write. I immersed myself in my work and went down for breakfast at half past eight. The GM was sitting with the others at table, and Barmy Chris and Maria were rattling on about hangover cures. When I went to the hatch to serve myself with porridge the GM joined me with alacrity, holding out his own bowl for a dollop. 'Thank you for being sensible for both of us, last night.' He spoke so low and fast I didn't take it in till he had turned back towards the table. He finished his breakfast with the same efficient speed and left the table with a brief 'Excuse me.'

Replies milled through my head, but on the whole I was

glad there hadn't been time for one, since none of them hit quite the right note. The right note, it seemed to me, was ironic dignity but any words I thought of sounded both arch and bitter. I admired him for acknowledging what had happened. I had assumed he would pretend it hadn't. Which made me dislike myself, for my meanness.

Querulous self-interrogation put paid to any further work; after sitting futilely at my desk for an hour, I gave in and went for a walk. The day was thick and damp and cold, with leaden cloud, and no movement in the air. The leafless trees jutted out from the sides of the gorge like skeletons arrested in a desperate dance. If I see a squirrel, I thought. Or a bird. Or anything alive. But there was nothing, nature was dead as I clomped dully through it.

On my return the house was silent (no Beethoven) and I took off my muddy boots and crept up the stairs. I was pulling off my coat as I went and when I got to the first floor landing I somehow managed to flick myself in the eye with the sleeve. You always know, the split second before you lose it. My contact lens was gone.

'Shit!' I dropped to my knees, peering at the swirling green and brown carpet. I heard the GM open his door.

'Alright?' he said.

'Contact lens.'

'Ah, bad luck. Which way did it go?'

I shook my head. 'It wouldn't matter only it's my spare. I lost the same eye in the bath last week.'

He knelt down on all fours and rested his cheek against the carpet, staring sideways across the pile. He began to inch across the floor. I ran my hands over my clothes then picked up the coat and began to examine it. He tilted his head up to look at me. 'Do you favour hard or soft?' with a grin.

'Ha ha. It's hard.'

'Good. Easier to feel.' He pushed his hands in front of him across the carpet. We searched for a while in silence. There were a surprising number of small gritty items in the carpet pile, we agreed the place needed a good vacuuming.

'It's gone,' I said. 'Thanks for looking. I don't want to interrupt your work.'

'Rubbish,' he said. 'It's here and we'll find it.'

'I *will* keep looking,' I said, 'because my glasses give me a headache. But I'd much rather creep about in my own time and not feel I'm wasting yours.'

'D'you think I don't waste it myself? This is a far better excuse for not writing than what I was doing before.'

'What were you doing before?'

We were gradually moving in a wider and wider radius around the spot where I had lost the lens. Your husband came to the edge of the top stair and felt along it. 'It could have flown downstairs,' he said. 'They're so light they can go anywhere on a random draught.'

'I know. D'you wear them?'

'My wife does.' He stretched out flat on his front and peered over the top of the stairs, slowly tilting his head from one side to the other. Then he descended a few steps and crouched against the stairs so his eyes were level with the carpet pile at the top. He scanned the carpet like a searchlight. 'Have you looked properly on yourself?'

I shrugged. I wanted him to go back in his room so I could be pitiful on my own. He came slowly up the stairs and towards me, peering at the floor all the way. Then he began to scrutinise me, starting at my feet and working up. I was embarrassed.

'Turn around,' he said. And then, 'Turn again.' Suddenly he stretched his hand towards my head. 'Ah ha!' He plucked the lens from my hair like a magician finding a red silk scarf.

I thanked him profusely and he asked me into his room for a coffee. It would have been churlish to refuse. I sucked the lens and popped it back while he poured coffee from a flask and grimaced. 'Sorry, there's no way of making fresh.'

'I know. You're lucky they gave you a flask!' I wandered over to the desk where his laptop hibernated next to a closed A4 pad. 'So how were you wasting time?'

'Texting jokes to my daughter.' I looked at him and he shrugged. 'She's unhappy at university. I've got a book, see?' He picked up a worn paperback from the sofa arm, and passed it to me. It was entitled *Best Jokes of 1997*.

I laughed. 'Was it a vintage year?'

'God knows. I always pick up joke books when I see them. You need jokes in speeches.'

'You're not going to tell me you write your own speeches?'

'Why not? From time to time.' He looked at me levelly. 'But not the jokes, obviously.'

There was a silence while we drained our coffee. Why was I so harsh on him? Your husband, the Great Man. 'I'm sorry,' I said.

But he wasn't paying attention. 'What do you do for headaches?'

'What?'

'Your glasses give you a headache.'

'Oh – they can start if off, yes. I need a new prescription. I get migraines.'

'Me too. Have you tried *Migraigone*?'

'No.' When I have a migraine I lie prostrate in the dark. People who can sit up and eat and watch TV say they have migraines. There's no point in talking about it.

'This stuff is good. If you take it soon enough, before the thing really gets a grip –'

'Right. Can you get it on prescription?'

'No. I get it from America. Hang on.' He went into his bathroom and returned with a box of pills. 'These are all I have with me but why don't I give you four, that's enough to see how you go on. You start taking them as soon as you sense it coming.' He slipped some pills into an envelope, wrote the name on it and passed it to me. I started to protest but he cut me off. 'I know how it feels. Nobody should have to feel like that.'

'Thank you.' I got to my feet. 'We should both do some work, I guess.'

He nodded. 'What are you working on?'

'A collection of stories.'

'Really? I like stories. Novels are too long. Tell me when they're published, I'd like to read them.'

'Right.'

I felt myself blushing. He knew I didn't believe him. Your husband knew just how mean I was. I moved towards the door and he stood up and followed me. 'Thank you for finding my lens,' I said. 'And thank you for the tablets.'

'Enough of the thanks,' he said. 'I like you.' He leaned forward slowly and kissed me. His lips were warm and firm and dry, they lingered against mine and I felt the sudden swooping intensity of skin, of flesh. I closed my eyes. I imagined the rosy stone gateway to a big sunlit house. I opened my eyes and the GM smiled at me, then he held the door open for me to leave.

Up in my own room I analysed the meaning of your husband's kiss. I considered its taste, its texture, its warmth, its promise and its lack of promise. It said things we had not articulated. It said them lightly, without assigning undue importance. And yet it honoured them.

*

Of course I told none of this to the GM's wife. But after a while, I did feel it deserved to be recorded. And when I'd finished, and revised it, I posted a copy to the GM at Westminster. I put my email address on the title page. He replied to me three days later.

> *My dear Lily B, what a terribly old-fashioned story! Beautifully written, of course, but no wonder you're not a best seller. Can't you spice it up a bit (and perhaps cut the references to my wife)? NB. My speechwriter has written this.*
> *GM xx*

The Disaster Equation

THE GIRL JOINED the boat at St Thomas. She was originally from Norway, and had been living in Charlotte Amalie with her boyfriend, but that had gone sour. Now she wanted to work her passage back to Europe. She was slight, no more than 45 kilos, according to Miles. She had long dark hair which she wore braided and pinned up, and her skin still had a northern pallor that looked almost ghostly in the Antilles.

'You have crewed before?' Miles quizzed her. 'There's only me and Danny-boy here, and he's still wet behind the ears.'

'Sure. Rotterdam – Madeira – Gibraltar on a private yacht, and Göteborg to the Arctic and back with Aurora Voyages.'

'See the lights?' Dan asked.

'Of course.' She sounded defensive but maybe it was her accent.

'I'd love to see them,' he said. 'Never been that far north. Are they as green as they look in the photos?'

'They're all colours,' she said flatly.

Dan showed her her berth and brewed up while she was unpacking. Miles ducked into the galley to raise his grizzled eyebrows at Dan and mouth, 'Frigid'.

Dan grinned. 'Ice maiden. Mysterious.'

She took her coffee up on deck and Dan followed, watching her appraising SeaBreeze. Dully weathered teak, shabby fittings, the upturned dinghy still awaiting repair, cooling system parts spread on a bin liner. He wondered how long she'd last. She looked at him and frowned. 'Miles is the boss?'

'Too true.'

'When must we leave?'

'When we're ready. Gotta do a few repairs, spruce her up a bit – back end of the week? If any charters come in he'll want to do them first, though.'

She received this in silence.

'You want some factor 30? Sun's pretty fierce today.'

'I prefer to cover up.' It was true, she was wearing loose cotton trousers and a long sleeved shirt.

'Yeah but you'll be in and out of the water.'

'I have sun cream.'

Her rudeness reminded him of a German student he'd known in Sydney. Maybe it was a Northern European thing.

'He is OK?' she asked, with a tilt of her head towards Miles, still below deck.

Dan shrugged. 'Likes his own way. But don't we all?'

She did not reply, and he wondered if she understood his English.

When Miles came up he'd made a list of the stuff they had to do before they could leave.

'Why you go Portugal?' asked the girl.

'Taking SeaBreeze to her new owner. I'm selling her. If that's alright by you.' Miles did not smile and Dan glanced at the girl but her expression was unreadable. She redeemed herself temporarily by volunteering to patch the dinghy.

'I have worked with fibreglass before.' Miles dispatched her to find the fibreglass kit in the stores, and although it took her a while (it was a shitheap down there, Dan knew – boxes of canned food, batteries, engine oil, spare line, it needed sorting) she came up with a box and laid the contents out methodically beside the dinghy.

The men were going to buy supplies and see if the cooling system valve had come. 'You can cook tonight,' Miles told her. 'This kid's cooking is shit. Kitchen needs a woman's touch.'

'Any special requests?' asked Dan.

'I am vegetarian –'

'Sweet Jesus!' from Miles.

'– But I don't mind to cook fish for you. Chick peas and beans will be good for the store. I can make fish and salad tonight.' Dan had to stifle a laugh at Miles' response. She appeared not to understand it.

When they returned the hole was neatly covered, inside and out, with overlaid fibreglass squares, and the smell of glue hung heavily over the deck. Dan came forward to inspect her work. 'Nice one. Want a tinny?' He passed her one from the new supplies. She thanked him gravely and set the beer down in the shade.

'We got you tuna steak to cook.'

Miles came up behind him, mobile clamped to his ear, and gesticulated for them to take the stores below. Dan saw that the girl had swept out the hold. 'Food this side,' she told him. 'Other supplies opposite. You can move this gear? It is too heavy for me.' She went off to start the cooking.

Dan and Miles were relaxing with a drink when she poked her head out of the companionway half an hour later. 'I am cleaning the galley. Where do you put different types of waste?'

'Davy Jones' locker!' said Miles. He raised his empty can to her, then deliberately hurled it over his shoulder.

'I am sorry?'

'Overboard,' Dan said. 'When we're further out.'

'Cans? Plastic?'

Miles rolled his eyes. 'A fucking recycler. That's all we need.'

'I will put a box for glass and cans,' she said, 'and a bag for plastics. We will not pollute the sea.'

Later Dan went down to the galley to look for a light. She had cleaned the stove and made a salad, and as he ferreted for matches she unwrapped the parcel of tuna. The metallic smell of blood pervaded the galley. She let out a little 'Oh!' and dropped down onto the seat.

'What's up?'

She was lowering her head between her knees. He heard her suck in a deep breath.

'You OK?'

She raised her head slowly. 'It is meat. It makes me –' She gestured.

'It's tuna. Fresh tuna. That's what it looks like.'

'But *blood* –'

Dan laughed. 'Bit different from that grey stuff in cans, eh? You need some help?'

The girl hauled herself to her feet and turned up the heat under the frying pan. 'No.'

He watched her scattering salt and pepper over the bloody steaks with an averted face, then stabbing the first one at arm's length with the breadknife, and dropping it into the fiery pan. 'I can handle,' she said. 'OK.'

After she had served them in the cockpit she went back down to the galley to make herself an omelette. They had almost finished by the time she joined them.

'Try a bit,' urged Dan. 'It tastes fantastic.'

'It was a living creature,' she said.

Miles snorted. He wanted to know about her experience of bad weather. 'Tropical storms? Hurricanes?'

She shook her head.

'Well you will. You're going to be fucking shitting yourself.'

'Ducky, ducky – language,' said Dan, in his best Edna Everage voice.

'I'm not your fucking ducky,' said Miles. 'Quack quack.' He laughed and slapped his thighs.

The girl said goodnight soon after and retreated to her cabin.

Miles rolled his eyes. 'Won't last.'

'Fair do's, she can cook.'

'No flesh on her. She's not strong enough, mate.'

'She did OK with the fibreglass.'

'You gonna cover for her? How much of those stores did you end up lugging down to the bilges?'

Dan remained silent.

★

When she climbed into her bunk (after inspecting the none-too-clean sheets) Anna could still hear them laughing and carrying on above her head. Miles, she thought, was a nasty old man. Dan was not so bad, but he was young, he couldn't be more than twenty-one, and he was subordinate. He would do what Miles told him. If she could have afforded to, she would have left. But she had no ticket home and she needed to get out. 'No choice,' she told herself. They were sexist pigs but she did not think they would hurt her.

In the morning both men were rather subdued. It was a still, sunny day; Anna was polishing the grab rail when Miles emerged. He shook his head. 'You can get your polishing gear out when we're underway. Nobody here we need to impress – only Mr Moneybags in Lisbon.'

Anna sat back on her heels and waited.

'You and Dan gonna go below and give her a good scrape today,' he said. 'Weed, barnacles, we're trailing a ton of shit.'

The wetsuit they offered her was too big, so she put a t-shirt over her bikini, to stop the BCD from rubbing against her skin. There was a belt with knife, scraper and torch attached. Needless to say, the batteries did not work. She could feel Miles' eyes crawling over her exposed flesh and in her hurry to get into the water, grabbed the first mask that came to hand. Once she was in the water it misted over and she realised it was slightly too big. She could see, but not brilliantly. They had agreed that she would take the port side, Dan the starboard. It was already clear to her that it would be a race – that they would judge her if she finished after Dan. The hull was thickly encrusted; it hadn't been cleaned for an age. She adjusted her flotation jacket until she could stabilise level with the keel, and taking the scraper in both hands, began to work. The stuff did not come away easily, and if you didn't get the barnacles at the first sweep they became almost immoveable. She'd never done scraping before, but she was reminded of childhood explorations in rock pools, wandering far from her brothers' clamour and gathering shells into her bucket. If you knocked a limpet sharply with the edge of your spade it fell off easily. Her father taught her that, in a rare moment of kindliness. If you only tapped it, it would redouble its strength and cling on 'like grim death', he had told her.

Her arms were aching after ten minutes, and she had cleared maybe two square metres? She was tempted to swim round and check on Dan's progress. No sooner had the thought entered her head than she sensed him behind her. Good, maybe he was finding it hard work too. She turned to face the dark shape in the corner of her vision, but it became a silver blur in the water, streaking away under the boat. Shape of an arrow. Two metres long. Fast. In her panic she didn't know how she got to the surface, only that she was gasping for breath and her heart was hammering in her chest when she reached the rope ladder, and that the weight of the tank, as she heaved up into the air, nearly pulled her down into the water again.

The deck was empty. 'Miles!' she shouted. 'Dan?' There was splashing behind her and Dan hauled himself quickly up and flung his mask on the deck.

'What's up?' The old guy appeared from the companionway.

'Barry,' said Dan. 'Fucking Barry's back.'

'Who is Barry?' asked Anna.

Dan peeled off his flippers. 'Barry the barracuda. He's been shadowing us since Santa Lucia. The biggest barracuda you ever saw.'

'Yes,' she said. 'I see him. Nearly two metres. I think it is a shark.'

Dan shook his head. 'We fed him scraps of meat and fish, it was good fun watching him dash after them – like lightning. He lives under the boat, he's followed us for days.'

'They're territorial,' said Miles.

'He was that close,' said Dan. 'Teeth like a pike.'

'Take a nasty chunk out of you with them,' said Miles.

'Well what we going to do?'

Anna loosened her tank and let it slide to the deck. OK, this wasn't her problem.

'Only one thing to do,' said Miles.

'What's that?'

'Harpoon the fucker.'

There was a silence.

'Well?' said Miles.

'Can't we just scare him off?' asked Dan.

'How? Pulling faces?'

'But – he's followed us across the ocean. We've encouraged him, for Chrissake, it'd be like harpooning your dog.'

'You want to encourage him to eat your arse?'

'How about we move on a few miles, see if we can shake him off?'

'We're not exactly hard to follow. Twat.'

Anna moved away to the opposite end of the boat, her flippers slapping loudly against the deck, and sat facing out to sea with her back to them. If they kill him, she told herself, I will leave this boat. They are a pair of bastards anyway. I will work in the bar till I save my fare home.

★

Dan watched the girl's retreating back. 'I've seen photos of divers surrounded by them.'

'You want to take that risk?' said Miles.

'It just seems a bit nasty to kill him.'

'Sweet fucking Jesus. We could have him for dinner. We'll get your ice maiden to gut him, that'll give her the willies.'

'He didn't go for either of us then. He just came up behind me for a look.'

'Kill him,' said Miles. 'Trust me, he's got a brain this big' – he held his thumb and forefinger half an inch apart – 'and the world he lives in is kill or be killed.'

'Thought you were talking about yourself there,' said Dan, attempting a grin.

Miles spat over the side and took out his mobile. 'I want the hull scraped today. And I want you and her to do it.' He tapped a number into his phone and went below deck.

Dan sat for a while, letting the sun warm him, feeling the pleasurable prickling of the salt drying on his back. Then he ambled over to the girl. She did not look up when he said 'OK?' but he sat next to her anyway. 'I reckon we should go down again,' he said. 'What barracudas eat is those little silvery fish that follow the boat. Jacks. OK, we've spoilt him with scraps but that's no reason for him to attack humans. And we must look just as big to him as he does to us.'

The girl turned to face him, squinting into the sun. 'You will not kill him?'

'There's no need. If we take it really slow – stick together, look out for each other – I don't think he'll bother us. He was just curious.'

There was a silence.

'You game?'

The girl stood up and pulled on her tank. When they were both geared up again, Dan unsheathed the knife from his belt. 'I'll go first. With this in my hand just in case. Remember to keep your movements slow and steady.'

She nodded. He took a couple of steps down the rope ladder. A momentary loss of balance as his flipper knocked the side made him grab at the rope with his right hand, and his knife splashed into the sea. It went spinning and glinting down through the water to the sandy bottom and before it landed the big fish had darted out from under the boat. Holding themselves motionless, the divers watched him. After a long moment eyeing the knife, he gave a lazy flick of his tail and swung back into the darkness beneath them.

'Shit,' breathed Dan.

'It's OK,' said the girl. 'You know, it is OK. He sees the flashing. Like those little fish he eats. When he checks it is not his food, so he goes away.' She selected a new mask and spat inside it and smeared the saliva over the lens with her thumb. She put it on carefully, easing it over her braids.

'What about the knife?'

She peered down into the water. 'I will fetch it. Here.' She passed her own knife to Dan. 'Move.' She fitted her regulator and lowered herself down past him, entering the water soundlessly.

Dan watched her adjust her flotation jacket and turn, swimming smoothly and strongly for the knife. He lowered himself silently into the water, hanging on to the bottom of the rope ladder. It felt cold after so long in the sun. The girl was a good swimmer. Trails of tiny silver bubbles span from her limbs, he saw every detail in close up and slow motion, then he realised he was holding his breath. She swooped on the knife, raising it balletically to her waist and slipping its silver light into the dark sheath. Beneath Dan there was a movement in the water. The barracuda's snout protruded out of the shadow of the boat. Dan tried to calculate whether he could reach Barry before Barry reached the girl. From the angle of her head Dan knew she had seen the fish. She was swimming slowly and deliberately now for the ladder, and as she came closer, Barry withdrew into shadow again. Dan gave her the thumbs up.

They started scraping near the ladder, close to safety – ripping the scrapers through the barnacles and weed as if they were ripping through layers of old wall paper. Blisters began to form in Dan's palms. The movement felt too much, but you couldn't do it weakly. He became aware of a murky shape alongside, growing larger, looming... He put his hand on the girl's arm to still her. Suddenly it was there, the barracuda's head, inches from theirs: his flattened disapproving face, his all-seeing eyes, the deep blue-grey of his side and the chalky whiteness of his belly. The pointed teeth of his upper jaw were fangs hanging over the lower. He looked like a giant piranha. For a moment the three of them were still in the water. The fish inched closer, seemingly inspecting their work. Then he was gone, and the powerful eddy of his turn was enough to knock the girl against the side of the keel. Dan steadied her, before swimming the circuit of the boat. He came back and gave her thumbs up. It took them an hour to finish the port side, and then they went up for a break.

'He's still there,' Dan said as he dragged off his mask. 'He's just sitting there under the middle of the keel, like a sentry.'

'No,' the girl corrected, 'not a sentry. He is our − overlooker, what do you call it? Overman?'

'Foreman,' said Dan.

Miles bared his teeth at Dan.

'This girl,' said Dan, 'this girl, mate, has more guts than the two of us put together!'

'The barracuda who has followed you, he is our luck,' she said. 'Now no harm will come.'

'Yeah, right,' said Miles.

The girl crouched to take off her flippers and Dan watched a trickle of water run from underneath her dark hair down the soft groove in the back of her neck. He laughed.

Miles' displeasure was not easy to ignore. Dan watched him staring pervily at Anna, but when the phone call about the charter came in, he beckoned Dan aft to discuss it privately, leaving Anna in the dark. In the old days they believed a woman on board was bad luck. But Miles couldn't imagine he stood a chance with her, thought Dan − he was old enough to be her father for Chrissake.

As the high of the barracuda moment faded, Dan felt complexity closing in around him. He was in some kind of equation, with letters and symbols that stood for things he didn't quite get; like the ones that used to baffle him at school. There would be parts in brackets involving not just numbers but fractions and letters added multiplied and subtracted, with little numbers above meaning 'to the power of', and you would get a load of this complicated stuff and then an equals sign, and one brutal little letter on the other side of it: X. Dan had a premonition. This X would be disaster.

Sure enough, after a couple of days, Barry vanished. They realised they hadn't seen him since they left St Thomas. Dan flung scraps from their lunch overboard but nothing happened: an hour later he went for a dip, just to check.

'Lost our luck already!' he joked to Anna as he heaved himself back on deck. But she did not smile. Maybe she thought Miles had killed him. Maybe Miles had? It would be unlike him to expend so much effort, though – more likely Barry had simply got bored: symbol for luck arrives (open bracket); symbol for luck departs (close bracket). But minus luck was always going to be more powerful than its simple absence. Once you had seen your luck, you knew what you were missing. Dan told Anna about the charter. Miles had agreed to take some holiday makers from St Kitts for a ten day cruise around the islands. It would delay their departure for Portugal. On the plus side, Miles would be forced to do the repairs properly, if they were getting paying passengers on board. And Anna and Dan would earn more, with the additional possibility of tips. He was irritated by the way she listened, with her face slightly averted, as if she didn't want to have to see him. What was wrong with her?

Then the dinghy went awol. It was on the day they came in to Soper's Hole on Tortola, where they were after a sail mender. It was a deep harbour and busy, they couldn't get anywhere near a mooring buoy. When Dan had seated the rusty anchor, he and Miles lowered the dinghy. They cleared customs and sped over to land in the golden afternoon light. They had different errands. Miles wanted stuff from a chemist, and Dan was looking for an impeller for the salt water pump.

It had burnt out thanks to a plastic bag blocking the intake. He also wanted to sprint to the market. Miles insisted on them having a beer in the flashy marina bar afterwards, then sat over his glass in heavy silence.

As they were climbing back into the dinghy they noticed SeaBreeze was dragging anchor. She was drifting towards the Irish schooner anchored nearby. They raced out to the boat and Dan started winching up the anchor, bashing the stiff chain with the hammer each time it stuck, and guiding the reluctant links into the locker. It was the devil to coil. The blisters on his hands popped and smarted with rubbed-in salt. The depth sounder was broken and he had to reseat the anchor twice, with Anna shifting the boat to what they judged was shallower water. By the time he was done (though not confident it would be OK even then) his hands were red raw. Miles'd got off the phone long enough to radio to the Irish, who were already moving to keep well clear. Anna suddenly pointed to the dinghy. In the rush, it hadn't been properly secured to SeaBreeze, and right now it could be seen bobbing on its merry way towards Little Thatch Island. Miles told Dan to lower the kayak and go after it.

The sun was already disappearing behind low cloud on the horizon. Long fingers of black shadow stretched across the anchorage, and a gusty off shore wind was building. Out towards the islands the water was inky, with little snappy crests of white.

'Miles?' Dan held up his hands. 'I'm fucked for paddling.'

Miles shrugged. 'Ask your girlfriend then.'

Dan took a breath before he answered. 'It's getting dark. And look at the waves out there.'

'Up to you. New dinghy'll take you a year, on your wages.'

At that moment the radio blarted into life again, and it was the Irish, offering to send their dinghy to fetch the errant one, 'before she puts the terror of God into some poor fella who'll be thinkin' you'se all are drownded.' The brogue and throaty laugh flowed like honey into the thin gruel of the mood on deck. Dan tried to catch Anna's eye but she was staring at her feet. There was a sour moment of silence as Miles shaped his mouth into graciousness.

'Ta. Much obliged.'

★

Next morning Anna was below the boat when Dan did something she found very strange. They'd been painting the cabins for the upcoming charter, and needed a dip to cool off. Anna wanted to look again for the barracuda. Treading water, she took a good lungful of air and dived. As she was arrowing down through the clear turquoise water Dan suddenly appeared, swimming strongly towards her, and as she paused to avoid kicking him, he passed her, swung round, and clasped his arms around her torso, pulling her to him in a strong brief hug. It lasted only seconds – she felt the pressure of his clasping arms and the warmth of his chest against her back – then he was gone. She twizzled round and saw him above her, head already breaking the surface. Her whole body felt the imprint of his. She was shocked by the precision of his movement; he had not grabbed or tugged, simply enfolded her entire body in his for one warm firm instant, easily, then let go. She kicked hard to shift herself away, not wanting to bob up next to him. When she broke the surface she dragged in a breath then swam strongly for the bow, rounding it to put a boat's width between him and herself.

What the hell did he mean by it? She checked the memory. He hadn't touched her breasts – she could still feel where his arms had clasped, below her bikini top, just above her waist, pulling her tight against his long bony body. Was it just a passing friendliness? She should swim back to the other side straight away, or he would be finding her quite strange, he would be asking himself what it was she was reading into his playful hug.

But as she swam round the boat she thought again. It was not a friendly hug. He had held her captive – effortlessly. Of course, he was stronger than her. If a man puts his naked skin against yours, if he presses himself against you, uninvited – this does not need analysing, she told herself furiously. He likes to pretend he is Mr Nice Guy, but look! She reflected on other things Dan'd done. He'd switched the contents of the galley lockers around. They kept bottles like oil and vinegar and soy in a high locker above the sink and she'd had to stand on a stool to reach them. He made no comment when he saw her doing this, but when she went to cook next evening she found the cans of beans and sausages and meatballs from the cupboard below were now in the top cupboard, and the bottles were within her reach. It was only when Miles complained about her putting things away in the wrong places that she realised it was Dan's handiwork.

And the cheese. Yesterday he had asked her what was her favourite food. Then after the dinghy had been rescued and secured, he had come into the galley with a specially wrapped goat's cheese. 'D'you normally buy this?' she had asked in surprise. Now she wished she had told him she hated it. What did he imagine? That she was his for the taking?

When she hauled herself up into the sunlight she moved straight to her mobile to send a message, blanking Dan completely.

*

Dan pulled on a t-shirt and got into the dinghy. Miles was there already, tapping impatiently on the seat. They were going to check out a sail-mender in Road Town. The day before, Anna had asked to come along for the ride: now she sat with her eyes fixed on the horizon as if Dan didn't exist. He took the tiller. As they entered the channel between Little Thatch and Frenchman's Cay he began to clown, zigzagging to meet the waves head on and bump across them. It was some relief to irritate Miles, and he hoped he was making the Ice Bitch feel sick.

Then pow! A flashing beast leapt into the dinghy. It slapped into Miles, sending him off his seat arse over tip. It writhed and threshed over him in the bottom of the boat, spraying blood. Dan cut the engine. His first thought was a shark. A shark had leapt into the boat and was eating Miles' face.

Anna grabbed its tail but she wasn't strong enough to hold it; Miles was trying to wriggle out from underneath, and Dan eased himself round and dragged Miles up onto the seat. Miles was gasping and swearing in strange high-pitched bursts, his white face was splattered with blood. It wasn't a shark but a king mackerel, four foot long, with a smaller fish clenched in its jaws. It was threshing like an epileptic and the blood of the smaller fish splattered the dinghy. 'Kill–' wheezed Miles. 'Kill. We'll eat him.'

Anna took the knife from the bait box. She was so contained Dan's heart lurched in his chest. He grabbed an oar and wedged it flat across the length of the creature, pinning it down with all his weight. He could feel the strength of its spine heaving and straining against the oar. She slit it quickly and precisely under the gills on both sides, and Dan felt it slacken, felt the energy draining from it: blood pooled in the bottom of the dinghy. Miles had slumped against the side, his face was an awful colour.

'Fucking mess,' he whispered. 'Drag it behind to bleed.'

Anna nodded and fixed a line around the tail, knotting it securely and tying it off on the rusty rear cleat. Then she and Dan together hefted it overboard, its blood smearing their clothes. Dan leaned over the side to see the line pay out and crimson bloom under the surface. The dead fish dangled behind them like a drowned man. Then suddenly, with an impossible shudder of energy, it heaved forward violently, jolting the boat and yanking the old cleat clean out of its socket – and disappeared in a trail of blood.

Miles had fallen off the seat. The boat looked like an abattoir. And there wasn't even a fish to eat. Miles was still swearing as he lost consciousness.

Then there was the journey back to Soper's Hole, thinking Miles'd had a heart attack: phone calls and sirens and trying to explain that it wasn't anybody's blood, that no one was *wounded*, that Miles had suffered a blow to the chest...

And more medics and a hesitant nervy doctor who stopped with his pressing hands poised over Miles' chest, and asked for an x-ray instead. Turned out the mackerel had cracked three of Miles' ribs, and somewhere along in the shenanigans one of them had punctured his right lung, which was now completely deflated. They took him off for surgery. Dan and Anna got a taxi back to the bloody dinghy, festooned with 10,000 glittering flies, and without a word rode it back out to SeaBreeze because it was too embarrassing to do anything with it under the disapproving gaze of the other boat owners.

So ended a second dinghy incident: Miles in hospital, and Dan and Anna left to sort everything for the charter. Which wasn't actually negative (except for Miles). Dan imagined being alone on the boat with Anna and his stomach gave a little flip. He told her to have first shower. He put her bloody clothes to soak with his and made them both a sandwich. Then they sat and wrote a list. Collect spare filters, laundry, food supplies, take on water. They would need some cash from Miles. Agree meeting time and place with punters in St Kitts; check they had all necessary charts; make arrangements for Miles to fly to join them when he was fit. Anna seemed stunned. She replied monosyllabically as they ate their sandwiches, then went to lie down. Dan held steady, kept his distance. There was time.

★

Anna dreamt about her aunt. She was back on the farm at the end of the fjord and the sun was shining. She and her aunt were walking hand in hand across the field; Anna was carrying the egg basket. They were going to collect the eggs, and together they were singing. Every detail of the morning was sharp and clear; the great grey-green rounded shapes of Husfjell and Svartesvassfjell watching over them; the elderflower bushes smothered in creamy blossom, and the tiny flies that buzzed there constantly; the smooth handle of the basket which had a broken reed sticking out sharply at one end, so you had to hold it at a tilt to avoid pricking yourself. The basket was big and deep, lined with an old scorched towel which had served as the cover for the ironing board. You could see brown iron-shaped imprints on it, from when her aunt had got distracted and left the iron face down for too long. Now it protected the eggs from rolling together and cracking. Her aunt would carry it back, it was too heavy for Anna when it was full. She could feel her aunt's fingers curled around her own, knuckles warm and knobbly like a pocketful of sea-rolled pebbles.

She lay still in her bunk and allowed the memory of her aunt to surface. Her aunt was tall and big-boned with a smiling face which curved inwards from her chin, like the face of the man in the moon. Anna stayed on her farm in the holidays. She always hugged Anna firmly, not too quick and not too tight. She was never in a hurry. In Anna's house everyone was in a hurry; her frustrated overworked mother, her squabbling brothers, her impatient father. Time was like stepping on sharp rocks – pick up each foot again, quick quick quick. Lost socks, spilt milk, a boy's shove or slap, her breakfast whipped away – 'You'll be late for school again' – and the savage scrape of the comb against her skull springing sharp tears to her eyes; 'Oh for heavens' sake, you cry-baby.'

Hop hop hop onto the next rock, get the day to pass. Time was red black hot sharp breathless.

At her aunt's time was slow and rolling, it lulled you along like a cockle boat floating on a gentle river. Colours were all the greens, gold and turquoise and inky blue. Colours of the fjord and the mountains, colours of the sea. She had not thought about her aunt for a long time.

She knew the answer without asking the question. Dan had the same lanky big boned structure. The same calm. Methodically she traced the link. His body pressed against hers in that strange underwater clasp. If she held aside her anger she could see. It could only have lasted seconds, yet it had felt perfectly poised: a point of stillness. Everything with Alexi had been breathless and desperate, always a drama. Always fighting or making up. Knife edge. Dan was balanced. But Anna knew she was doomed, by all she had inherited from her parents, to hot sharp rock days, not to slow and rolling. You were one or the other, you couldn't choose. She knew the kind of men she could have, and the kind that could have her. And they were always fast and furious. Kindness was not their agenda.

Resisting the urge to launch herself at the day's list, she lay back on the bunk and allowed herself to trawl through memories until she netted another object as tangible as her aunt's bony knuckles. A thick blue flannel, wrung almost dry, neatly folded in half and rolled into a plump sausage. 'Here, press it against your eyes,' said her aunt, 'then the shampoo won't sting.' Her strong fingers massaged Anna's head, and she ran her thumb gently up and down the groove in the back of Anna's neck, till Anna felt like purring with content.

Hairwash at home was a torment. Her harried mother slathering shampoo on to her head and violently kneading her scalp, while the soapy water ran into her eyes and made her shriek. 'Be quiet! Be quiet now!' hissed her mother, digging her nails into Anna's skull. 'Or I shall give you something to cry about. Boys, stop fighting!' Once Anna had tried to reproduce the rolled flannel at home, laying it flat on the toilet seat in order to fold it neatly in half.

'I haven't got all day!' cried her mother. 'Head over the sink. Now!'

There was the sound of Dan's door opening, and his footsteps moving up onto the deck. The chartering couple's children could have Miles' cabin. Anna mentally added cleaning it to her list. She put on her oldest trousers and shirt, twisted her braids around her head and went up to the galley. Dan had made real coffee, for her too, but there was a nasty tomato sauce smell. He was stirring a pan. 'There's only a bit of bread left,' he said. 'I thought you'd like it for toast. I'm making a can of spag.'

'You have spaghetti for breakfast?'

'Why not?' His eyes were the same blue as his t-shirt. She felt breathless with anger.

'Why are you kind to me?'

'Why wouldn't I be?' he laughed, and headed up on deck with pan and fork in one hand and his coffee mug in the other. He was trying to trap her with kindness. If he knew her he would not do this.

★

Dan could see Anna was edgy. After they had made a new list of jobs, he kept out of her way. They both worked flat out all day and by Friday they were almost on course. Then Dan blew it. He was hurriedly letting down the dinghy to pay a final call on Miles before they left anchorage, and it started to drop too fast. He leapt to push it away from the stern but it smashed into the transom then smacked lopsidedly into the water. A dark crack snaked right across the bottom of the little boat, from Anna's neat repair, to the stern.

Dinghy fuck-up number three.

Money for a new dinghy would only be earned by the charter. But the charter couldn't happen if there wasn't a functioning dinghy onboard. Anna went across the harbour in the kayak to break the news to Miles, and to see if he had any hidden reserves of cash, while Dan ignominiously rowed the slowly-sinking dinghy to Bertrand's to see if anyone there was up for repairing it. Even if they were, it wouldn't exactly be sea-worthy. A day passed. He tried round the marina to see if anyone could lend a dinghy for a fortnight. He phoned the punters and described Miles' accident in detail. He told them he might be a day late but could give them two extra days at the end in lieu.

This meant they were still in harbour when the storm warning came. Tropical storm Erika, winds 50-63 knots, heading for the British Virgin Islands. If it hadn't been for the dinghy, they'd have been a hundred miles clear to the south on the way to St Kitts.

At first Dan thought nothing of it. You got storm warnings all the time, they changed course or they fizzled out, the forecasts always made a drama of it. But the guy at Bertrand's was busy getting boats out of the water, when Dan paddled back over to see if there was any joy with the dinghy. 'Had one of these mothers three year ago almost to the day. Took off most of the roofs in the place. Enough swell in the harbour to smash your hull.'

'Serious?'

'Serious.'

Dan saw that events had conspired, one after another, to keep them here. Not just to lose them the dinghy (dinghy to the power of 3 in the equation), but to keep them here to be smashed to matchwood by a tropical storm. Steeling himself Dan went to see Miles, who was now sitting up with an impressive bandage strapped around his chest. Miles was surprisingly calm.

'You've lost the charter. You fucked that when you fucked the dinghy. Now this storm. If it stays on course, the advice'll be to stay here, but frankly it's shit. SeaBreeze is seaworthy. In a crowded anchorage where every Tom Dick and Harry's bolted for cover, they'll be running foul of one another. You need to get out into deep water – get out fifty, sixty miles south. You may run into some heavy seas but you won't be crashing her against the breakwater or some other prick's precious schooner. And if you keep a good eye on the forecasts and track Erika's path, you've got time to get clear away. You've got room to manoeuvre, out at sea.' He leered. 'In more ways than one.'

'We leave you here?'

'Nah,' said Miles. 'You row me out on a stretcher so I can roll off my bunk in a tropical storm and crack the other side. What do you think, dick head?'

Dan paddled back to the boat and told Anna the plan.

'We have no dinghy,' she pointed out.

'No. Just the kayak.'

'So if SeaBreeze goes down –'

'Frankly, if the seas are that bad, the dinghy'd be useless.'

After a moment she said, 'OK'.

They checked batteries, lifejackets, whistles, flares, everything they could think of. Dan got the projected path of the storm up on the computer. It was inbound from the Atlantic on a curve, and Tortola was directly in its path. So if they sailed south, keeping west of St Croix, they should be able to get well clear. The faster they got out the better.

The sun was shining, there was a deceptively gentle swell: the calm before the storm. They weighed anchor and headed out to sea.

'If it is foolish to stay in harbour,' Anna asked him, 'how come all the other boats do this?'

'Maybe they don't realise they'll get more damage there.'

But when Dan thought it through he saw this was typical Miles. Damage in harbour would be to boats – crunching against one another or the quay. It would be expensive and annoying but no one would drown. Out at sea there was less risk of bumps and scrapes. But if they were swamped by a big sea, that would be the end of the story. For

143

Anna and Dan. Miles would lose his boat but he'd get lump sum insurance for that, and it would save him taking it to Portugal to sell. Miles was risking their lives in order to avoid scratching his boat.

Dan was tempted to turn back. But everything felt unreal. The clear sky; the glassy sea; the unsettling presence of Anna; the gap where the dinghy should be. If they continued their course, disaster would come at sea. If they returned to harbour disaster would find them there. Whatever Dan chose, he would be wrong.

Updates showed the storm following its predicted path. Dan kept up a steady 6 knots away from it. They were burning up the fuel but frankly, that was the least Miles could do. Erika was forecast to hit Tortola in the early hours of the morning. At 5pm a low bank of cloud appeared to the south, and what little wind there was dropped away. Dan asked Anna to make them both a sandwich and then get some kip; they would take watches through the night, he would wake her at 2. Once she had gone down to her cabin he felt a little more relaxed. It was good they were outwitting the storm, rather than waiting in harbour like sitting ducks.

But as the fast tropical dusk came down, his mood changed again. Anna didn't like him. He had been too pushy – he winced as he thought of that hug, and of the way he had scrubbed her clothes with his sore hands to get the mackerel blood out. What was the point? Anna could leave anytime. The person he was with was Miles, who was proving himself a bastard yet again.

Radio contact was breaking up. The last clear info he got was, winds hurricane cat 1 on the Saffir–Simpson scale. Tropical storm Erika seemed to be breaking up into a series of heavy, possibly cyclonic, thunderstorms, no longer hooking north in the same way. He looked at the charts. 'No longer hooking north in the same way.' So, no longer heading for Tortola. Adjusting the radar to 24 nautical miles, he knew before he saw, with the uncanny foresight of a nightmare, that the batch of storms were coming straight for the boat. They had sailed out to meet Erika like a long lost friend.

The wind was picking up – best he could do now was to run before the storm and hope to escape the worst of it. Directly above and to starboard, the sky was dotted with stars, but something massive was coming up from the east – black cloud moving, heaving, coiling, even as he watched. The drum roll of the thunder became continuous. It was about five miles distant and closing fast, seething and swirling in on itself under the lurid strobe lightning its own violence produced. He turned away unwillingly as something tugged on his arm. Anna, mouth wide open, gesticulating – her words snatched away by the wind. He realised he was an idiot, they couldn't run before this, they'd dis-mast her. They must get the main sail down and lash it to the boom – this was all happening much too fast. He and Anna battled together frenziedly to get the job done, then she tugged him below deck and shouted, 'We must rig up life lines!'

Sudden rain began to bucket down. Dan dragged out the box of heavy weather gear and shoved some at Anna, pulling trousers and jacket over his shorts. He fetched the two new lifejackets with harnesses they had bought for the punters, and they put them on top. The boat was beginning to pitch. Anna's mouth was moving but he heard nothing now except the thunder, he was inside a gigantic electric bass pounding and vibrating his every fibre. He lurched up on deck behind her, and secured the hatch. Anna was fastening the life lines right down to the bow and across the stern. She had the same determined focus that she had displayed when dealing with the mackerel in the dinghy – her thin fingers threading the line around the cleat, once round each side, twist, round again to lock under itself. She was quicker than him, he stumbled beside her, paying out the line, clutching her tightly at the elbow, because the wind was getting strong enough to lift her off the deck.

When the lines were rigged they clipped into them. Suddenly there was nothing else to do. High erratic waves slapped SeaBreeze on all sides, showering the deck in spray and making her shudder; flying fish slithered across the sloshing boards. The roiling mass was bearing down on them. They stood together at the helm and stared at it. There seemed to be a centre – they could glimpse, by the erratic firing of the lightning, a twisting column of steel in the middle of the heaving clouds. A waterspout? Dan opened his mouth to ask Anna and a gust of wind blew into him so hard he choked. Would they be safer below? No, whatever was going to happen would happen up here first, and if it was a gigantic pillar of water it would be better to be sucked up and washed away, than to drown ignominiously jammed below deck.

Anna tugged on his arm and he looked down at her. With her right hand she was describing a curving motion. Curve. Curve. She jabbed a finger impatiently at the storm. He looked up, trying to block out the drama of the lightning, the sickening rising and curling over and under of the boiling black cloud, and to gauge the movement of the whole. Had it stopped getting closer? Certainly it wasn't bearing down on them with the same speed. He lined up the flickering steely column at the centre, with a port-side stanchion. As he watched, the storm moved to the right of the stanchion. Without getting any bigger, without coming any closer. It moved on slowly to the right. Anna pulled his head down to her level, and her hot breath forced itself into his ear. '... changing direction...?' He nodded. They stared.

The storm was passing them, set on its own course, like a giant container ship powering past a raft – churning up the sea but passing, no longer heading for them. The SeaBreeze still sprang and reeled and juddered at the continued slapping of the waves; random waves with no rhythm or pattern to them, like the blows a punch-drunk boxer might hail upon his opponent when he finally gets him down. So strange and sudden and choppy were they that she didn't pitch or roll, she lurched – jumped – slammed, she groaned as they shoved her all ways at once.

Dan and Anna crawled onto the coach roof and slumped

down. They stared at the storm as it continued to swirl in and over itself like a creature devouring its own entrails. It was moving away.

It began to rain again. The waves still snatched and slapped at the boat, but with decreasing force. 'It's going,' said Dan, and Anna glanced up in surprise at the loudness of his voice.

'Do you feel deaf?' she asked.

'I don't know. I don't know what I can hear.'

'You can hear me.'

'Yes but there's a roaring –'

She nodded. 'I have that too. I think is not the wind anymore. Is like after a concert.'

Dan nodded. The rain stopped.

They sat, Dan's arm still tight around Anna's shoulders, watching the seething shape of the storm move on until it was no more than a black ball rolling towards the horizon. Above them, the clouds were racing after it, and the starry face of the sky was clearing.

'It's gone,' she said, unclipping her safety line.

'It's gone.' Dan unclipped his.

'Did you think we will die?'

'I wouldn't have fancied our chances if it'd hit us.'

She took a moment to digest this. 'It was a waterspout, no? At the centre?'

'I think so.'

'It could lift us up, like–' she gestured.

'Yes.'

There was a silence, then she gave an odd little laugh. 'Well.'

Dan ran his thumb gently up and down the little groove in the back of her neck, under her wet hair. 'Bit of an anticlimax, eh?'

'Anti-climax?'

'You think something will happen, then it doesn't.'

She was quiet for so long he thought she would not reply, then she said, 'No. Something happened.'

'Yes?'

'We remained alive.'

'We remained...' He was trying to see her expression, and she turned to face him fully.

'Alive.'

He realised that he could kiss her. That they would kiss.

Dan saw that he had misunderstood that equation, as he had so often done at school. X was not disaster. He unbuckled Anna's life jacket, and she helped him get out of his. As he knelt to roll her damp trousers down her legs he was buoyed by a wave of such gratitude that his eyes blacked out for a moment. When he could see again, Anna was naked in front of him. Her body gleamed like a pearl in the starlight.

'Wait, you'll be cold.' He ran down to his cabin and brought back his sleeping bag and blanket; laid the bag on the deck and draped the blanket over her shoulders. Then their arms went around each other and she pressed herself against him. X = X rated, thought Dan, before he stopped thinking. X = kiss.

When dawn came there was a moderate landward breeze. They pulled on dry clothes, hoisted the sail, and made for Soper's Hole.

Ivory Bird

I WAKE UP to a stink of alcohol. It smells like someone has poured wine over me while I slept. I pat the duvet: dry, that's a relief. It's not me. I haven't been drinking; I feel perfectly fresh, I've slept a deep and soothing sleep. Of course I have – I'm in Adam's bed! Not on Mum's saggy mattress or the thin hardness of the bed at work: I'm in Adam's state-of-the-art posture-pedic bed, where every spring is designed to support and yield, to ensure all-night lasting comfort. I give a little bounce to prove it. Lovely. Weird that it smells, though. I didn't know Adam drank. I reach out for my mobile and check the time. 6.50. Perfect. How nice it is to lie here, seeing the pale green light filtering through Adam's lily-leaf curtains, anticipating his fluffy sheepskin rug under my feet. I think I'll just hop out of bed and make myself some tea. There'll be some lovely kinds to choose from; last time I was here I had Harrods Breakfast tea. I'll just tap it into my phone: How I love flat-sitting for Adam. It's like the poshest hotel –

Yeah but isn't it where he lives? *You are doing him a favour. D'you think he's ever considered paying you?*

It's like the poshest hotel only nicer, because Adam himself has chosen the rugs and pictures and antiques; or else his ancestors have passed them down to him. Each beautiful object has its own story, as if it was made just to be displayed here in Adam's flat. Even the modern things he's bought for himself, the special kitchen gadgets and the discreetly angled lamps, they fit in – perfectly!

I bet you could buy things that matched too, if money was no object. Not everyone buys all their household goods from Age Concern, you know? Some people can choose any colour of reading lamp they want, not just between scratched red with a Batman logo, or dented white with a wonky switch.

I love it. I love the glowing Persian rugs and the blue Delft tiles and beautiful Wedgwood china.

Well ask dear Adam if you could stay. Why not? Hasn't he got a spare bedroom? You could be surrounded by luxury items 24/7. If you put a gold clothes peg on your nose you could even toss the odd cracked ornament to a beggar.

I'm so lucky to have a godfather like Adam! He's kind, he's thoughtful, he even remembers my birthday. I switch on the burnished bronze lamp and swing myself out of bed. Help! My feet land on wetness! Oh no – there's dark red liquid splashed across the snowy white. Spilt wine – I knew it. But I don't even remember opening any wine last night. I cycled from Women's Aid after my evening shift, it must have already been 10.30 when I arrived. All I did was unpack my bag and crawl into bed. I step over the rug and crouch down, looking for shattered glass – but thankfully there's none. Nothing broken. But how can you get red wine out of sheepskin? It's ruined, I'll have to buy him a new one. I'll never be able to afford it. Run to the kitchen for paper towel. Oh my God. What on Earth has happened? The kitchen is in chaos! Someone's yanked open the fridge and thrown everything across the floor – they've smashed jars and bottles and sloshed stuff up and down the walls!

The contents of Adam's fridge? Jars of organic hand-picked wild fruit jam and appellation pâté and finest sundried tomatoes in virgin olive oil? Pots of crème fraîche and probiotic farm fresh low fat yoghurt? Dearie dearie me. How wasteful.

Oh my God. Whoever did this may still be in the flat. I freeze, straining my ears. There is nothing but the steady drone of the open-doored fridge. I pick my way carefully across the floor and swing the fridge shut. Then I creep back into the hall and stare at the front door. Closed and locked. How did they get in? A window? Where are they? They came close enough to my bed to spill wine on the rug – I'm suddenly shaky at the knees. What if they're still here? I should phone the police.

Good idea. The police will check for fingerprints. They'll be sure to catch the villain.

God, I could be trapped. If they're still in the flat they'll hear every word. Move quietly, hush. I'm putting my phone on silent.

If I was you I'd get out. Before things get worse: go while the going's good. Let Adam call his own police.

Slowly and quietly I open the sitting room door and peer in. The mantelpiece is empty! The mantelpiece where Adam's old grandmother clock always sits, flanked by his two Chinese ivory birdcages. He loves those cages – he's told me how they were made. Each one's carved from a single tusk, complete with bird inside – workmanship so exquisite it must have taken the carver years to make a single one.

They have to kill the elephant to get the tusk. You do know that, don't you? Poachers slaughter 40,000 elephants a year, by quite horrific methods. Elephants in the wild will probably be extinct by 2020. But hey! – ivory ornaments and jewellery are an excellent investment, especially antique and highly crafted items.

I hurry across to where the contents of the mantelpiece lie in a heap, as if they have been swiped off with a single wild sweep of someone's arm. The clock's casing is cracked open, its insides are still. I reach down and pick up one of the ivory birds: her cage lies like shattered bone around her. Why would anyone do this? Stealing I can understand, but wanton destruction?

There are all sorts of weirdos in the world. I guess some just like to wreak havoc.

Poor little bird. She can't stand up without her cage. I glance around the room. The botanical prints I love dangle crookedly from their hooks, glass shattered. But the prints themselves aren't damaged, I don't think – oh, thank goodness! I move closer to make sure.

You know what? You might pocket a few things yourself, before you call the police – Adam won't be any the wiser. He'll just assume they've been nicked with the rest.

Shut up. I must sit down a moment. I need to think. What happened? How did they get in? Open the curtains, check the windows – all properly locked. Crunching across the floor (what on Earth is that? Lumps of blue and white china. The willow-pattern bowls!) I cross the hall again to the bathroom and open the door. It gets worse. My nose nearly goes into orbit – battle of the pongs! Calvin Klein, Yves St Laurent, Sanctuary – shower gels, body lotions, skin cleansers and toners, shampoos, conditioners – someone's squashed and squirted them in all directions, they're dribbling down the mirror tiles, pooling in the bath – oh my God, and pills peppered across the floor like bullets after a shoot-out!

Eat your heart out Jackson Pollock.

I can't believe the mess. The cost! There must be hundreds of pounds worth of –

I wonder what'll happen to Adam's dry/greasy combination skin? Without the correct unguents in the prescribed sequence? He might get a blemish. Without hypo-allergenics he might erupt in wild skin disorders – rashes, spots, stars and stripes, oozing pus-filled boils...

What is wrong with you? They must have been drunk – stoned – out of their heads, whoever it was who did this. That's the only explanation. I need to find out how they got in. I return to the kitchen and check the window – locked. I go back into Adam's bedroom; this room has got off lightly, thank heavens – it must be because they found me sleeping here. They must have been watching the flat and seen him leave. But not noticed me arrive. Well, it was dark and raining, yes, it would have been easy for them to miss me. So they came in – the vandals, the hateful destructive idiots, thinking the flat was empty; came through room by room, wantonly destroying things – until they came to his bedroom and discovered me curled up in bed. Then they were so surprised they spilt their wine over the rug and beat it, before I woke up.

You must have slept like a log. Like Sleeping Beauty!

I can't believe it. Usually the smallest sound wakes me. Am I ill? They must have come through the front door... But it's Yale locked. No one could have got in without a key. Unless; what about the credit card trick? Isn't there a way to slide a credit card down a Yale lock and open it? Or what if someone had a key? What if Adam's given a key to a neighbour? So they can pop in and water his plants. And maybe the neighbour has a grudge – or is even mad – maybe the neighbour hates Adam's guts –

Homophobic, probably.

I don't believe anyone who knows Adam could have done this. He's the gentlest man alive, no-one would lift a finger against him. But – what bothers me is, wouldn't a thief, a robber off the street, wouldn't they steal valuables? Things they could flog? It's all still here; flat screen TV, DVD, laptop... Why would anyone do this?

If his neighbour was jealous – jealous of all Adam's lovely things – maybe he'd just want to smash them.

I need to ring the police. This is vandalism, pure and simple. Someone has got in and destroyed stuff, wantonly, someone has –

The neighbour had to smash them. He couldn't steal them because they're unique; the police can trace antiques – china and clocks and ivory birds.

And I'm the one who's responsible. I'm Adam's god-daughter! He trusts me with all his lovely things. He asks me to stay when he goes away, because he knows I'll appreciate them and look after them. He loves the way I leave his flat spic and span!

He thinks he's doing you a favour: you poor kid, working in that shitty hostel – he's giving you a glimpse of higher things, refining your taste, surrounding you with objets d'art. *Plus you are cheaper than a burglar alarm.*

OK. It could be worse. I can clean up. Nothing major's broken, only the – the clock, and the birdcages, and the bowls. I don't think anything else is broken. Thank God they didn't get into the china cupboard. So if I go on sleeping at the hostel and at Mum's, and I don't rent a room, then, my take-home's £705 a month, I could pay him back, maybe £150 a month? OK it would take a long time but even so...

People like Adam are insured to the max.

But who could it have been? The police need to see the scene of the crime, the police can prove that someone got in. I'll call them first, then tonight I can come back and clean. I just need to scoop the stuff up and get a bucket and mop and wash the walls and –

Adam surely has a cleaner?

I can scrub the tiles and the bath, I can –

Imagine: an eager little Polish girl who's desperate for work. This'd be what – say eight extra hours? At eight quid an hour, on Adam's munificent rates? Think how much that would mean to her.

Adam'll never speak to me again. He'll be heartbroken, furious –

Look, you'll be redistributing wealth. Adam doesn't need it, the Polish chick does. You should make more mess for the cleaner. More mess, more hours. More!

Adam will disown me!

Ahah. Now we're coming to it. Now we're getting to the dark heart of the matter. She's got her beady little eye on inheriting. Who else can old Adam leave it to? No children, no siblings: who but his lovely obedient god-daughter?

Look, I stay at Adam's because I like it. I love Adam, I love taking care of things for him. It would be disgusting to expect a reward for that, it would be grotesque. I despise people who do things for material gain.

Good. Well we agree. What if Sleeping Beauty had a nightmare, that all these worldly goods were hers? And they were piling up and burying her alive, with value and taste and antiquity and carefulness and delicate aromas and gleaming surfaces and too much fucking privilege? Maybe she nearly vomited up her own intestines in self disgust. So she did what needed doing.

No. I can't bear it if he thinks – if he suspects… He must never ever think I'd do a thing like this.

How's a girl to prove she really doesn't give a fig for his goods? And that she loves him for himself? How's she going to prove she's on the side of the angels? Sing it loud and clear: property is theft!

I need to clear my head, I need to work out what to do. All the jars and tubes and stuff – if I check all the names and go to *Superdrug* – No, no, somewhere posher, *John Lewis*, I could replace most of them from there, if I used my holiday money –

No. That's not what we're going to do. No no no. What we're going to do is to prove it's Adam we care for, and not his worldly goods. No cupboard love for us! We are not hypocrites, skivvies, lovely girls. This is our manifesto. We're going to paddle across the kitchen floor and have a look in the china cupboard. Oh yes we are. We're going to have a smashing time!

You Want?

IT HADN'T SNOWED in Nîmes for thirty years, according to the guard. But as Karl's train approached the city now, it crawled past snow-filled vineyards and olive trees splattered white. Karl disembarked into a raw damp cold that shrivelled the skin on his face. The train was over an hour late; it was fortunate he had allowed a two hour connection time for his bus. But the bus information attendant, snug in her glass enclosure in the elegantly restored vaults of the station, informed him that all buses had been cancelled because of the snow. For two days, minimum.

Karl found this hard to believe. Traffic crawled along the street in front of the station; the gutters were awash with icy slush but the road itself was clear, as were the other roads he had noted from the train. 'Two days? You're sure?' She was.

He would have to hire a car. But the Europcar representative, inside his own glass cubicle in the archway he shared with Hertz, wanted 230 euros. And the car must be returned to Nîmes. It was absurd. Karl had no reason to come back here; he was flying home from Lyon St Exupèry. He was damned if he was giving these sharks 230 euros.

Taxi. Taxi was a better option, obviously, for a one way trip. He strode out to the vehicle which stood throbbing opposite the main entrance. His tap on the window elicited a bored shake of the head. An oaf in Wellingtons and a grey knitted hat called out something unintelligible from his commanding position in the middle of the road. It transpired this taxi was reserved; the queue was at the other end; many people were waiting, monsieur. Backing away in embarrassment,

Karl stepped into the deep pool of slushy water that lapped at the kerb and only just preserved his wheelie-case, containing his laptop, from being submerged. A dozen or more people were hanging about the other end of the station entrance but there was no obvious queue to join. He memorised their faces so he would know who he came after and not make a fool of himself again, checked his watch, then concentrated on wriggling his sodden toes. No taxis came: the one that was reserved continued to pump steaming exhaust in their direction. He calculated that it was nearly two weeks since he had heard from Johnno. Maybe there would be an email tonight.

Almost an hour later Karl heaved his suitcase into the boot of a taxi and, as he slipped into the warmth, checked the price to Le Vigan. 280 euros. Impossible! The driver shook his head. The distance was long; road conditions hazardous; many people were seeking transport, because of the snow... 'It's a one-hour drive,' Karl said. 'eighty kilometres, max.' The driver shrugged. Karl got out of the taxi and removed his case from the boot, stepping into the ice water again as he did so. Greedy bastards. Greedy rapacious bastards. A few inches of snow and they thought they could exploit everyone to the hilt. Well, they could try it on some other mug.

He dragged his case back into the station and considered his options. The buyer was due at the house at 2pm tomorrow. He did not sound like the kind of man who would be put off by a little snow. Karl needed to be there before him: the shutters would be swollen with damp, he'd have to bash them open with the hammer wrapped in a towel. There could be puddles, rodents, crumbling plaster... OK, car hire. Nothing else for it.

But the Europcar man shook his head with indifference bordering on contempt. There were no vehicles remaining. Demand was very high due to the problems with the snow. The Hertz lady similarly was désolée to inform him that she had no cars left. But might she compliment him on the excellence of his French? Did he know that, because of the snow, the airport had been closed and all passengers diverted to Marseilles? Also that the rail lines were blocked between Montpellier and Perpignan? The demand for rental cars was incredible. She had never in her entire life – Karl thanked her and made his escape. What a filthy pointless incompetent dump. It was already half past five. He would have to stay the night.

Carrying his suitcase this time, he picked his way across the half-flooded road in front of the station and headed into the side streets to the right, where he had noticed a few small hotels on previous visits. The first one, La Vigne Fleurie, had a room at 55 euros: he took it. Gradually, creature comforts were restored; a warm shower, clean socks, hair-dryer applied to shoes. He would nip out later for a drink and a burger, there was a stall opposite the station. If they were capable of functioning in the snow. He sat on the bed, wrapping the duvet around his legs. There was still the problem of tomorrow. If the buses really were cancelled for two days (surely not? But why would she lie?) then he would still need either a taxi, or hire car. He was filled with rage. Barefaced robbers, whichever way he turned. He made a plan of action: one, ring Europcar and make a one-day reservation for 8am. Two, ask the hotelier to recommend a taxi firm and get a quote for a valued customer. Three, check the bus station first thing in the morning and if nothing doing, go with whichever of the other two was cheaper.

But it was still infuriating. He couldn't plausibly light a fire at the house now (needing to stay the night would have provided his excuse); he would have to rush frantically to clear and disguise whatever faults were most evident; he would be horribly out of pocket on this trip. The buyer might not buy. And if the rapacious bastards still demanded the same prices in the morning, he would have to pay up, in which case this hotel was an added cost. What he should have done was take the car at the first price. What he should have done was check the weather forecast. What he should have done was come down with an extra day in hand, for such an important appointment.

The house had to be sold: he needed to finance the renovations at his aunt's old place. Both houses were depreciating by the day, falling into ruin. He must make a sale. How else was he to escape an old age of penury rotting in some council care-home? Or indeed pass on anything worth having to Johnno? Forty years of work and he had sweet FA to show for it, not even a pension. Managing two ruins in snatched days between translation jobs created a tightening band of pressure which bastards like these screwed ever-tighter; why couldn't they just let a man go about his business? This evening he would have to plough on through *Le cours supérieur du Dessin d'après modèle*. It had taken him the entire journey, London-Paris-Nîmes, to translate the twenty-one page introduction. From now on there were illustrations so it would be quicker, but even so.

The rage and pressure were familiar, and the recognition that they were familiar − a near constant state, in fact − generated still more rage and pressure, which in turn led to insomnia. He was tired, yet he never slept. Which naturally led to rage... He lay down on the bed and pulled the duvet up to his chin.

Rapacious. It was a word his wife had used. He turned it in his mind, waiting for it to yield. Yes. The first time they had come to France together − her very first time, when Johnno was a baby − she had called the woman at the Chambre d'Hôte *rapacious*. He had been a little shocked and had wondered if she were xenophobic. Then the woman had asked him...

Within its cramped confines his mind, like a captive worm, sensed the aperture and began a long slow delicious extension towards and through it, escaping into memory. He remembered their drive from the ferry, with sunlight splashed across the wide open countryside, and sudden rows of sentinel poplars, light shade light shade light, lining the straight road. The glorious freedom of being back in France, country of his childhood. Elizabeth sat beside him, breastfeeding Johnno and exclaiming at the quaintness of villages and church spires. He remembered turning into the swooping drive of their first night's stop and them both laughing aloud as the place came into view: a collapsing farm-chateau, magnificently dilapidated. They were paying a pittance for the night. A whippet-thin woman in a silk headscarf answered the door and showed them to their room. Curtains of balding velvet hung to the floorboards; ancient dining chairs were heaped at one end; and a double bed, a single, and a baby's cot were ranged randomly in the space. It was big enough to be a ballroom. The linen sheets were yellow with age. The bathroom, at the end of the corridor, contained a stained toilet and a cracked sink with one functioning tap.

'D'you think we should complain?' asked Elizabeth, and he had laughed.

'I think it's rather charming, don't you? Better than some bland hotel chain.'

Their evening meal, tout compris, was a morsel of pink and salty ham, with a potato each followed by salad leaves. The lean woman ate with them, as did an older, totally silent man, who must have been her father. He poured one careful glass of wine each. The woman pointed out to them the virtues of simplicity in cooking, and promised them cheese and dessert to follow, in the French way. The cheese was a wizened goat's cheese from which she cut them tiny slices, like a child dividing a cupcake. The taste, she insisted; you must savour. It is of the region, incomparable! They nibbled obediently and admired. The pièce de résistance was a plate with four peaches 'from our orchard'. The peaches were very small with softly wrinkled skin which reminded him of the furry cheek his grandmother used to present for him to kiss. When Elizabeth bit into hers she found a worm. She set down the offending fruit and the woman calmly passed her a knife. 'It is best to cut the fruit, Madame, to avoid pests – you see?' She carefully demonstrated how to cut a peach with a knife, then popped a slice in her mouth and nodded at Elizabeth. 'Délicieux.' Elizabeth wildly caught his eye and for a second they teetered together on the brink of hysteria.

Back in their room they filled up on the shortbread they had brought as a present for Karl's aunt. He played devil's advocate: the farm was clearly ruined, perhaps the old man had gambled it all away, and here was the daughter holding onto her pride, trying to keep the place going on such small cash offerings as she could screw from paying guests. 'She must think we're idiots,' insisted Elizabeth. 'She knew we'd be too polite to complain.'

'Well she offered us the best they had – they ate it themselves. Délicieux!' They laughed so much that Johnno began to whimper in his cot.

'Rapacious,' said Elizabeth, wiping her eyes. 'That's what she is, rapacious.' She sent Karl to ask for some warm water to wash the baby.

He made his way down the staircase and along a dark corridor, looking for the kitchen. 'Madame? Monsieur? Allo?'

Her voice called out impatiently, 'Oui?'

When he pushed open the door she was bent over the sink, tugging at a recalcitrant plug. Her bare legs beneath her skirt were lean and sinewy. She freed the plug with a tut of annoyance and turned to hear his request. Their eyes met. And there was something in her eyes – a look, a flicker. He told himself she was nearly old enough to be his mother. She nodded towards the kettle, then she swiftly picked up a tray of clean glasses and he held the door for her to pass through.

Alone in the kitchen he relaxed, inhaling the steamy soapy air. It smelt wholesome and familiar, like kitchens of his childhood. On the gas the kettle was barely warm. He waited in a trance for it to heat up then took it out into the corridor.

A door to his left, which had been closed before, stood half open. As he drew level the woman moved forward from shadow into the doorway. Her dark hair now framed her face.

'Tu veux?' She sounded almost careless.

He stood like an idiot, steaming kettle in hand, staring at her.

'Tu veux?' she repeated impatiently. Time hung.

He remembered shaking his head and smiling foolishly; only registering that he had seen the bed behind her after he had stumbled away, apologising and declining, hurrying as if afraid she might pursue him.

He imagined her, as he had done many times since, standing in her bedroom doorway with one hand at the top button of her blouse (it had hovered there when she accosted him, this detail came to him later) watching the bungling retreating back of the Englishman, her lip curled in amusement.

He carried the hot kettle to Elizabeth and didn't tell her what had happened, sifting and re-sifting the encounters in kitchen and corridor, imagining his way into saying 'But yes!' and slipping through her open door. Stripping her clothes without a word. Her body would have been as hard and smooth as polished wood. He imagined her hip bones jutting under her skin, the hollows at her collar bones, her long neck extending as she rolled her head back into the bed, arching beneath him.

When Elizabeth had washed and fed Johnno and laid him in his cot, they made love in the lumpy double bed. He felt her softness under his hands like billowing silk, like clouds, and regret and shame and anguished embarrassment spurred him on, so that Elizabeth gasped and laughed and said, 'Hurrah for holidays!'

She was quickly asleep. He lay staring at the cobwebby ceiling until Johnno grizzled in his cot, releasing Karl to tiptoe over and pick him up. The child snuggled in, and Karl carried him back to bed and lay holding the little boy close to his chest. He remembered the heat of his son's body, the silky softness of his head against Karl's throat, the still weight of the child as he relaxed into sleep. He remembered slipping into a moment, a blissful moment of peace. Of simple love.

The moment glows. Waking, he feels it recede, disintegrating like the fragile ash of a sheet of paper in a fire. Johnno is in America now, bumming around with his feckless band, emailing Karl when he remembers, with accounts of amazing or terrible gigs. Elizabeth, whose body was always soft and who became flabbier with time, divorced him fourteen years ago. She has a new husband now, according to Johnno. And he is here in snow-bound Nîmes, late, irritated, pressurised, sick to the gills of himself. What is wrong with him? What is behind his own trip but rapaciousness and greed? He catches a glimpse of himself, a petty Englishman whinging about the greed of foreigners, ridiculous in his rage and his demands. Ludicrously striding into the gutter of icy slush.

Tu veux?

He wants. Oh he wants. But what does he want?

He calculates his age, which is no longer a thing he automatically knows. Sixty-one. He has what, maybe ten good years left? Will he waste it in rage? He calculates his own obsessive, depressive, painfully self-conscious personality. Humiliation is his greatest fear. It has always held him back.

But now his thoughts return to the woman. Is she still alive? She would be old now, a bony old woman. Did she actually, as they sat over their goat's cheese and peaches, look lustfully upon him? Or did she make advances to all her male guests, in the expectation of being paid? Was her offer simply the usual way she supplemented the housekeeping? He has had his share of successes, but he has never flattered himself that women are falling over themselves for him. There was something about that moment in the kitchen, though. She heard him enter the room but she didn't turn, she stayed bent over the low sink, her arse towards him, her strong bare legs braced to take the weight of her lean. Wasn't there something in the look between them in that moment she turned, when she realised he'd been looking at her legs, when he realised she realised?

Even so — if it were true — it could still be that she was only asking him because she thought she could make money. Of course she wasn't going to make a fool of herself by propositioning men who never even *looked* at her.

More intently now, he replays the scene. Imagines her, entering her bedroom with that tray of glasses (but how strange! Why take the glasses to her bedroom? It must have been a split second decision, she must have thought he was right behind her and that she wouldn't have time to put them away.) She must have set the glasses down and hurried to the mirror to pull off her scarf and run a hand through her hair. Then she would have moved near to the doorway, listening for him. And he was taking his time in the kitchen, waiting for that kettle to boil. She might have glanced at the bed to check it was tidy. Darted back to switch on the lamp and switch off the unkind overhead bulb. Putting her hand to her throat, she might have fiddled with her top button — undone it then done it up again — just in case. When she heard him finally swing the kitchen door open and stride down the corridor, she must have taken a deep breath before judging her moment and stepping into the doorway. Her throat perhaps was constricted with nerves at the sight of him coming towards her — so the words came out quite toneless. Perhaps she could hardly even recognise them as her own. *Tu veux?* And maybe she did, just a little, want him. And maybe she didn't, only wanted his money. But either way she was standing there, older than him and on display, offering. And he stared, and shook his head, and rejected her.

He has always told himself she watched him go with contempt, but now, patiently reviewing the scene, he acknowledges he didn't look back. For all he knows, she retreated immediately into her room. Isn't the most likely thing, that she would flinch backwards and close the door as quickly as possible? Isn't it likely she would want to hide? That she might crouch by the bed, shrinking into a knot of anguished embarrassment, leaning her burning face against the mattress? If she needed the money, there would be the wretchedness of not getting it – but beyond that, the humiliation of having exposed herself to his contempt. His hasty rejection must have made her think he couldn't even imagine her in that way; wrong-footing her perception of his look in the kitchen.

He hadn't seen her again. In the morning it was the old man who brought them coffee and bread. Karl had been relieved not to see her, because of his own embarrassment. But now he realises *she* must have been quite desperate to avoid *him*.

There's enough in it to make him push back the duvet and swing his feet to the floor. Has he been misrepresenting her all these years? A sudden release of pity washes through him. He sees the woman crouched at the side of her bed and longs to put his arms around her, to offer her innocent comfort.

It is strange. He stretches. He feels loose-limbed, almost giddy. Strange how much he cares about her. Slowly he puts on his shoes and coat and lets himself out into the dark street, nodding bonsoir to the patron. He walks round to the front of the station, crunching through the frozen snow. The burger bar isn't there so he goes into the Café de la Gare and orders a glass of red and a croque monsieur. The air is heated by an electric fire mounted on the wall, and the place smells of wine and scorched dust and wet wooden floor. He seats himself at a dark table in the corner and tunes in to the guys at the bar. They are arguing about global warming. One of them repeats a phrase stubbornly, like a mantra: 'Snow does not come from heat. Snow does not come from heat.' Karl and the waiter exchange a grin.

When he goes back to the hotel he'll check his emails; there could well be one from Johnno. He holds the woman in his thoughts, tenderly. He's very tired. He thinks that he might sleep, after all, tonight.

The Anatomist's Daughters

WHEN MY SISTER rang me she was worrying about a skeleton.

'A human skeleton?'

'Yes.'

'Why have you got a skeleton?'

'I thought I could use it in some way – make casts of the bones –'

My sister Tamsin is an artist. She's made exhibition pieces out of a giant clam and a sheep's pelvis, so a skeleton didn't seem very strange. 'Well what's the problem?'

'I don't know. It's in my kitchen. I don't know where to put it.'

'In the closet,' I quipped. 'Keep the skeleton in the closet.' I tucked the phone under my chin while I uprooted a thistle; I was still gardening, in the last of the light. I asked her where the skeleton came from. She had got it from Chris who did his medical training in Melbourne back in 1980. He was splitting up with his wife; his med school skeleton had been kept in their garage. He told Tammy his wife had screamed at him to 'take that damn ghoulish thing away too!'

'Where did *he* get it?'

'I can't hear, talk into the mobile!'

'Sorry, I was just getting a weed. I asked where did –'

'They all had them then – anatomy students, they had to buy a skeleton to study –'

'It's illegal to trade in body parts.'

'Now. I suppose they have plastic ones these days.'

We talked some more about the skeleton and I suddenly

visualised it, hanging there, listening to her talking to me. I found myself entering into her predicament.

'It's not hanging, it's not all strung together,' she said.

'You mean it's just a heap of bones?'

'There's a hand connected up, and a foot, and a few of the vertebrae. The rest's –'

'The knee bone's connected to the – ah – thigh bone,' I sang.

'She's a person, Kerry. She was in an old banana box, all cobwebby and dusty. When I opened it up and saw her skull... I had to polish her and wrap her in pillowcases to make her feel better.'

'Her?'

'Chris told me she's an Indian woman.'

'You could bury her,' I said stupidly.

'And if someone digs her up –'

'Ah. A murder rap. You can't get rid of her.'

'No. But I can't just keep her under my bed.'

'Where are the skeletons all the other medical students used to have?'

Neither of us could imagine. You don't go to the doctor's and see them displayed in the waiting room, alongside the doctor's certificates. Or in junk shops or on eBay. Or maybe you do, I've never looked for a skeleton on eBay.

'Dad must have had one.'

'Yes. I remember seeing it at his lab.'

Our father was a professor of anatomy, before he died.

'Where did they all come from?'

'India. All the skeletons in Australia are Indian,' she told me.

'But how did they get them?'

'Bought them from med school suppliers. Who bought them from agents in India –'

'But where did *they* –?'

'Dad said they fished them out of the Ganges.'

We laughed then. It was so exactly what he would have

said. The combination of slimy corpses, casual racism, and the trashing of religious sensibilities made this his favourite sort of utterance.

'Well,' said my sister. 'At least you made me laugh.'

I thought about our father as I finished my gardening. He would have scoffed at Tamsin. He had no patience for anything psychic or spiritual: he was a rationalist to his core, a despiser of sacred cows. He liked to think of himself as a rebel and identified with every kind of outsider. But he also despised stupidity, and since religion and superstition were, to his mind, stupid, his attitude to most people was one of contempt.

I pondered his character as I worked, then felt angry with myself, and sat on a crate and rolled a cigarette. He was dead and couldn't defend himself. I hauled into my mind the things I loved about him; his passion for books and ideas, his sense of humour which was a scalpel he wielded against every kind of self-inflation. His expert gentleness when we were little; he could soothe a grazed knee, get a comb through tangled hair, comfort with the laying on of hands. He was the best teacher in the world: able to render complex ideas simple without distorting them; a lover of plain English, a great democrat in his teaching. A mountain of good qualities against the mole-hill of his failings. Why was I so bitter?

For childish reasons. For childish reasons, although I was an adult.

Tamsin rang me again a couple of days later. I was driving home from the shitty call centre, I had to pull over to talk to her. 'D'you want to come round at the weekend?' she asked.

'What's up?'

'I want you to meet Indira.'

'Indira?'

'The skeleton. I'm reassembling her. I'll have her strung together by Friday.'

'I don't mind coming to see *you*, but –'

'You think I'm being stupid.'

'I think you're being irrational.'

'I can feel her watching me. It's as if I've let a genie out of a bottle, her presence is expanding.'

'Get rid of her. Take her in to the Anatomy Department.'

'She wouldn't like it.'

'Can you hear yourself?'

'There's so much sadness. She's been ignored for so long.'

'It's *bones*, Tammy.'

'I'm not being funny, she's in my house. I have to figure out a way of living with her –'

'Get a pet. If you need something to love, have a baby or get a pet, and stop being such a fucking flake.'

There was a little silence, then Tamsin put the phone down on me.

Later that week I lost my mobile. I'd stopped at Kulkami Reserve for a walk on my way home from the call centre. My mobile was in the pocket of my denim jacket. It was warmer than I expected and I ended up carrying the jacket slung over my arm as I climbed up Mindiyarra Hill. In the distance I could make out a mob of kangaroos idling in the spring sunshine, on the flank of the hill that leads down to the creek. I decided to go down that way rather than back along the path. To begin with I was scrambling through rocky outcrops; then the slope became more gentle, with coarse tufts of grass underfoot. The kangaroos didn't move off till I was pretty close, and I saw a couple of joeys hop back into their mothers' pouches. That always makes me smile.

I didn't feel for the phone until I got back to the car. Then I realised what an idiot I was. The most obvious place for it to have slipped out was while I was slithering down the rocky area near the top of the hill. It was already half past five and I was meeting Mike at six thirty – and, doh, couldn't phone to say I'd be late. I set off at a run back through the kangaroo pasture (they'd vanished, not a one of them in sight) and up the side of the hill till I came to the area where rocks take over from grass and scrub. Then I realised the impossibility of it. There was no path through the rocks, that's why I'd had to scramble. I stopped. Red rocks and their black shadows on all sides; between them a multitude of cracks into which a small object, dropped, would immediately vanish.

The lost phone bugged me all that night. It was partly the cost of a new one; mostly, the hassle of having to go into town to buy it. Losing it disconnected me from everyone I knew. I imagined the phone, lying on a stony patch of ground, bleating and going onto answer-phone; people leaving me messages I could never pick up.

That gave me the idea. If I borrowed Mike's phone and retraced my steps, I could ring my own number. The sound of its ringing would lead me to it. My shift at the call centre didn't begin till ten, I'd have time before I started.

In the morning he was grumpy about lending his phone. 'I feel lost without it.'

'That's how I feel.'

'I might get an important call.'

'One of your other women?'

He laughed and pushed me back onto the bed and we rolled there together for a minute, warm and close. 'Why is sex more enticing when there's not enough time?'

'Because you like to know you can get away. Shoo. You'll be late for work.'

We left his house at the same time, and I drove straight out to the reserve. The early sun was still low in the sky, making the red rocks glow like embers and intensifying the smoky green of the gums. I dialled my number on Mike's phone then held it away from my ear. Silence. In the distance a magpie warbled. I thought I'd retrace my steps so that I could leave the top of the hill at the same point I had done yesterday. Maybe from the top I would be able to identify my route down.

I dialled and listened repeatedly on the way up. Nothing. At the top, the same. The morning sun was beginning to bite, it would be hot today. I sat on a rock and rolled a cigarette and stared down at the jumbled, stony hillside. It was already nearly nine. I didn't want to go to the call centre anyway. Of all the crap jobs I've had that's the crappest. Jabbering at idiots all day long, you don't know them, they don't know you. I decided to try and find myself some sort of outdoor work, gardening or agricultural, something that wouldn't be so – contaminating.

Our father cut himself off when we grew older. Left our mother, left his university post, took himself up to Darwin. I don't know how he lived up there, we were never invited to visit. My mother assumed he'd gone to another woman but I'm not sure that was true. He sent me and my sister a letter saying he wanted to concentrate on making sense of his own life, now we were grown up. I know the letter by heart but that doesn't mean I understand it. He talked about having no more to give us, and said his job with us was done. He recommended that we be kind to our mother (to whom he was sending a monthly cheque) and he hoped we would be happy.

As if. For a long time we were angry, and that settled into a lingering resentment. We would have conversations about how we wouldn't visit even if he invited us. My aunt talked about male mid-life crisis. But time ran on and we never heard from him, not even on our birthdays. It was a complicated stew of feelings; anger and hurt at his rejection, and an embarrassed kind of shame at his behaviour, which was so aberrant, so unfatherly that we felt the need to conceal it from our friends. In my darkest heart I understood that it must be our fault, that he must be more disappointed in us than any other father ever was in his children. It was easier to pretend that he was dead, than to reveal that he simply did not want to see us. In our rare moments of success we felt truculently satisfied that he was not able to bask in reflected glory: in periods of failure and despair we observed bitterly that this was all due to his unnatural behaviour. I used to fantasise about a reconciliation, and how he would try to make it all up to us.

And then we heard that he had died. He was diagnosed with a brain tumour, and they tried to operate and he died. He died on the operating table with a surgeon probing the unfathomable circuitry of his brain.

His death was hard to bear. He had removed himself even further, rendering himself permanently inaccessible, removing the possibility of us ever understanding or of his ever being able to make amends, even if he had wanted. How can people do that? Just die, absent themselves, cease to be answerable? Leaving all those question marks hanging in the air? At his funeral we were stunned and dumb.

Sitting there on Mindiyarra Hill I felt an urge to talk to my sister. But I didn't want to use Mike's phone; finding my own was somehow dependent on not making a proper call from his. I thought of Tamsin wrapping the bones in pillowcases, and wondered how many spare pillowcases she had, and why she chose them rather than old t-shirts. I thought about the Indian woman and wondered if she had children, and if they had been to her funeral.

I once visited Bombay. I stayed in a cheap hotel opposite the back entrance of a hospital. When I woke in the morning there was wailing under my window, and a small crowd with garlands of orange flowers taking delivery of a corpse. It was a woman in a sari, who they carried at shoulder height in a noisy procession down the street. I remember being shocked at the lack of concealment. I caught myself thinking stupid things – that an open corpse on the street is unhygienic, and that I wouldn't want everybody looking at me when I was dead.

Now I wondered what they had done with her body. You don't get a skeleton from cremation. To get a skeleton you must clean the flesh from the bones, by worms underground, or weather and vultures in the air. Or by immersion in a vat of chemicals. What family signed up for an acid bath?

People do leave their bodies to science. But if *all* the medical school skeletons were Indian... I found I was having gruesome, Burke and Hare thoughts, of relatives not consulted, of absence of donor cards. Of fishing bodies out of the Ganges. I rubbed out my cigarette butt between finger and thumb and dialled my number. Nothing. I got to my feet. It was easy to identify the spot where I had begun my yesterday's descent, to the left of a large jutting rock, and down to where the ground became stony and loose underfoot. Since it was too steep and slippery to go straight down, I must have chosen a diagonal across this. I slithered to the nearest sizeable rock, perched and dialled again. There was a click. I looked at Mike's phone. It gave one little exhausted beep and switched itself off.

I was so angry I nearly smashed the thing. Here I was on the exact rocky pathless stretch where I knew damn well I'd lost my phone, and I'd used up Mike's battery calling in all the places where I knew it *wasn't* lost. When the rage faded I put the dud phone into the zipper pocket of my combats, and considered running back to the car. I'd only be half an hour late for my shift.

A great flock of galahs came wheeling and clattering overhead, and as their racket passed over I heard another sound underneath it. A tinny electronic four note ditty. Close enough to touch. I leaned over the rock and looked down into the shadow on the other side. My phone lay exposed like a piece of evidence on the bare ground. I got it on the seventh ring, just before it went to answer.

'Kerry?'

'Tams! You've found my phone for me!' I told her about my lost phone. She listened, sympathising and laughing in the right places. Her voice was warm and bright in my ear. My sister, connected on the end of the line. I apologised for calling her a flake.

'It was when you said have a baby –'

'I'm sorry, I'm s –'

'– you sounded like Dad.'

'I know.'

There was a little pause then she said, 'Alright.'

'Can I come over tonight, and make acquaintance with Indira?'

'It's not a joke, Kerry.'

'I'm serious.'

'OK.'

'OK. I'll bring a bottle of wine.'

I walked back down to my car, my phone clutched tight in my hand. As I passed the kangaroos I shouted 'Whoopee!' but they just twitched their ears and carried on nibbling the grass.

The Runaway

THERE WERE FIVE cigarettes left at 1am. Eleanor took a couple from the pack and slid them behind the postcard leaning up on the mantelpiece. The sound of footsteps in the street froze her in her tracks for a moment, until they had passed the gate. Then she picked the third cigarette from the pack, struck a match, and lit it.

A kind of terror behind the inhaling and the waiting, in the dim room lit only by the glow of the bedside lamp coming through the open bedroom door. This feeling and the smoke hitting her lungs reminded her suddenly of standing on the top diving board at the pool, the sickening lurch of terror and then the sudden burst of hurtling delight, the flying. Perhaps you can't have delight without terror, she thought.

Which was rubbish because what delight was on offer here? The possibility of his coming back? At best that would be accompanied by a dull relief – relief that he wasn't out even later, that he wasn't incapably drunk, badly injured, in bed with someone else, arrested, dead. But the relief could only be provisional because already he had been out too long, too late, to be up to any good. And what was far worse anyway was the fact that she had told herself she would not do this. Gareth's comings and goings were his own affair. It was ridiculous and pathetic to be pacing the room at ten past one waiting for a twenty-three year old to come home.

She hadn't wanted him to know she was up, if he came back; the light from the bedroom wasn't enough to show through the living room curtains, and she had imagined scuttling back to bed and pretending to be asleep when she heard him on the stairs. But now the room was full of smoke, she might as well have a drink. She switched on the standard lamp and poured herself a whisky. He could be in a club. They stayed open till two, two-thirty, three. But he hadn't enough money. Someone could have paid for him. Of course.

She settled in the corner of the sofa. It would be better if he didn't come back anyway. Far better. Time for this ridiculous business to end. Everything in the room seemed particularly rich and still, lovingly illumined by the lamp; the coffee table stood squarely on its own shadow, as if posing for a photograph. The folds in the curtain – a faded beige velvet, in daylight – were deep and sculptural, as if carved in stone. The anemones she had put in a tumbler on the end of the mantelpiece were in that final stage of contortion before the petals start to drop; heads flung up, down, sideways, one writhing down over the edge of the glass then snaking upwards again; an ecstatic still life. Alright, she thought. This room. Me in the corner of the sofa, holding my glass. Is it a happy picture?

No, because it's waiting. She tried to think of the painter whose work it would be; the anemones made it difficult, they were too extreme. Subtract the anemones, and it could be Hopper. Whose rooms do wait; whose everything waits: street corners, beaches, expanses of sea through doorways – waiting, with a desolate and expectant kind of dread, and a knowledge that the waiting will go unanswered. What was it Hopper was waiting for? What was the absence he was framing? Oh for God's sake, she told herself impatiently, deliberately lighting another cigarette although it was only twenty to two. She had meant to ration them to one an hour. The cigarettes must last until he came home. Well, when the cigarettes were gone, he would come.

The absence... Jeffrey had written her a letter. It had surprised her, he was not the sort of person who wrote letters – although that was a stupid thing to say, how did she know what sort of person he was, she had lived with him for twenty years and still had no inkling of what he really, honestly, thought about anything. The more you saw of a person the less you knew them, it was a fact, and the reason of course that you could still (yourself) not know what you (yourself) were going to do, was because you knew yourself too well. Whereas someone who had only met you six weeks ago could easily predict your behaviour.

He had mentioned absence. In his letter. *In view of your continuing absence from the family home.* He wanted to put things on *a more regular footing.* If she had any regrets, if she thought she might have made a mistake – if she returned before the end of June, no more would be said about it. They would draw a line under this unhappy chapter. But if she wished to continue in *this course of action,* he felt it would be appropriate to contact a lawyer about settling their financial affairs.

It was a polite and slightly pompous letter. Such a decent man. Would I have preferred it, she wondered, if he had come round with half a brick and tried to beat the living daylights out of Gareth? That would have been unfeasible anyway, given Gareth's advantages in height, age and physique... but still. It might have shown he cared. On the other hand, his kindness and courtesy over the years, his continual attempts to jolly her along – did these not constitute much more potent and enduring evidence of care? Of course but I can't be bothered with it. It's too bad. It's just too bad. And the *absence.* What did he mean? Did he mean the same thing that was missing from this room right now?

It was unlikely. She had bought a print of a Hopper picture once, the lit bar at night, plate glass up against the black night air, three figures held in the cage of light. Jeffrey had pronounced it *rather depressing.* He had asked her not to hang it in the dining room. In fact it had ended up on the landing, between the boys' bedrooms; a spot where it could easily be ignored.

Was the absence in this room simply Gareth's absence? She wasn't sure. If he came back now, drunk and angry, and threw himself into that chair opposite, demanding a cigarette

181

and wanting to know why the Inquisition was up – the curtains with their mysterious folds would still stand in the light behind him; the coffee table would still squat, patiently, over its shadow on the floor: no, the room would still be waiting, waiting for something – bigger, she supposed. Bigger and better.

In fact there was something quite horrible about Gareth. Something frightening. When he knew he had behaved badly, his reaction was of hatred and anger. So he would come in and sneer at her for waiting up – maybe even lash out at her with his fist again. She supposed he was testing her, proving that she loved him no matter what he did – unconditionally, absolutely; well, that would be a psychologist's explanation.

But was it accurate? The still, mysterious room seemed to be drawing thought out of her, pulling unexpected things from her head into its space. It was perfectly possible that Gareth was testing her, but benign understanding of his traumatised psychological state was not actually the reason she was sitting here waiting to be hurt again. Oh no. It was for herself she was here, she realised, with a sense of suddenly remembering something vital. It was nothing to do with love and understanding. It was for herself, because she was waiting for... She was wanting, her heart was fluttering with the expectant thrill of it – she was *wanting* to be hurt. Yes, by what he would say, by what he would reveal about what he had been doing. Even, could it be, physically? Would that be the fulfilment? – of the expectation, the nervous dread-like thrill, that had been inside her since she woke?

What a preposterous thought. She was seriously telling herself this was what she had set up for herself? Why on Earth would anybody do such a thing?

Because I deserve it, she whispered aloud into the room – pulling a face at the melodrama of the words as they came back to her own ears.

Why?

She got up and paced to the curtains and back, to shift herself out of the shadow of the shape she had been sitting in, to make herself different. The only obvious bad thing she had done was to leave Jeffrey and the boys. Some might say she should be punished for that. But surely it would be more logical to return to them, than to stay away, seeking punishment?

No, it wasn't that. Anyway, she didn't want to return. That wasn't the reason she should be punished. This was the reason. That when she married Jeffrey; when she had the boys; for twenty years – she had led a life of complete dishonesty.

This thought sprang out of her head into the room like a healthy young horse leaping a gate. Shockingly, hugely, it was there, prancing about, striking the earth with its hooves, filling the air with the stench of its hot breath and shimmering flesh. But how? How was I dishonest? She was cowering before it – she backed into her corner of the sofa again, reaching tremblingly for the last cigarette (But there are two behind the postcard on the mantelpiece). The horse kicked up its heels and arched its neck, snorting, delighting in its new-found space, happy to be alive.

You pretended a part of you didn't exist. You wanted Jeffrey to like you, you wanted to be a good mother to your sons. You behaved as you should in those roles, you behaved, as you felt, appropriately. You acted the part. And the feelings you deemed inappropriate, you disallowed.

That's not true, she countered, her confidence coming back. That's absolutely untrue, I had screaming rows with Jeffrey, I threw plates of food.

No, replied the horse patiently (though its front hooves were pawing the ground). You threw things if he tried to help you – as he saw it – if he tried to improve on your wifely/motherly attempts. Because you felt (quite rightly) that that was a criticism. And you could not bear to be criticised by him because you had given up so much in order to achieve that motherliness, that wifeliness.

This is romantic crap. Eleanor stood up and reached for

one of the cigarettes behind the postcard. I'm supposed to believe that for twenty years of married life I've been suppressing some wild passionate part of my being, which has now at last made a bid for freedom?

That's right, said the horse. And because you've denied it for so long, and because it is so *sweet* (and here the horse bared its teeth, which were long and yellowish, in a horrible kind of grimace, so that it was impossible to tell if *sweet* in fact meant its opposite, or not), it is now seeking revenge. It wants to punish you – or, I should rightly say, you want to punish yourself, for denying it for so long.

This argument was becoming almost enjoyable. Ludicrous, but absorbing. You mean to say that Gareth is the embodiment of the wild suppressed part of my nature, come back to punish me?

Of course, said the horse irritably. I should think anyone would want revenge if they've been shut away from the light for twenty years.

Gareth is himself, stupid! cried Eleanor, filled with triumph at noticing this flaw in the argument. He's a separate person, he's got his own reasons for existing and behaving –

But to you – said the horse, he is what you need him to be.

Eleanor looked down for a minute, concentrating on lighting the last cigarette – and when she looked up, the horse was gone. Cigarette smoke hung in heavy drifts across the room, which was as empty and still as if no-one had moved in it all night. There was the sound of feet running down the street. They slowed and turned at the gate. They went quickly up the steps; the sound of a key twisting impatiently in the lock; the door slammed shut. Oh God, he'll wake the people downstairs. The feet ran up the stairs. Eleanor's heart leapt.

'Still up?' he said. 'What you doing?'

'Drinking.'

'Stinks of smoke in here.' He crossed to the whisky bottle, raised it and inspected the level critically. 'You drink too much,' he said.

The blast of night air he brought in with him and the energy and bulk of his body filled the room, deflating Eleanor in her place on the sofa like a shrivelled balloon. She stared at him helplessly.

He threw his jacket on the other end of the sofa. 'I need a piss.' He went into the bathroom and slammed the door. Eleanor stared at his jacket, one sleeve was half inside-out. It would still be hot from his body. The flush sounded and he reappeared, lounging against the doorframe.

'Well?' she asked.

'Well?' he grinned.

'Where've you been?'

'You still my probation officer?'

'No.'

'OK. I've been' – he counted the list off on his fingers – 'mugging old ladies, dealing crack, fucking a minor, TWOC-ing, watching porn, gambling, lobbing bricks through plate glass windows – is that enough?'

Eleanor took a last puff of her cigarette and carefully ground the stub in the ashtray. It would be sad (if she believed it) to contemplate that a liberated, wild and passionate part of her psyche could muster no more interesting behaviour than to time its return home so that it coincided, to the dot, with the smoking of her last cigarette. 'You didn't have to come back,' she said.

'Didn't you want me to?'

'Only if you wanted to.'

'Well I did. OK?' He shifted impatiently.

Suddenly the abyss yawned again at Eleanor's feet. She felt herself swaying, teetering on its edge, filled with swooning longing for the downward plunge. She made herself speak calmly.

'I don't like to think you're humouring me.'

'If I was humouring you I would've come back earlier, wouldn't I?'

'It's a question of trust –'

'Of you not trusting me.'

'I do trust you but you want to make a fool of me – to, to prove something –'

'To prove what?'

There was a silence.

'Eh?'

Eleanor nipped the inside of her lip between her front teeth. The bright taste of blood released her. She didn't have to do this. 'I don't know. I don't know what.'

Another silence. She could move away.

'Look, I'm too tired for this. I'm going to bed.'

'Fine.'

She stood up but he made no move. She went past him to the bathroom, cleaned her teeth again, then got quickly into bed and turned off the light. She lay straining her ears to hear what he was doing. There was movement across the room, then the clink of the whisky bottle. It's OK, she told herself, burrowing a dent into the pillow. In the morning I'll ask him for his key back.

She must have fallen asleep then, because when she opened her eyes it was dawn. He was kneeling on the side of the bed, bouncing up and down slightly to wake her.

'Ello,' he grinned. 'Fancy a fuck?'

'I hate you.'

'Yup.' He grinned again. 'Well?'

Eleanor laughed, and raised herself up on one elbow to meet his kiss.

Lucky

THERE WERE SEVEN tests. If the 8.20 to Victoria was on time. If there were no empty seats. If I saw the weird couple. If I could get across the station concourse without them making any change-of-platform announcements. If the beggar was in that doorway just round the corner from the post office. If a pigeon walked across the pavement in front of me without me dodging to get it there. And if I arrived at work before nine. Check check check check check check check! He loves me.

Each day I make it more difficult and each day it's proved – apart from Tuesday which was crap in every other way as well, what can you expect, it would be unbelievable if it *did* always work, there has to be an exception to prove the rule. Like spelling.

He brought the report back in to me at 3.07pm. 'Well done Janine, you've done a good job.' He smiled. 'Apart from the usual problem. Have you turned that spell-checker off, or simply converted it to your own personal language?'

'It's on,' I said. I was trying to stop giggling. 'There wasn't a single underlining. Honest.'

He laughed that deep brown glow in his eyes it warms you through to your guts. 'Creative spelling. I love it! OK, I've underlined in pencil here. Can you get it in tonight's post?'

He was starting to go. Like the sun disappearing behind a huge dark cloud taking all his lovely warmth away. 'Dr Anderson –'

'Yes?'

'I – d'you want to see the corrected copy?'

'No Janine, I trust you.'

Of course he does. He trusts me. He closed the door gently and you could hear my heart banging like a drum, sometimes it's dangerous I'm afraid the others will notice – the bitching the gossip, they'd have a field day. You only have to listen to the way they talk about Fiona. Tina was on the phone though and Laura was taking her printer to bits, the paper feed was jammed again. They don't notice. Because they can't imagine. They can't imagine he'd like someone like me. They think they're so great with their wonderbras and lipgloss and step-ladder shoes, they don't even ask me what I did on Saturday night.

Well fuck them. They know nothing.

Once he sent me a note. *Jan – articles from BMJ on post-abortion depression, May 95-97, by 10.30 if pos? You're wonderful.* I keep it folded up in my pocket. I can feel it through my jeans, secret against my thigh.

You'll be wondering how it started. I'll tell you. It's good to tell someone at last, it's been like this secret balloon inside me, this lovely growing swelling thing that makes me so huge and light I sometimes think I'll burst – burst with happiness or just take off and float into the sky. The secret wants to burst out of me I want everyone to know.

It was instant. First sight, on my second Monday there. He came into the office. 'What's this? Can't a man turn his back for an instant without everything changing?' He smiled at me. He's got grey hair but he smiled right into my eyes and I had that feeling you get in a high-speed lift when it suddenly plummets 20 floors and you think Omygod.

'This is Janine,' said Laura. She kicked Tina under her desk then she said, 'She's filling in for Fiona.'

'Welcome Janine filler-in-for-Fiona,' he said. 'You let me know if they're not looking after you.'

My hands were sweating, I couldn't hit a single key right. I had to get out a pen and fiddle about pretending to make a note of something. He went over to Tina's desk asking about some letters, his voice is deep and soft and furry my ears can pick it out anywhere it's right close up to them, in a crowd I can sometimes hear it too, low and close murmuring beside me as if it'll keep me safe from everything. When he'd finished at Tina's desk he came back past me and he slowed down he couldn't walk past me he couldn't help himself he had to stop.

'You girls get younger every week. How old are you Janine – or is that an offensive question?'

'No.' I was afraid I would giggle. It's horrible. It comes out sometimes and then they laugh at me, they used to laugh at school. 'Eighteen.'

'As old as that!'

I was giggling. I couldn't help it. He would hate me and think I was an idiot. He started to laugh. 'She's a giggler!' he said to Laura and Tina. 'Wonderful! A dose of that all round every morning and you'd halve the NHS waiting lists!'

He went then and I was giggling so hard I was gasping for breath, I could feel my face like a beetroot. But the other two didn't notice, they were whispering together, Fiona this and Fiona that, he can't wait till she gets back. He's been to see her twice in hospital. I wasn't interested in Fiona. I knew he liked me. You can tell.

You know it but you don't believe it. You have to keep checking, you don't dare to let yourself think it might be true. That someone like him could fall for me. But everything that's happened – every single thing – reinforces it.

The library. I go to the library for my lunch. Often I think I won't, I think I'll go to a wine bar where there are foreigners or business men doing deals but in the end I go to the library. The others send out for sandwiches but I don't like sitting listening to them, I like to go somewhere where I can watch people without them feeling sorry for me and trying to drag me into the conversation. In the library you go through the revolving door and past that expensive card shop then down the stairs to the café. I like the posters down the stairs, all the plays they have on there, one day I'm going to go to that theatre. One night, I should say. I bet it's different at night full of glamorous people holding drinks from the bar, chattering away, reading their programmes. Maybe I'll go with him!

At lunchtime you can sit by a pillar or the wall, usually you can get a table to yourself and there are invisible people there, old codgers with lots of coats and a cup of tea, sometimes studenty types I suppose they use the library, or ordinary people, fat with a shopping bag. There's a man with glasses who always reads a book, everyone ignores each other and you just queue and pay for your sandwich, none of that embarrassing waiter business. You can buy theatre tickets there – I've seen where they do it. Also the toilets are good, very big with gigantic mirrors, there are four cubicles and when you come out it's like you're a film star reflecting back and forth and back and forth in the mirrors in front and behind.

He came into the library café. July 2nd. July, the seventh month. I still don't know... did he follow me? I can't believe he did but how else did he end up there when I was there, what are the chances of him going where I was going at lunchtime with the whole of Manchester and all the important people he has to meet for lunch and the girls asking if he wants a sandwich when they pop out – *how* did he end up there with me?

I was in the right hand corner by the pillar near the stairs and he came down the opposite stairs. We saw each other straight away. Instant. He smiled then there was a little frown, I was afraid he wasn't pleased to see me. But he didn't have to look at me, it's easy enough for people to pretend they haven't seen you isn't it? They do it all the time. Or he could have just smiled and waved from a distance. But no, he came straight to my table like he was drawn there by a magnet. 'All on your own Janine? Not having lunch with the other girls?'

I shook my head. I was afraid I might giggle.

'Is everything alright? You all getting on OK in the office?'

He was so kind he is so kind. He's the kindest person I ever met. 'Fine thank you. I just —' I didn't want him to think I was stupid but I couldn't think what else to say. 'I like it here.'

'It's a marvellous building isn't it? A jewel in the heart of the city!'

He understands everything I think.

'I'm waiting for a book from the depths. May I join you?' He went to the counter and when he was there he turned back to me and made sign language pointing to the teacups then back to me. I mouthed back *coffee* and he smiled and I felt as if I was melting into a puddle. I *was* melting into a puddle it was awful my nose started to run and I had to swallow my mouth was full of saliva I was all warm and watery inside I was afraid I might have wet myself. I didn't dare to look at him until he was sitting down, he ate his sandwich in seven bites. Seven is my lucky number.

'D'you use this library?' he said. I shook my head and he leaned forwards. 'Have you ever been upstairs?'

Upstairs. I can't believe he asked me that. 'No.' The giggles were rising in my throat nearly choking me.

'Well if you've finished come with me and have a look. You might want to use it one day.'

He stood up and drank his coffee in three gulps. It was coffee. The same as mine — not tea. We went up the marble steps together there are 26 to the ground floor, I stepped on each one at the same time as him. We moved at the same speed.

'Wonderful institution, public libraries,' he said. 'But we must use them. Use them or lose them, eh Janine!'

He says my name so beautifully. I was giggling and he laughed too, he *joins in* my giggle. I thought I would never tell anyone because people would probably sneer, my mother would say something terrible and crude like he's a dirty old man or something because he's about 20 years older than me but she doesn't understand anything. Now I have to tell someone but you won't laugh because you can see he's not dirty he's kind, he's kind to a person like me when he doesn't have to be, he notices me he talks to me he looks at me he *loves* me.

We turned round the corner and went up the next lot of steps. 35 (definitely lucky – the sum of my birth day and month, the 27th of the 8th). There's a desk where you get books stamped then he turned through an archway into the centre of the building and I followed him between two tall bookcases in to the middle where it opens up. He looked at me to see if I liked it. It opens up under a vast round white dome smooth as an egg, with a glass circle at the top. Around the edges, gilt lettering; SHE SHALL BRING THEE TO HONOUR WHEN THOU DOST EMBRACE HER. SHE SHALL GIVE TO THINE HEAD AN ORNAMENT OF GRACE. Me. Me and him. It must be. He *knows* it. Brilliant sunlight pouring through the glass dome.

'It's beautiful,' I said and he patted my shoulder his fingers touched my blouse.

I can feel the shape of them still on my skin I could draw round it with a biro today if you wanted me to show you. It was only for an instant and he went ahead of me towards the round counter in the middle of the room he moved away pretending it was nothing. He had to, in a public place like that we had to be careful.

My legs were trembling I sat down at the end of a long table, there was a young black woman writing away at the other end with a pile of books around her. I can come here. This magic place he wanted me to know about. All the round walls are lined with books and mustard marble pillars and tall bookcases come inwards like rays of the sun and there are big metal cabinets with newspapers and maps in, and quiet voices and pages turning. Our special place.

He picked up a book from the counter then he went

round to a photocopier, I watched him fish in his pocket for change. I wanted to run over and do it for him, I could have done that. He copied two pages then he took the old book back to the counter. He handed it to a librarian and she smiled at him – I couldn't see his face, his back was to me but I saw the way she smiled at him and I thought Hah! You don't know. Forget your smiling like that you slut, it's *me* he loves.

He came back with his papers he was looking at his watch I counted his steps, 17 from the counter. 17. 'Shall we be getting back? It's nearly 1.30.'

We didn't talk on the way back, we didn't need to, we each knew what the other was thinking. He stepped in front of me and held the lobby door open for me and the security man saw us come in together smiling and happy a couple.

He's married. You guessed that. I know everything about him. The others talk; he's got two kids at university. His wife's a doctor, his name is Paul. They talk about him and Fiona but they know nothing. Paul. In my dreams every night he's smiling – he's reaching out to touch my shoulder – he's leaning towards me and his voice is stroking, tickling, inside my ear.

Sometimes I don't see him for days. But I know he's here. Inside the building, talking, smiling, thinking of me. We can feel it – each other's force field. I know when he's in the building and when he's out, I don't have to see him to know that. Tina had a phone call for him and I said He's not in – and she rang through to his office because she didn't believe me. But I was right.

They had a kind of party. It was to launch something – a booklet, *Maternity Care in the 21st century*. We were invited to stay for a drink after work. Tina dared Laura to ask Paul if Fiona was invited and they laughed like a pair of hyenas but I ignored them. I didn't know what to wear. They dress up like secretaries, he knew I wasn't like them. He knew I was different. I was afraid his wife would be there and that I might let something slip. If I met her I might start to giggle – I wouldn't be able to help myself – she would stare at me and she would begin to realise – she'd quickly understand that this is why Paul has been so strange lately, so dreamy and absent-minded, smiling to himself and humming a little song. Because of me.

I worried about it all night, the fear of it kept me awake. I didn't want to make things difficult for him. That was the last thing I wanted. And I had nothing I could wear.

In the end I decided not to go, when the others finished at five and locked the office I put on my jacket and went down the stairs. They got in the lift, they didn't bother to say goodbye.

As I was going across the lobby he came bursting in from the street carrying a huge bouquet. 'Hello,' he said. 'Coming up for a drink?'

'I have to go home.'

'Oh that's a shame.' He wanted me there. He knew how much I wanted to be there. 'Well have a carnation. I'm sure the chairlady of the AHA won't miss one!'

He pulled out a long-stemmed bright red carnation. As red as blood as red as my heart thumping Paul Paul Paul. It's a promise. He knows why I'm going home. He knows we will be together one day – soon. I keep the carnation pressed inside *Rebecca*.

Fiona was coming back to work the week after that so my job ended but on my last day I saw two magpies when I was walking to the station – two for joy! And they gave me a card signed by everyone in the office and he'd put *Thanks for all your hard work. Good luck, giggler! Paul* X With a kiss. He had to be careful because everyone would see the card, but even so, he put a kiss.

I'm working in the accounts department now at Debenhams. It's seven minutes to the library, I go there every lunchtime. I don't like it so much since they redecorated, the café is navy blue and yellow, a depressing combination. There are even blue lights, they seem to shed darkness. It's been a long time since I saw him, I think that's why I'm bursting to talk about it. Sometimes I go upstairs to the big white domed room and sit at a table and look at a book. That's where we'll meet again. He knows I'm here. I can sense it. Soon it will be July, our anniversary.

The Road

A YEAR LATER she was driving alone at night when a vision of the Indian suddenly came to her. He was squatting on his haunches at the roadside, head in his hands, his thin bare brown knees bent double like a cricket's. He was frozen in an attitude of complete despair. A yard away from him the traffic thundered past.

The memory was so vivid that the hot damp smell of the coach she'd been in, and her own peeled-eye head-achiness, came rushing back. She could feel herself burrowed into the corner seat, the stiff velour pricking through her thin cotton blouse. She was twisting to keep the squatting figure in sight; she had a sharp physical sense of the heat and proximity of the passenger beside her.

Back in the car in Yorkshire, in the dark and steadily increasing rain, Liz flicked the windscreen wiper lever for more frequent wipes. She worked out that it was actually two weeks since her sister Mel had gone into hospital. What the hell had gone wrong now? Why couldn't her mother keep her up to speed? She must know what was happening. Liz remembered that she had left Ben's jacket at her mother's. She drifted back to India.

They were driving from Bombay into the hills; rainy season, low skies and thick wet grey air cloyingly warm; the atmosphere itself was sweating. The road was a slash, a scar across the green, stretching for mile after mile. It was a steadily moving procession of vehicles relentless and unceasing as ants; ancient lorries, cars, coaches, taxis, more vehicles than you could count or imagine nose-to-tail patiently toiling in both

directions. Remorseless and tragic as trains of refugees
patiently making their way across the land to alien camps and
rootlessness. A gigantic two-way traffic jam that led from
Bombay far far inland, far into the heart of the country.

The hotel she'd stopped in had been just off the road.
An ugly out-of-season place with a faded slopping swimming
pool, its surface smudged and stippled by fine rain. At night
the air-conditioning rattled and she had got up to turn it off.
But then the distant continuous throb of the road came into
focus; all night they drove, all day and all night, never lessening,
never stopping.

The squatting Indian was the photo she had missed. The
best picture of the trip. Photos of the road itself failed to
capture the enormity of it; turned out to be simply shots of
vehicles.

The squatting Indian. Behind him his lorry lay like a
swatted insect; sprawled, twisted half off the steep edge of the
road. The cab still clung with two wheels onto the tarmac;
the wagon part behind was flipped onto its side, underbelly
exposed to passing traffic. The coach window was too smeary
for her to use her camera.

'If they swerve a little – one wheel goes too near the
edge of the road and –' The woman in the seat in front of her
was leaning back and staring. 'It happens all the time. They
get tired and they fall asleep at the wheel.'

'It doesn't look too bad. They'll be able to tow it back
onto the road.'

The woman in front shook her head. 'Haven't you
noticed the others?'

It came to Liz that she had. She had noticed the hulks
and wrecks of vehicles littering the roadside, some of them
picked clean of tyres, doors, windscreens, seats, engines;
haunting the edges of the road, the leavings of vultures. 'Don't
they repair –?'

'Once they're off the road they've had it.'

'But surely it would be worth –'

'To who? No one's got insurance.'

'They don't belong to firms?'

'The drivers own them. It's their family's living. If it goes off the road they can't afford the recovery costs – the towing and all that. Nine times out of ten they leave it. Take the bits they can sell and…'

'I thought he was waiting for help,' said Liz.

'Nobody will help him.'

Liz could see that it was true. That was why he squatted there so bowed and still. He was not waiting. There was nothing to wait for. She tried to formulate a comment that would be rather comforting, along the lines that he was lucky not to be injured. Her brain rejected it.

But she had done well in India. She had moved (she had been told) beyond the obvious, the picturesque, the heart-string-tugging. It had been clever to go in the rainy season and mute the prettiness. The money from the Indian pictures had made the price of the trip five times over. And two magazine covers, and her name getting known.

The beggars, the cripples, the wide-eyed children ragged outside restaurant doors – she had rejected all such soft targets. Made choices instead like the solitary gardener, gnarled and stick-thin in tattered shorts, cutting the lawns in front of the Prince of Wales Museum. The glorious colonial Indo-Saracenic building (1905, commemorating the first visit of King George V) towered behind him, and he crouched in the centre of the opulent jewel-green lawns, clipping each blade of grass by hand with shears the size of nail scissors. His brown bony figure was dwarfed by the palatial museum, isolated in a sea of green. Her pictures had a cool intelligence, the *Independent* said.

Just before dawn she had photographed the homeless who slept underneath the flyover on Marharishi Karve Road, lying beneath or slumped against the crash barrier, wonderful in shades of grey before daylight could find any trace of colour there. They were like scruffy roosting birds with rags for feathers, the solid round of a head or the pointed skinny angle of an elbow or knee protruding. The quiet monotones of the pictures captured their abandon in sleep, they lined the road like whole and peaceful corpses. Her pictures allowed India dignity, the review had said. The dignity of difference.

Now she had more assignments than she could handle. Now the children spent all their holidays with her mother and she left Jeff to make his own arrangements about when he would see them there.

It was already ten to midnight. When she got home she must pack and order a taxi for the morning. There was no time now to visit Mel in hospital, but she could ring from China; she could do an Interflora from the airport. And Ben; well, she had told Ben when she was leaving. If he chose to go on sulking that was up to him. If there was no message on the answer-phone she wouldn't ring him. Flashing her lights at an oncoming car who'd failed to dip, it occurred to her that Ben was probably over. He couldn't keep up. Jealous of her work, demanding proofs of affection like a spoilt child. The China trip would take her away from him for four weeks. Time to move on. New country, new places, new pictures, new man. Why not?

Unbidden in the dark the squatting Indian lorry driver reappeared. The great lost picture. The picture of a lifetime – tragic and simple enough to be beyond sentiment. The road had carried her past it. It was a horrible voracious thing, that road.

Birds of American River

KANGAROO ISLAND IS separated from Cape Jervis, on the southern coast of Australia, by seven miles of warm blue sea. The straits are full of sharks, dolphins, seals, squid, and an abundance of smaller fishy life. On the ferry I read the *Whalewatch* notice, which told me that female whales and their pups pass this way in winter, en route for their northern feeding grounds. Here's one old female won't be passing this way in winter; I'll have to take the whales on trust.

I thought it would make a good prison. Probably did too, in the old days. Just the place for a penal colony: sharks come cheaper than a boundary fence.

They put me out of hospital like you put out the cat at night, knowing it'll be back. My neighbour came in with meals. My son and his wife came to stay. My old friends rallied round. My daughters phoned from Sydney and said they had told their father, and please please would I talk to him. They heaped their grief and concern upon me like so many pillowcases of dry white feathers, till I was damned near suffocated. Each one had his or her own fondest imagining, of how I'd want to spend my last – six months? six weeks? They're cagey about giving you dates. It all depends. And the bargaining games that you play, like 'swap you a month of bed-lingering for three good strong days on my feet and eating', are not with the doctors who seem to hold the key, but with some bastard who won't even show His face – never mind His hand.

Last year Arlene offered me and Matthew use of their holiday shack at American River on Kangaroo Island. It was far enough away to shake them all off, but not so far that I wouldn't be able to get back if. When. The consultant was kind; he told me, full and square, and gave me time for questions. 'I don't know how fast it'll grow. Come back when you need us.'

I'll go. I don't fancy pain.

So I rang Arlene and got the key. Begged her not to worry about the smallness, untidiness, bareness, general lack of suitability of the place for dying in. Declined all offers of companionship. And set off for American River.

A ferry always uplifts me. It's having my feet not planted firmly on the ground, that's the joy. I'd rather come back as a bird or a fish; wouldn't you? Call what we can do motion? Watch a dolphin, or a swallow. Seal hunters named it American River a century ago. Knowing this, I imagined darkness, spicy with pine forest; an ice cold river; silent, fur-wrapped men, their breath crystallising in the air.

I couldn't have been more wrong. American River, on the sheltered northern side of Kangaroo Island, lies warm and open as a child's palm. There is neither river nor forest; a lazy indentation in the coastline has formed a lagoon, where pelicans and black swans float like toy boats on a mirror. In the distance the far shore of the lagoon is white sand and green scrub, pretty as a pirate's island. The seal trappers have gone, and American River now boasts a hotel, a bottle shop, a deli and a post office. There's a single block of modern ranch-style houses, and, on the lagoon side of the road, a shanty village of holiday homes. They call them shacks: they're made of hardboard and corrugated iron, and either mint green paint was on special, or they had trouble getting any other supplies, because every crooked lean-to is painted that colour. Most sit in their own small yard of dust; it is too dry for grass. A few big gums have been left between the tiny lots, and an implausible row of three city neon lights grace the central track.

Inside Arlene's shack I opened up the windows – it was stinking hot – and bashed a couple of the screens back into place. I checked there was rainwater in the tank; no need to turn the pump on. Then I drove to Kingscote for a boxful of groceries. By late afternoon I was done.

I walked down the dirt track towards the lagoon; the shore was only a few minutes walk away, but blocked from view by the huddle of shacks. Walking slowly past them, I realised that not all were holiday shacks. There was suddenly the interesting, poverty-stricken impression you always get where houses which were built to be temporary have become permanent: ramshackle additions and repairs, areas fenced off with chicken wire, a trough of glowing well-watered petunias sitting in the middle of a bare yard. At the fronts, built in to the shabby plywood verandas – or boxed in at the sides from uprights and chicken wire – were bird cages. A community of bird lovers? At the last one, where a long-nosed, foxy dog came rushing to the fence to sniff me, I noticed top-notch pigeons at the nearer end, galahs in the centre cages, white yellow-crested cockatoos at the far end. Nothing rare or strange; there were a bunch of galahs and cockies in the big gum behind the shack, they could've caught them in their own back yard. The yard was fully fenced – with an old fridge and the door of a car plugging weak spots – and the earth packed and trodden in a way which suggested poultry. I could see half a wooden railway truck behind the house, so I guess they kept chooks or turkeys there. But why the wild birds?

The pigeons were croop-cruuing, that close nostalgic sound which conjures damp early-morning mist, back in the England of my childhood, and neat grey slates on a church spire. The galahs and cockies sat hunched at the backs of their cages, staring balefully. I moved on.

Past the end two shacks the track widened into a dusty turning-cum-parking area, from which a footpath led on to the foreshore. I scrambled down and sat on a boulder. There were some spoonbills and a crested grebe floating close in to shore. Behind them the early evening sky was light blue paling to yellow, and the lagoon blue-green, darker where weed hung close beneath the surface. Above the glassy lagoon floated the strip of opposite shoreline; above that, impossibly, more sea and an even further shore. A black dot in the sky, moving in from the other end of the lagoon turned into a dash, and then into the outstretched wings of a large bird. A primitive shape, like a pterodactyl – great pointed beak and broad oar-wings, gliding rather than flying; doing the occasional flap to lift it onto a higher air current, but mostly riding the thermals. An airborne pelican joyriding the sky with a wingspan wider than a man's arms, his great white back exposed to the sun and never a fear of Icarussing down.

I watched him a long time, half wanting him to head for water, to watch that impeccable glide-down to splash; and half wanting him never to come down, but to go on effortlessly gliding up and up the whorls of hot air, till he disappeared altogether.

As I walked back to my shack I glanced into the cages at the two middle houses. The first was just one big batch of galahs – seven or eight in there together, with space enough to flutter round. The second had smaller birds; some honey eaters, other bush-birds I couldn't name. There were empty stubbies on the veranda steps, in clusters of threes and fours, left where they'd been set down by their drinkers. I was going to cook myself tea, like any other holiday maker in the evening after a stroll. I was going to eat as if I meant to live. What else can you do?

But I didn't feel like it yet. I poured myself a beer, put on some stinking mosquito repellent, and dragged an ancient armchair out into the yard. It was a funny place to sit, blocked in on one side by a ramshackle weatherboard garage, and on the other by an ingenious system of four corrugated tin rainwater tanks, which provided tapwater in descending order. Above the roof of the next shack I could see the tops of two of the great gum trees. I sat down in my chair and took a mouthful of too-fizzy beer. All I could taste was mossie gunge. Everything was wrong.

I went back in, poured the beer down the sink, and had a shower. It was a home made affair with a water heater you had to switch on while the water was running. When I switched it off from under the water-stream a fair sized yellow spark streaked out at me and made me laugh aloud. You can't get me – I'm already spoken for!

When I was dry I put on my long skirt and blue silk blouse. I went in the bedroom and got what I should have got first, the bottle of Black Bush Matthew brought me for Christmas (What was I saving it for? The wake?) and a pack of cigarettes to keep the mossies off. The ice cubes I'd put in the antique fridge weren't quite frozen, but I picked off the top slivers of ice and floated them in my whisky. Then I went back out to my chair. I'd only been ten minutes, but the sky was a lot darker; the gums above the shack roof were blackening now against the sky.

Suddenly there was a great squawking and kerfuffle overhead. A whole flock of galahs came wheeling in across the sky, did a couple of turns and settled heavily and clumsily into the gums, like fruit awkwardly re-attaching itself to trees it's fallen from. The dark pink undersides of their wings glowed hot against the sky, although the sun was already too low for colours. They filled the air with their excitable cries – flapping each other off their unstable perches, and gadding about to find another roost. A bunch of white cockies came in straight after; some came flapping down to the telegraph wires, where they squawked and screeched themselves into a fine old frenzy.

I lit another cigarette, and drained my tumbler: the sky was near black, I could see the first two stars. Birds still jockeying for position launched and twirled from the trees like exotic blooms; their racket crescendoed and I realised that an answering cacophony was coming up from the caged birds all along the track. Then, as suddenly as they'd started, they stopped. A single, indignant squawk from one: an answering shriek from another – and silence. Done.

I watched the sky as one by one then two by two then score on score the summer stars came out, and the good warm whisky soaked through all the little holes in my body, and I felt more unimportant, and everlasting, than I had done for a while.

I slept late; it was hot when I woke up. I was hungry and made a lot of scrambled eggs, which would have been nicer on toast, but there was no grill. Arlene had left an old exercise book of instructions on where to go and what to do, so I looked up swimming beaches and decided to head for the nearest. Nothing strenuous (I hadn't swum since the operation) but I was longing to be weightless again, and graceful. I walked down to the deli for a newspaper to take; at one shack, an old guy with a face like a dried apricot was pouring water into a dish in the galahs' cage. The door was wide open. I paused to watch and after a minute he looked at me. 'G'day.'

'G'day.' He carried the water jug back to the steps and picked up a bucket – there was food in it, fruit and household scraps. The galahs were hunched and motionless against the back wall of the cage.

'Won't they fly out?'

'Pardon?' He set the bucket down and turned slowly to deal with my question.

'The birds. Aren't you afraid they'll escape while the door is open?'

He grinned and moved his head very slightly to the left, a slow and energy-conserving no.

'Why not?'

'Scared. They scared to fly.'

'Why?' Hunched against the wall and glaring, they looked like convicts waiting to be shot.

Without any perceptible movement the old man's

mouth and shoulders indicated a shrug. The birds in all the cages were still and quiet. At last he said, 'The space, mebbe. And the wild birds. They'd go for 'em, no worries. Mob 'em, peck 'em to death.'

I looked at the birds, and they looked at me. 'How do they know?'

'Ah.' He seemed to smile. 'They know.' He turned to fill their food bowl slowly then stepped out backwards. The birds made no move.

'They aren't hungry,' I said needlessly.

'This protects 'em, see,' he said, tapping the chicken wire he had just pulled across. 'Keeps 'em safe.' He gave a single nod and moved back and up the steps to the flyscreen door.

While I waited there, not one of them moved; and they were as still when I came back that way with the newspaper in my hand.

An hour later I was swimming in the clear sea, watching shoals of small pale fish beneath me against the near-white sand. I saw two little puffer fish as well, and a kite-shaped ray idly flapping along the bottom. I should have brought a snorkel mask. A V of Cape Barren geese passed over, honking. Then I sat in the small shadow of my car, regretting the hot metal but lacking any better shade, and cut a hunk of hot bread and sweating cheese to eat with a couple of apples. I'd brought one of the knives from the shack, to cut the cheese; it was a surprising knife to be there, really. I guess the previous resident had left his cutlery behind. Did he die there? If he lived there alone; if it was his only house. He would have died there. People die in houses. Babies are born in them. You buy a house and all you know is the number of bedrooms and the price. The knife was old and solid, with a square yellowed bone handle. I read the name engraved on the blade; *Made in Sheffield for Richard C. Ford, Orroroo.* It was a good knife: the handle solid and comfortable to the palm; the long blade scratched and slivered thin with years of use and sharpening.

I was hot, even in the shade; hot and pleasantly exercised for the first time in weeks. On my shoulders and back the skin was prickling with dried salt water. I could feel each pore it expanded in. Quite soon I was too hot, so I went back to the shack which was even hotter and sat in the ancient chair on the shady side of the shack, and tried to read. But the book was boring and the chair not comfortable and I could taste the dust rising in the heat from the ground, and I thought for the first time that it was bloody stupid to be on Kangaroo Island pretending to have a great holiday alone.

You start the morning full of life, full of joy – and as the day goes on – well, it just runs out. At last the hot afternoon was done for, there was that scarcely perceptible shift in the atmosphere that means everything's changed, night's coming, and I found the energy to walk down to the lagoon again and watch the black swans and the pelicans gliding about like they'd been paid to do it. A white faced heron stood like a stump pretending I couldn't see him. There was a cormorant too, diving for his supper. I tried holding my breath while he was underwater, but had to give up long before he reappeared. How come a bird's lungs can hold more than a human's? He brought one fish up held sideways in his beak and tossed it – once – twice – before he caught it just the right way round to swallow; then down it went, head first, one gulp. At the edges of the lagoon the water was black silk; and in the centre, pearly grey, with the last reflected light of the sky. As suddenly as the previous night, the birds began to shriek and flap: I watched flock after flock of them come in across the lagoon, galahs, rosellas, cockatoos, all squawking and filling the quiet night with their mad racket. As I walked back along the track in the clear darkness I could hear the shrieks and squawks of the caged birds too; excited at their mates' party, even though they were too scared to join it.

Then I sat in the yard again, smoking and watching the stars come. The mosquitoes were hungrier than last night, queuing up for a stab at my neck and wrists and ankles. I was maddened to tears by them, 'Leave me in peace you little bastards!'

There will be all the peace I can handle.

My first real fear. Not panic or irritation or unfairness. Real gut-fear. The shack wall behind me, the dark lean-tos on either side, the patch of black sky high above. A dark wooden box, measuring no more than your own height and width. Underground, forever.

I wanted to throw up but I couldn't. I couldn't stay in the yard, I was hyperventilating and my hands and feet were tingling. I got through the shack (small, dark, enclosed) out onto the track.

A swarm of moths around each of the three street lamps, flinging themselves against the light and falling. Dead quiet everywhere now, the birds are all asleep, the people all inside. Only the faint sound of laughter and voices from the other side of a lit window.

I pick my way, stumbling once, and squat beside the lagoon. It is hardly visible, but spreads a hundred soothing noises of its own into the darkness, lappings and ploppings and suckings at the shore, sounds I never even knew were there in daylight. Swans and pelicans are floating out there, asleep on the black water.

I think of the scruffy captive galahs, hunched up against the back of their cage. Like me. Angry, afraid.

I can't fly, no more than they can. I lack the − faith. Wouldn't you −? Wouldn't you have to believe in God and Christ and all the holy fucking angels, before you could take a leap into blind space?

Except I have to leap anyway. He's coming, to shake me out of the cage. To uncurl my toes from the perch.

If birds can fly...

If birds can fly... Can I begin to believe that death is freedom?

I find that I am laughing, in the noisy gentle darkness, laughing aloud. I can just hear my kids' disgust: 'And you know what? She turned religious, for Chrissake, just before she died. She upped and told us she believed in God!'

Well, laugh. Why not?

Ped-o-Matique

THE BOOTS TIGHTENED their clasp around Karen's ankles. They began to vibrate. Karen tensed for a moment against the unfamiliar sensation, finding it oddly intimate. She half-tried to remove her feet, but they were firmly clamped in position. Relax. She drew a deep breath and settled back into the squashy comfort of the leatherette chair. She had a full half hour before she needed to be at the gate. *Spoil Yourself*, the instructions urged. *Enjoy Ped-o-Matique Free Foot Massage.* Time to relax.

She began to review her list. She had forgotten to change her dollars into euros, but there would be time for that in Paris. It was surprising how much there had been to do. At first, a six hour connection lag between flights had seemed intolerable, and she had scoured the net for something better. But direct out of Adelaide, Quantas and Malaysian Airlines were equally bad. Once the wait in Changi Airport had become inevitable, it began to acquire a dreamily elastic nature, in her mind. She might go for a swim in the airport pool, after visiting the fully-equipped gym. She might take the free bus tour of Singapore, laid on for transit passengers. She might take the opportunity to 'be enchanted by our themed gardens from the serene Bamboo Garden to the ancient Fern Garden.' Or even visit the cinema.

In the event, this yawning gulf of time had been all too easily filled. Leaning forward in her seat, she studied the buttons on the machine and switched VIBRATE to *Fast*. The vibration sent tremors all the way up her legs to her thighs. Embarrassed, she glanced at the other passengers gliding past

211

on the travelator, and at the group further down near the Palm Tree internet access site. It felt almost indecent, to be sitting here in public receiving such sensations.

Since landing she had phoned home to check that Zac was happily tucked up in bed; picked up her emails and sent a message to all her students reminding them that she would be absent this week; found a chemist that sold melatonin, for the jet lag; found a quiet seat in a restaurant and spent two hours re-revising her paper for Monday afternoon; bought an irresistible shell mobile for Zac, a length of batik cloth for Faye, and a green silk blouse which she hoped would look smarter than her turquoise shirt. Finally she had selected a postcard of a smiling lion and posted it to Zac with lots of kisses. He was too young to understand, but Faye could tell him Mummy had sent it. And now she was treating herself to a foot massage, which, according to the notice, entailed the benefits not only of stress relief and improved circulation, but also reduced the likelihood of deep vein thrombosis on long haul flights.

Leaning forward again she switched off VIBRATE and selected MASSAGE. There commenced a slow rhythmic squeezing of her feet. She flicked the switch through *Low* and *Medium* to *High*. The squeezing intensified to an almost alarming level. It began by tightening over the toes, and moved swiftly upwards, tightening in turn over the arch of the foot, the heel, the ankle, the lower calf, clasping her so tightly it was almost painful, before repeating the sequence. She switched her choice back to *Medium*. It was almost like dancing, she thought. Passive dancing. The machine danced your feet for you. How did it know how much to tighten, considering the different shapes and sizes of everyone's feet? Hers were small: if someone with big fat feet were as tightly squeezed as this, bones would be broken. It would be like Chinese foot-binding.

Karen checked her watch. Fifteen minutes till she needed to be at the gate. She had not really succeeded in relaxing yet. Her stomach was churning with anxiety, as it had been ever since she climbed into the taxi and waved goodbye to an oblivious Zac, wriggling in Faye's arms. But it was ridiculous. He was nearly eight months old. If she could leave him to return to work, as she had done when her maternity leave ran out, then she could certainly leave him for five days to go to a conference. Everyone thought so. She was fortunate, her Head of Department was really behind her career. He had encouraged her to submit an abstract for Paris, he had been more thrilled than she was when her paper was accepted. And Zac couldn't be in safer hands. Faye was her favourite post-grad, quiet, responsible, thoughtful. Karen had it all. A baby and a career and no man to tell her what to do.

She was tired, that was all. She had forgotten how to relax. She tried to remember the meditation instruction from her old yoga class. 'Focus on the moment,' the teacher had said. 'Our minds are always running to the future or the past. Gently draw your attention back to this present moment in time. Try to live in this moment.' The kindly Ped-o-Matique squeezed and caressed her feet, and she laid her head back on the head rest and closed her eyes, and told herself 'I am living, I am living, I am living in this moment.' But what time was it now in Australia? Zac might be waking up and crying for her. He would be shocked when Faye picked him up. She hoped Faye would hear him from the next room. It had seemed rather much to ask her to sleep in Zac's room, as Karen herself did. But it would be terrible if Faye were a heavy sleeper. Karen imagined Zac screaming, red hot with distress.

Forcing her attention back to the machine, she glanced at the controls; she had not yet tried MASSAGE and VIBRATE together. Switching MASSAGE to *Low*, she pressed VIBRATE. Now that definitely was the best of all – the movements felt less mechanical and more random – she upped MASSAGE to *Medium*, oh yes, very nice. Her feet were tingling and fizzing with life; she imagined them sparkling with tiny champagne bubbles. The squeezing movement just below the ankle felt particularly good. There was something wonderfully soothing, almost caring, about it. She thought about P, whom she had loved and who was married, and the way he would clasp her ankles, gently and firmly, when she bent up her knees either side of his head. He used to hold her securely, manipulating her into another position when they were both ready, the movement continuous as a ballet. When things were good, they seemed effortless. She was dancing and being danced at the same time.

Karen's feet felt wonderful. She was already looking forward to using Ped-o-Matique on the way back. Briefly she allowed herself to imagine coming back. It was only five days. In five days time she would be coming back! It was no time at all to be away – Zac would probably hardly notice. She had agreed to go to Paris because they all said she must, and because it would have been childish and ungrateful not to. But it was a strange thing to have to do, to fly to the other side of the world to talk to people she didn't know, when they could just as easily read what she thought in a journal. Of course, she knew academic dialogue was important. Conference attendance was essential, if she wanted to further her career. Networking, her Head of Department told her; networking is vital. But that meant hanging around at coffee time or in the bar before dinner, striking up conversations, trying to ask intelligent questions. When all she would be able to think of was running back to her room and ringing Faye to check on Zac. She was already eight hours flying time away from him. And there were another fourteen to go. How could she bear to be on the other side of the world?

Karen tried to remember why she had agreed to go. When she said she didn't want to, people had been incredulous. It was an honour – an accolade! It showed she was a real high flyer. Ha ha. And why would anyone in their right mind *not* go to Paris? Lucky her! Even her mother said it would be good for her. 'You spend too much time in that flat. You need to get out and meet people.' Her mother wanted her to meet a man. But I've met the man, Karen said to herself. I've even had his baby.

How could she relax? How could she relax when she allowed everyone around her to push her into doing things she didn't even want to do, which were allegedly for her own good? 'It's a subtle straw that bends and doesn't break,' she recited to herself. It was an old saying of her grandmother's and it meant that you should bend to the prevailing wind. You should go with the flow. Or was it a '*supple* straw that bends'? That would really make more sense, because how could a straw be subtle? Was she subtle? Was she supple? Was she doing the right thing? They should have Ped-o-Matiques for every part of your body, she thought; hands, arms, shoulders, neck, head. A head massager was what was needed. Something to pummel and smooth all these anxious rebellious thoughts out of her head.

It was time to go to the gate. Leaning forward, she switched MASSAGE to *Off*. The machine seemed to hesitate, then continued its slow, rolling, juddering squeeze. She switched VIBRATE to *Off*, and the juddering stopped. The squeezing continued. She stared at the controls. Both MASSAGE and VIBRATE were off. She switched MASSAGE to *Low* and then *Off* again, to be sure. The rhythmic squeezing continued without pause. Feeling a little foolish, Karen checked the sides of the machine for the on/off power switch which she had clearly forgotten. But there were no switches on the sides. Leaning right forward, she glanced under the chair. Nothing. She double-checked the machine again. MASSAGE: *High, Medium, Low, Off*. VIBRATE: *Fast, Slow, Off*. Vibrate was *Off*. Massage was *Off*. She switched them both on and off again, just to be certain. Ped-o-Matique continued imperturbably.

There must be something wrong with it. Karen stared at her legs, which disappeared at mid calf into the black pulsing oversize boots. It should be possible to wriggle out between squeezes – the thing was only on *Low* after all. She tentatively flexed her right foot but the toe-squeeze tightened on it instantly. She concentrated on the movement of the squeeze. Squeeze toes, squeeze instep, squeeze heel, squeeze lower ankle, squeeze ankle, squeeze calf, squeeze toes. The movement was a rolling one, so as each portion of foot or leg was squeezed, the hold was already tightening on the next. The toes were being squeezed again before the calf was fully released. The instep was being squeezed before the toes were free. Given the crushing strength of the thing, attempting to jerk her legs out might result in serious injury. In fact it said as much on the warning plate, which she had not previously noticed. *Safety warning. Do not attempt to remove feet while Ped-O-Matique is in motion.* It was clearly powered by electricity, so there must be a switch. But where where where was the switch? She must keep a lookout for an airport employee who knew how the damn thing worked. Several had already walked past; another would come by any minute.

What on Earth was it that made that rolling squeezing motion? Springs? Paddles? The image of a bread-making machine sprang to Karen's mind; its action whilst kneading dough. She remembered how she used to make bread, back when she was a student. She had enjoyed kneading and pummelling. When she had been working too long on an essay and her mind wouldn't stop racing, the feel of the soft elastic dough under her palms, and the pungent scent of yeast, grounded her. Once she began lecturing and doing her own research, of course, there was less time for bread-making. So her mother kindly bought her a Bread-Maker. The timer was a real boon, she pointed out: Karen could pour in the ingredients before she went to bed, programme it, and wake to delicious warm bread. But the machine took up an inordinate amount of space in Karen's small kitchen. When inactive, it reproached her; if she bought a sandwich she felt guilty. Its open maw devoured a torrent of ingredients, and she realised her housemates had eaten up the loaves she used to bake. Her freezer filled with quarter-eaten loaves, and she came to understand that the machine had appropriated the only aspect of bread which she truly enjoyed; the yield and stretch of the dough under her fingers. Now it languished in the cupboard under the sink and she only got it out when her mother was round. Perhaps it would come into its own when Zac was old enough for solid food.

Karen glanced at her watch. The gate had been open for ten minutes. She shifted the MASSAGE switch through all four positions again, and rammed it to *Off*. No change. It was embarrassing but she couldn't wait any longer.

'Excuse me. Excuse me!' The Chinese couple walking past glanced at her and smiled without slowing their walk. At the Palm Tree internet station, everyone was engrossed in their screens. There were no more pedestrians at that moment; she would need to attract the attention of the people on the travelator. 'Excuse me! Hello! Hello there!' A few people turned to stare in her direction. They wore the tranced expressions of people riding a conveyor belt.

'Hello, excuse me!'

A plump grinning boy waved at her and shouted back, 'Hello!'

'Help, please! I'm stuck!'

The passengers on the travelator stared at her blankly while they were carried down towards their gates. There was no way off the moving walkway until the toilets, 200 yards or so down the corridor. Why would anyone take the trouble to get off and walk back to see what she wanted? There must be a power switch. She carefully checked the machine again then thumped it hard and hurt her hand.

'Hey! Help! I'm stuck!' she shouted loudly, but the emailers continued slaves to their machines. 'Help! I can't get up!' One of them glanced up from his screen, then shook his head fractionally and continued tapping on his keyboard. Maybe he didn't speak English.

Eventually someone who worked here must pass:

security, cleaning staff, check-in girl. But eventually was no good. The gate had already been open twenty minutes. It would close in half an hour. At 23.50 the flight for Paris would depart. 'Help! Help! Help!' Now she was yelling and people glanced up then quickly away. For God's sake, what did it take? Must she drop down dead at their feet?

Karen realised how utterly stupid she had been to time going to the gate so finely. What had possessed her? Why had she not gone straight there? How could she be in the airport for six hours waiting for her connecting flight, and then miss it? Suddenly she remembered her mobile. Thankfully, she drew it from her bag. But who to ring? No one at home could help her. The relentless mechanical squeezing of her feet was making them ache. The machine was grabbing each foot in turn in one spot after another, tighter than handcuffs, holding her fast: it was beginning to make her feel giddy. For a moment of pure terror she imagined being trapped here forever, and never seeing Zac again. What was the international emergency number? 111? 999? She didn't even know. And was it an emergency? Did she require medical attention? No! She tore through her travel documents, willing a number for the airline. The only one was the Australian booking office. Well they could ring Singapore for her. She tapped in the number, feeling the sweat prickling in her armpits, and a niggling pressure in her bladder. The phone went straight to answer. Staring at it in rage she noticed the time. It was 00.18 in Australia.

Closing her eyes against the horror and the shame, Karen began to scream. When she looked again, two middle-aged women with rucksacks were hurrying towards her.

'What's the problem?'

Thank God, Americans. 'I'm sorry, but something ridiculous has happened.' After she had explained, the pair of them tried all the controls, crawled around the chair and neighbouring wall in search of a socket or an on/off switch, and suggested she try pulling her legs out between squeezes.

A few other people drifted over from the internet station, and began to make helpful comments. Some who spoke English suggested finding the on/off switch, unplugging the machine, or quickly pulling her legs out. A man advanced offering to help her yank her legs free.

'Please,' she begged the American women, 'please run and find someone who works here, for me.' The American women had an anxious debate about the time of departure of their own flight, then one of them set off at a half-run in the direction of the shopping mall. A young Indian woman in the growing crowd said that there was a real massage place a little further down, and she would ask the man there. A kindly elderly couple said they had to get on to their gate, but what was her departure gate number? Because if they passed it they could tell the staff to hold the flight for her. 'Your baggage will already have been loaded,' they pointed out. 'And they won't fly with unaccompanied baggage. It would take them a lot longer to unload it all and find yours, than to switch off the foot massage.' Karen told them her gate number. It would be closing in four minutes. Her feet were hot and throbbing and she was beginning to feel sick. People were starting to pull up the carpet tiles behind the chair, looking for a switch.

She remembered how P had changed, early last year. He had started grabbing and shoving and making bruises on her arms. Shifting her about to suit himself. With hindsight, of course, she should have ended it straight away. Instead of anxiously wondering what was wrong, thinking she needed to be different, appeasing him. He was trying to end it, she understood that now, and two miserable months later he finally did finish with her. Because she had been too stupid and blind to take the hint, she had allowed him to use her, to the greater misery and self-disgust of the pair of them. If she had only come out cleanly and said *It's not working any more*. Then he wouldn't have had to operate his scorched earth policy. He wouldn't have had to make himself hateful. But while they were in that downward spiral she had never seen it clearly.

Maybe she was still getting it wrong. Did he really start to hurt her because he knew he would go back to his wife, and he felt guilty? Or did he decide to go back to his wife because Karen herself was too passive? Didn't it take a victim, to make a bully? Where did the imbalance begin, and the effortlessness end? Maybe it had never even been effortless, only seemed so to her. Maybe for him it had all been effort. How could she trust her own judgement?

Time passed. Karen's confused brain began to sound other alarm bells. If the thing had gone completely haywire, maybe it would give her an electric shock. How many volts of electricity were behind that pulsing, squeezing, insanely repetitive movement? She jerked at her legs in terror and was rewarded by a savage clamping onto the wrong part of each foot and ankle – a jarring pain which winded her. It took all her concentration and a couple of rounds of the massage to force her feet down into their original positions again. People peeled away from the crowd to catch their flights, and new people joined. They made helpful suggestions like 'try switching it all on and off again,' and, 'try whipping your feet out of it.' The Indian girl came back with the man from the massage shop, who felt all round the chair for a power switch and shook his head in disbelief. 'Hang on,' he said. 'I will ring security.' He hurried back towards his shop. The American woman appeared at a run and nodded to her friend to set off for their gate. 'I've told them on the Info desk. They are trying to get hold of someone in maintenance. They are trying to get someone out to you.'

'Thank you, but did they say how long –?'

The breathless woman shook her head and began to trot after her friend. Karen glanced at her watch. The gate would have closed by now. The flight would be taking off in ten minutes. If there was really no switch, they would need to turn off a whole circuit to stop the machine. It would disrupt lighting and flight departures boards. They wouldn't do that in a hurry. Maybe they would need to dismantle the machine around her feet – the bruising, crunching, pummelling machine. It wasn't massaging anymore, it was masticating. It was chewing up her feet and legs – she imagined them when they were finally extricated, limp and mangled, boneless, hanging uselessly from her knees. Maybe they would end up cutting her out. She had a sudden lurid vision of the girl in the old story of the Red Dancing Shoes. Those shoes would never stop dancing, and they danced the poor girl all the way to the executioner's house, where she had to ask him to chop off her feet with his axe. It was the only way she could be still.

A woman was kneeling beside her patting her hand and saying 'Never mind.' Karen realised she was crying. She also realised with acute embarrassment that the crying had set off another fluid release. If the seat was electric as well as the foot thing, she would certainly be electrocuted now. She found herself beginning to laugh.

The affair with P had ended so wretchedly, it had taken her a long time to become aware of the astounding symptoms of pregnancy. She was never going to see him again. But she was expecting his child. By the time other people started noticing, it was six months, and the fact of the child had become inevitable. It was what her body was doing, just as it had grown and shed milk teeth and replaced them with bigger ones, and even, in time, wisdom teeth. She had Zac, who was hers, and nothing to do with anybody else.

A small Singaporean man in blue overalls was coming towards her; the crowd parted to let him through. Karen started to explain but he shook his head, No English. The woman who was patting Karen's hand, and who seemed to have developed a proprietorial interest in her, began to ask the crowd to leave. 'Please, if you can't help, why don't you move on? Can't you see you're upsetting her?' The man in blue overalls took up more of the carpet tiles, then spoke at incomprehensible length into his mobile. When he was done he smiled and nodded at Karen and began to walk away. The sharp aches in her feet had now become duller and deeper, as if the bones themselves had started to hurt. Most probably her feet would be extremely bruised and swollen. When she finally got them out, she probably wouldn't be able to get her shoes on. How could she possibly go to Paris? In clothes she had peed on, with damaged feet that couldn't fit into shoes?

A young woman in smart airport uniform was hurrying towards her now. 'Please Madam, very sorry. The boys from maintenance are here. This will be no problem. Please to relax.' She shooed away the remaining onlookers. Karen watched in a daze as the man in blue overalls directed two men in brown overalls to prise up a block of flooring in front of the Ped-o-Matique. They probed amongst a nest of wires. After some discussion one of them inserted a long thin pair of pliers into the tangle, and decisively snipped one wire. The Ped-o-Matique gave a convulsive shudder and fell still. It held Karen clamped tight at heel and ankle, but now it was still she managed to twist and wriggle and wrench her feet through the tight part, and haul them out to freedom. They felt ready to explode.

'Oh my god, my god!' she heard herself crying, and thought angrily that she sounded melodramatic, and she hoped none of them were religious. The man in blue overalls nodded and smiled. The girl from Information squeezed her arm. 'I am very sorry for this trouble and any inconvenience it may cause,' she assured Karen. 'If there is anything I can do to assist, not a problem.'

Her feet were free. She wasn't trapped. She was free!

'I think I've missed my flight,' said Karen, feeling her toes with one hand and assessing the size of the wet patch with the other.

'I can seat you on the next Paris flight. It is not a problem.'

'It'll be too late. My reason for going to Paris is – is tomorrow.'

'Tomorrow?' echoed the girl.

'Yes. I think I should return to Adelaide.'

'No problem. Not a problem at all,' the girl smiled. 'I will check availability.' The men in brown overalls were replacing the floor block, and recovering it with carpet tiles. The man in blue overalls came up and spoke quietly to the girl, nodding at Karen as he did so.

'He says,' the girl translated, 'he is very sorry for this machine fault. He says, he will look into the problem deeply.'

'Thank you,' said Karen. 'I think I'll just sit here for a minute. I'll follow you to the desk.'

'Not a problem,' said the girl. 'I will be seeing you.' The girl and the man in blue overalls set off back to the concourse, followed by the two men in brown overalls, carrying their toolbox. Karen relaxed back into her wet seat. She felt almost happy enough to dance.

Hitting Trees with Sticks

As I am walking home from the shops I pass a young girl hitting a tree. I should say she is about ten years old. She's using a stout stick, quite possibly a broom handle, and she is methodically and repeatedly whacking the trunk, as if it is a job she has to do. There is a boy who stands and watches her. The tree is *Prunus subhirtella*, flowering cherry, growing in the strip of grass that separates the pavement from the dual carriageway.

I know that when I speculate about such things, I am on treacherous ground. But as I look at her I do have a flicker, like the quick opening of a camera shutter, of Henry crouched on the bonnet of the old green Ford, bashing it with a rock. We were at the farm then, so he must have been nine. The flicker is not so much of what he did (because of course I remember the incident perfectly well) as of my own furious older-sister indignation.

Watching the girl today I feel simply puzzled. So many things are puzzling. The only thing that is certain is that I cannot trust myself to get it right. That flicker of indignant fury runs through my veins like a shot of cognac. Wonderful. I can walk on with a spring in my step. Hitting trees with sticks makes me think of the way they sometimes feed remains of animals to the same species; pigs, for example. Hitting the poor tree with wood, making it beat itself. It is against nature, it adds insult to injury. But maybe I am missing something.

When I come to unlock the front door, I can't find my keys. I find a set of keys in my bag but they aren't mine. Mine have two shiny wooden balls like conkers attached to the key-fob; boxwood and yew, golden and blood-red. I've had them for years. They came from trees that were uprooted in the great gale. There is no fob at all with these keys, they are simply attached to a cheap metal ring. I search carefully through my coat pockets and the compartments of my bag. I check in my purse. My own keys are definitely missing – and as for these new ones, I have never seen them in my life before. It is worth trying them, obviously, since they must have appeared in my bag for a reason; and lo and behold, they open my door.

All I can think is that Natalie must have put them there when she had an extra set cut. She must have forgotten, and hung onto the old ones by mistake. I have to have a little chuckle over that, since she's always so keen to point out my lapses of memory.

The post has come while I was out. There's a reminder from the optician, and a letter from the council. Of course the optician's is right opposite the council offices, so you'd expect that really. Fortunately my old glasses are still on the table. The council writes about the almond tree.

Your tree which stands 0.5 metres from the neighbouring garden, no 26 Chapel St, is aged and diseased, with consequent danger of falling branches. Our inspector is unable to recommend a preservation order. A tree surgeon will call on Oct 29 to fell this tree and remove the timber. Thank you for your co-operation.

Their thanks are a little premature, since I have no intention of co-operating. I find the whole thing perfectly extraordinary. Last spring the almond tree, *Prunus dulcis,* was smothered in blossom; the petals carpeted the garden like pink snow. I can only assume they've made a mistake. Well, clearly they have made a mistake, because nobody has been to inspect the tree. I'd know if they had because I would have had to let them through the house to get into the garden.

There is always this nagging doubt, however. I have Natalie to thank for that. I know she has my best interests at heart but one can feel undermined. Frankly, one does feel undermined, to the point where I find it safer to tell her very little about my affairs, to save myself the confusion and humiliation of her interference.

I let myself out into the garden to be perfectly sure. It is not a patch on its former glory but there are a few sweet roses still, Rosa Mundi and Madame Alfred Carrière. And at the edge of the lawn the dear little autumn croci, my last present from Neil. Every year they pop up again to astonish and delight, palest mauve against the green. Now, the almond tree. Undoubtedly it is alive: the leaves are turning. There are a couple of bare branches over next door's garden but those leaves may well have dropped early. It might be an idea to take a look. I am in the process of dragging one of the garden chairs to the fence when I hear the doorbell. It rings repeatedly, as if an impatient person were stabbing at it without pause. I have to hasten to the house, there isn't even time to remove my muddy shoes. The doorbell won't survive much more of that treatment.

At the door there's a woman in jeans which are too young and too tight.

'Meals on Wheels. Was you asleep love?'

'I beg your pardon?'

'Meals on Wheels. Been ringing for the last ten minutes.'

'I think you've made a mistake.'

'Mrs Celia Benson?'

'Yes.'

'Let me bring it in, love, it'll be stone cold.'

'Certainly not.'

'It's your *dinner*, love. Shepherd's pie.'

'There's been a mistake. Is it for number 26? They're away, you know.'

'I'll tell you what, you give your Natalie a ring. She'll remind you. And let me just pop this on the kitchen table.' She pushes her way in and deposits her tray, leaving the kitchen filled with the thick odour of school canteen. Is it possible Natalie has ordered Meals on Wheels without consulting me? Even for Natalie, I think that would be going a little far. What on Earth am I supposed to do with it? There'll be some poor old dear somewhere down the road waiting for her dinner, while this sits here getting cold. I should ring Meals on Wheels, I suppose. That will be the best way of clearing up the muddle.

When I go to pick up the phone, it's not in its cradle. Somebody has moved it. Unless of course I left it by my bed. That's quite possible, I do take it up with me at night, and I'm not always one hundred percent about bringing it down again in the morning. You see I am aware that I'm not perfect at remembering. Painfully aware, you could say. In fact it's only as I'm making my way upstairs that I remember the girl. There is a girl who stays in the back bedroom. I have a feeling she's not very well, but how she has slept through all this racket I can't imagine. Her door is slightly ajar, so I can peep in without disturbing her. But she's gone. She must have slipped out while I was in the garden. Yes, her bed's empty – she's even made it and pulled up the covers before leaving. She's not a spot of trouble, that girl, she's so quiet and tidy you'd hardly know she was there. I can scarcely remember the last time I spoke to her. My legs are playing up, so I sit on her bed and try to remember; it is important to try. As Natalie says, in her rather brutal way, use it or lose it. I do remember looking in the room just before I went to bed. And she was sleeping then, I saw her dark hair on the pillow. Now I would only have looked in if I was checking she was there, which would suggest that she returned fairly late, after I had eaten and while I was watching television, and that she slipped quietly upstairs without me knowing. It would have been the uncertainty which led me to check on her.

When I stand up and look out of her windc
is drawn to the almond tree. Its leaves are turning,
yellow and some are red. But there's a suspiciou
branch above the fence. I hope it's not diseased. Som
left a garden chair next to it, right on the flower bed
have to go and move it when I've had my dinner. I
cheese salad sandwich, but when I look in the breadbii
astonished. There is no bread at all, not even a crust! Ir
there is a neat brown paper parcel. It looks the sort of p
which might have been delivered by the postman; bro
paper, sellotape, edges neatly folded in. But most curiou
all, there is no address. It is much too small to contain bre
so what is it doing in the breadbin? I wonder if I am th
victim of some kind of practical joke. Or – I hope I haven
done something foolish. How could this have happened?

Whatever it is, it is important Natalie should not find
out; unless of course it is another of her attempts to be
helpful, backfiring. I have to hunt for the scissors to get
through the sellotape, it really is extremely well wrapped.
Inside the brown paper is a layer of newspaper, and inside that
a layer of bubble wrap. It makes me think of pass the parcel.
Imagine my astonishment at discovering inside – my
doorkeys! They are definitely mine, they have the two shiny
wooden marbles from the yew and the box; front door, Yale
and Chubb, back door, Chubb. I am happy to see them, and
I pop them into my coat pocket directly, in order not to
mislay them. Then I sit down to my dinner which is rather
cool by this point. I eat half the shepherd's pie but leave the
peas. I have never been able to understand the attraction of
mushy peas. I can't think why they gave them to me, whoever
it was, the person who made my dinner. They have been
quick about it, I must say. Tidy too; I wonder if it was the girl
upstairs? I could ask Natalie – or perhaps just leave a thank
you note by the cooker, that might be the best plan, cut out
the middleman.

I put the kettle on and then I realise the phone is

nging. It is rather difficult to hear when the kettle is roaring
way, so I turn it off. Definitely the phone is ringing. But when
go to pick it up somebody has moved it. It isn't in its cradle,
t is nowhere to be seen. I look on the table, the dresser, down
the arms of the sofa. It has simply vanished. When it stops
ringing I turn the kettle back on and to my annoyance the
phone starts up all over again. I have the sudden inspiration that
someone may have put it in the breadbin; but no, the breadbin
is empty. That in itself is strange, because I must have been
shopping this morning. I take the weight off my legs and try
to remember what I bought. Bread, obviously, since I have run
out; and very likely fruit, because the fruit bowl is empty. I
probably bought a nice little piece of cod or chicken for my
tea. Where is my shopping? Is it possible someone has nipped
in and stolen it? I know that is unlikely. In fact, that is the sort
of thing I am quite determined not to think, because it is
paranoid, and whilst it is one thing to be forgetful, it is entirely
another to be paranoid and irritating to others. As I have said
to Natalie, if I ever get like Grandma, shoot me.

All I need to do is apply a little logic. It is almost certain
that I have been to the shops, since that is my routine; therefore
it is entirely likely that at some point during the afternoon I
will come across my shopping. The telephone recommences its
ringing and I recall that I have perhaps not fetched it down
from beside my bed. I am toiling up the stairs to see, when the
doorbell rings.

It is Natalie with her mobile clamped to her ear. 'Why
can't you answer the phone, Mum?'

'Why are you phoning me when you're standing on my
doorstep?'

'I phoned you from home this morning, and then I
phoned you from work. I've been phoning you all day, you
never answer. I thought something was wrong.'

'I've been out.'

'Where?' She follows me into the kitchen.

'Shopping.'

'Yes but you must've come back hours ago. You've had your lunch! What's this?' She picks up a letter and begins to read it. 'Thank God, at last they're dealing with that wretched tree.'

'What does it say?'

'Haven't you read it?'

'I don't believe I have.'

'They're going to chop down the old almond tree that next door keep going on about. You should ask them to chop some other stuff while they're out there, that garden's like a jungle.'

I am not sure who 'they' are, who plan to chop down my tree, but Natalie can be a little impatient so I shall wait till she has gone, then read that letter for myself. I ask her if she would like some tea but she is in a hurry.

'Mum, where's the phone? That's why you didn't answer, isn't it.'

'I don't know what you mean.'

'Where's the phone?' She presses her mobile and the phone begins to ring.

'Please don't do that, Natalie.'

Natalie goes upstairs and after a minute the ringing stops. She comes back down with the phone. 'You need to get an extension. Then you won't have to keep moving it.'

'That's rather an extravagance, isn't it?'

'Mum. I have to come and check on you because you can't answer the phone because you don't know where it is. If buying another phone stops that from happening, won't it make life easier for the both of us?'

'There really isn't any need for you to check on me, you know.'

Natalie opens the fridge. 'What are you having for tea?'

'Chops.'

'Where are they?'

'I haven't unpacked my shopping yet.'

She sits down at the table. 'Look, I worry about you. You

forget things. I know you want to be independent but sometimes—'

'What do you want me to do?'

'Get another phone. I'll get it for you, you can pay me back. Alright?'

'Alright.'

'Good. Shall I unpack your shopping before I go?'

'It's fine thank you. I can do it myself.'

'OK. I'll call in tomorrow after work. See you Mum.' She kisses me and lets herself out. Lucky about that shopping; now, I have to find it, quick sticks, before it slips my mind again. I have an inkling I've put it in the breadbin – but no. It isn't in the fridge or the cooker; I wonder if the girl upstairs has taken it to her room by mistake? But a thorough search upstairs draws a blank. I have to sit on her bed for a little rest, I really am feeling quite done in.

When I come back down to the kitchen I notice a letter from the council on the table. They want to cut down the almond tree! It was here when Neil and I bought this house in 1951. It must be nearly as old as I am, I should be very sad to see it go. But I must concentrate on the shopping. I might have left it in the garden. My legs are painful and it seems to me that the joy has rather gone out of the day. Maybe I could go to bed early and not bother with tea.

No, that would not be sensible. It is important to have a routine. Break your routine and where are you? Adrift on a wide wide sea. I let myself out into the garden; it is already dusk, with a chill in the air. Someone has left one of the garden chairs on the flowerbed near the tree. I move it, and then I have a good look under the bushes for my shopping. If it isn't there it's nowhere; and that's what I am forced to conclude. That shopping has vanished. It is a relief to feel certain about it. At least now I can sit down in the warm and stop worrying. But when I try to go back inside the door won't budge. I know I haven't locked it. I check my pockets – no keys. That proves it. But it is definitely locked. I sit on a garden chair and try to decide what to do. Who has locked me out? Whoever has done it might well be a robber; might, even at this moment, be going through my things. I peer into the sitting room but it is too dark to see.

Well, if there is a robber, let him take what he wants and go. My main concern is that Natalie shouldn't know what has happened. But how am I to get out of the garden? I can hardly stay here all night! I wonder if the girl upstairs has come in. I knock on the back door, then tap on the sitting room window. There is no reply. Then I hear the phone begin to ring. I hope she might answer it, but it rings and rings, more than twenty times. Who could be ringing me? Natalie. I am decidedly chilly. I feel around in the blackness of the garden shed and manage to lay my hands on the picnic cloth, which I wrap around my shoulders. It's an old Indian bedspread, there's not a lot of warmth in it, but it smells rather sweetly of grass clippings. The outdoor broom topples over, so I take it for a walking stick. I hobble back to the sitting room window and listen to the phone ringing again. I expect she will come round in a while. She will be cross with me.

I don't want to be any trouble and everything seems to conspire against it. I can see I am nothing but trouble. Perhaps I can make them hear me next door. But when I look up at their house, I remember they're away. They leave that bright bathroom light on to fool robbers, though any robber worth his salt wouldn't take long to work out that the bathroom light has been left on for a fortnight. They think nothing of wasting electricity, the bulb must be 200 watts. It shines straight down onto my almond tree, as if it were the star of the stage. That tree has been nothing but trouble.

When Natalie comes, she'll not only be cross about the phone, she'll also be cross about the tree. It has been diseased for years. If it wasn't for that tree I would never have had to come into the garden in the first place. The trouble it's caused: the letters, the telephone calls, the stream of people coming and going about that tree, it is extraordinary. Why can't they just chop it down and have done with it?

I am a patient woman, I believe I am. I try to be patient. Not like Henry, he always had a horrible temper on him. I can see him now, hitting and hitting that old green Ford, just because they wouldn't let him ride the tractor. But I have to ask where it has got me. Look at me now, trapped in my own garden in the cold and the dark, with my swollen legs really quite troublesome, having to face Natalie being angry with me yet again. Natalie is angry. *I* should be angry. First Grandma, and now this. I have to wonder, you know; is she me? Am I my mother?

I think about being angry. I think about feeling a hot flicker of rage, coursing through my veins like a shot of cognac. I think I *am* angry. Really, I have had enough of all this, I have had it up to here. Grasping the garden broom firmly I stride over to that wretched tree. It's time I taught it a lesson. I raise my broom and begin to whack it, good solid ringing blows on the trunk. Yes! My anger is warming me through and through. It is time that old tree knew it was beaten.